I0846535

"*A Private Haunting* is a sometimes beautiful and eerie book which looks at the strangeness beneath modern life in a style reminiscent of Alan Warner or Jon McGregor. The author knows how to peer into the lives of his characters with an unsparing eye, finding the warmth and horror that surrounds us all."
—Alan Bissett, author of the *Moira Monologues*.

"In this taut, terrifying tale of loss from McCulloch, readers are never sure whether one or both of his lead characters is a cold-blooded murderer, a victim of unfathomable tragedy, or perhaps both. Surprising bursts of humor lighten a narrative that is otherwise suffused with death, sorrow, guilt, and madness."
—*Publishers Weekly*.

"*A Private Haunting* is a captivating triumph that confirms the arrival of a blistering new talent on the literary scene." —*Daily Record*

"This is a literary work of art, a rare contemporary artistic gem, a beautiful rendition of love and pain delivered with a sometimes caustic, sharp, sense of humor. *The Accidental Recluse* is an unforgettable tale of sorrow and laughter. A beautiful tragicomedy, highly recommended." —Tony Nesca, *Screaming Skull Press*

"McCulloch's characterisation of Johnny is complex but handled with as light a touch as the lean, tight storytelling which makes *The Accidental Recluse* such a pleasure to read... McCulloch resists the easy route of sentimentality and showy, crowd-pleasing catharsis. The climactic confrontation with the ghosts of Johnny Jackson's past is, when it comes, wilfully underplayed, and all the better for it." —Alistair Mabbott, *The Herald*

"*The Accidental Recluse* has brilliant portrayals of a childhood in Scotland in the 1950s and the hedonism of 1960s London. In Johnny Jackson, McCulloch has created a multifaceted, utterly ambiguous character who leaves the reader thinking about his story long after it is over." —*The Scotsman*

"*The Accidental Recluse* continues to showcase McCulloch as a novelist with a genuine flair for originality and a distinctive and entertaining narrative storytelling style. An engaging read from cover to cover, *The Accidental Recluse* is unreservedly recommended." —*Midwest Book Review*

Editor: Krysta Winsheimer of Muse Retrospect

Book Design: Gary Anderson

Cover Design: Rory Ambrose

ISBN: 979-8-9904851-5-0
Run Amok Crime, 2026
First Edition

Run Amok

Riprap

Tom McCulloch

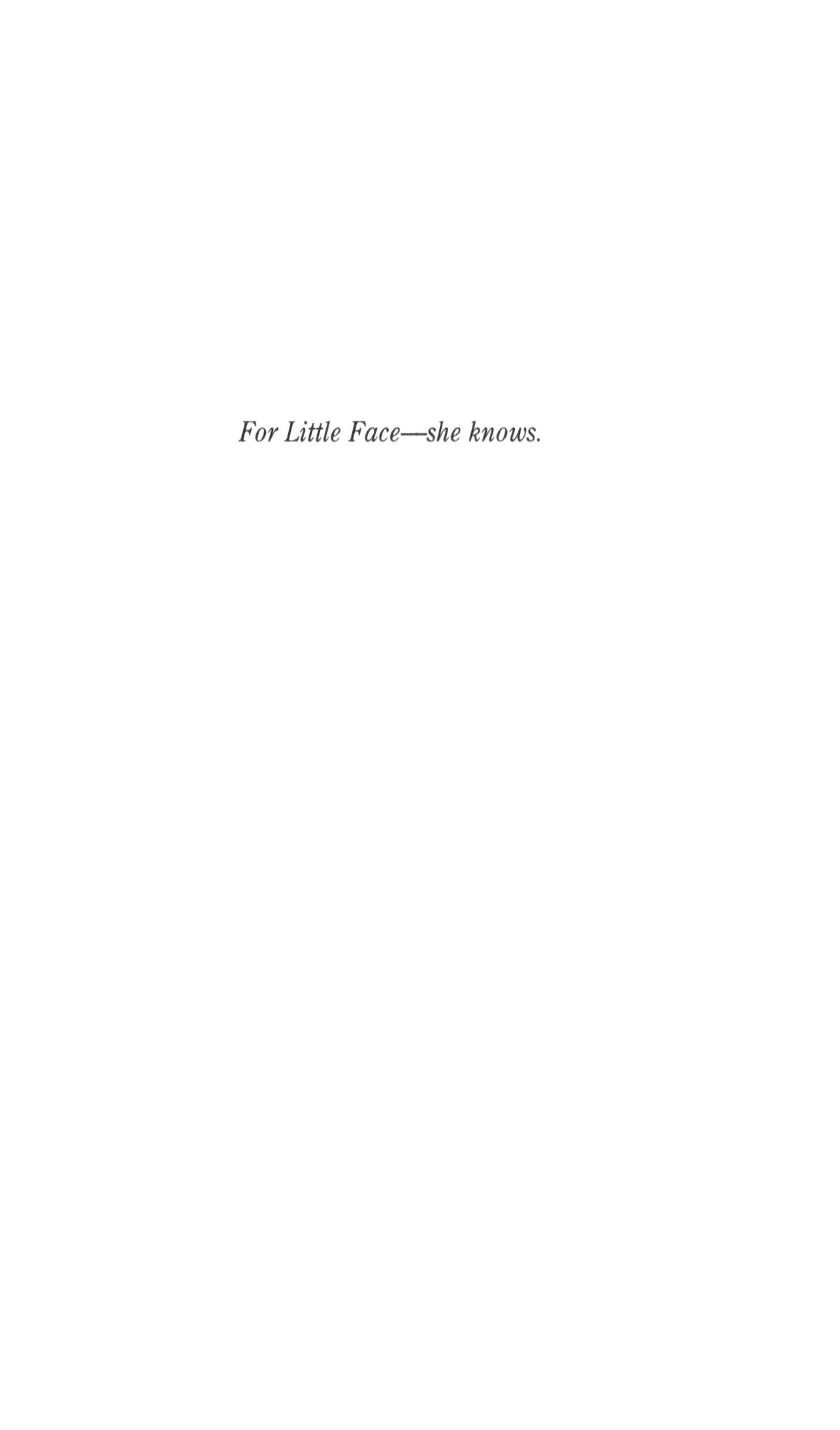

For Little Face—she knows.

Riprap (noun):
loose stone used to form a foundation for a breakwater or other structure.

"Truth is what most contradicts itself. What a farce it all is."
—Lawrence Durrell, *Balthasar*

I shot a cow once.

I know.

When you're the one dying, you tell me what pops into your head.

I tell you, it sure is something. I must be so quiet to look at, so still on this hospital bed.

You know what, though?

Down here? Down here it's deafening.

Girls are not supposed to shoot cows. No one is supposed to shoot cows. Apart from the specially licensed. Cow shooters must exist. After all, there's nothing new under this sweet 'n' easy sun of ours.

What's the word? Ennui. Sounds like a cockney dad with a speech impediment shouting for his son:

"Oi, Enwee, get in 'ere, ya little bleeder!"

Ah, ennui, all your vistas a-seen and all your boulevards a-traipsed, nothing remarkable about cow shooters, no, no.

Remember those careers days at school? A tired, sour-smelling library hardly anyone used and a rickety table placed deliberately between two walls of imposing photographs. On one, year group after year group in sombre, wide-angled rows. On the other, the portrait procession of identikit, bat-like rectors, the same thinning pate, piggy eyes, and dandruff-dusted gowns. Under the weight of that photographic gloom sits the similarly despondent guidance teacher who went to the same school, years back. He remembers being on the other side of the table, staring at another teacher like the girl now looking back at him.

Patricia.

Patti.

A Letham.

Will he treat me differently? *Could* he? Like my venerable grandfather, he's a man of principle, a union man, though his collar isn't blue, more whitey yellow. So, stand your ground, Mr Turner, puncture those dreams 'n schemes with the flair you employ with *all* the duds.

But Mr Turner manages to reassure himself, never easy, every day. He tells the bathroom mirror, "I am a professional." See his shoulders relax as he looks away from the windows where the rain runs like tears and opens the Good Book, *Universal Job Tables, 158th edition.* Closing his eyes to *feel* the judgment, he traces a finger down a random page before abruptly stopping.

There! He straightens his spine, becoming ever more crooked, and tells me:

"Cow shooter."

It's less workaday than nurse at least.

The nurses who come and go as I come and go from dreams that may be reality, but all is provisional anyway.

I hear tell I should be waking.

Not dying.

Zat so. Gimme a bloody …

My eyelids.

Let them fall like iron curtains before they notice me looking. They being the nurses but sometimes the doctors, *los especialistas*. They come and go as I lie unmoving in my bed.

It's raised too high!

The pillow's straining my neck!

Yet being unable to speak, I cannot actually protest to the voices sometimes close and sometimes so far away. These are not moments to try to open my eyes. I have no desire to look up at medically masked faces staring down at me with their beady peepers.

Like this pair.

How on earth did they ever become nurses?

Man, can they talk.

Let's call them the Two Fishwives!

*"Patti Letham, eh? Remember her at school? She was told she'd be a cow shooter." "Really?" "I ain't lying. Some folks have all the luck. Some folks are priv-il-*eged. *I just got nurse. Leisurewear model was a close second." "Ah, the shell-suit years. Dangerous times, my friend, a lit ciggie and you might have gone up like a Roman candle." "What is a Roman candle?" "Dunno." "Sally Higgins got nurse too. Whatever happened to her?' "Married into greasy money. Johnny Atkins, remember his fast-food van, Cabin Feeder?' "Oh yeah, bought another and another and then a top-end burger restaurant in Edinburgh. Always had ambition that boy, a proper* on-tray-pren-oooor. *Once sold me a five-pence bag of crisps for twenty.'*

I could do with some muck. It's unlikely the food being piped into me is cheeseburger slurry and—

Again! It's happening again! I am being searched. Hands are

moving my arms into strange positions.

It's the other nurse.

Katie.

Why does she creep up like this? Lukewarm water on my chest. A gentle patting dry from a towel that I imagine is faded blue, thrown afterwards into a stinking laundry trolley and wheeled into the bowels of the hospital by a catastrophically disillusioned young man from West Africa.

I am eased onto my side.

Water on my thighs. A seeping into the bum crack. Katie never dries me properly there. Katie Jones, who I recognised from a voice that now and then says "there, there," as if I am a child or a geriatric. Yet one's absence of speech means that one cannot, much as one wants to, much as one feels one's mouth shape the words, one simply *cannot* say … dry the crack puh-*leeze*.

Katie:

"I didn't think you were going to make it."

And she vamooses as suddenly as she appeared. I have been returned to my back, crack water soaking into my alarmingly big nappy. The room is silent but for the wheezes and beeps of the machines that make me think of sci-fi movies, the USS *Patti* drifting through endless black.

Able to move a little more.

Able to hear, but I've always been able to hear.

The Two Fishwives, say. Their piss-taking is relentless, an intravenous monologue. The voices slip fortissimo to pianissimo as I blissfully sink. Then the name that brings me back up, up…

Hector.

"Oooh, our bonnie boy!" "That's the one, he came back this morning." "Was he in uniform?" "I told you, detectives don't wear uniforms." "He's persistent." "He's a copper, a man of routine." "Sure, I'd give him a *proper* rooting, what does he want anyway?' "What do you think, he's waiting for Patti to wake up." "Well let's just let him in." "Ehh, you wanna explain *that* to Sister Sledgehammer?' "What's the point in asking any questions, it's pretty bloody obvious what she did."

But Hector's already been here talking to me.

Months back or maybe a week.

A day ago?

He waited until the night. I like the night. I think I know when it's night, it's fuzzier, another kind of sleep, who knew there were so many; it's all of a spectrum, narrow yet boundless. I can go anywhere. I can walk out of here and down to the sea, the fuss of the waves as I stare into a red rising sun, the milk-water sea a pathway to the centre of everything.

Yonder's the path Hector came a-moseying along, a silhouette drifting into town, up to this Victorian hospital on the hill, through the corridors, the night terrors and generator hum, passing the nurses at their ill-lit stations, who sensed something passing yet turned to empty space.

Hector looking down.
I feel his presence again:
"Funny how it all works out, eh Patti?"
And:
"I see myself years from now, flicking through these chapters of your life. You know what I'll be thinking? How everything unfurled the only way it could. It's cause and effect, eh? Causeway and effect."

Granny Causeway

"You look like her," people would say to me when they still said such things, when I was much younger and Granny C. had been dead for some years, yet close enough in remembrance to be seen in me.

It still made me feel proud.

I walked down to the shore. I sat and closed my eyes. I saw her in that so-familiar pose from the framed photograph on my mantelpiece:

She's wearing a long tweed skirt and a draped green cardigan, me a pair of old Levi's and faded blue parka. But our hair is ever the same, long and white, soft blowing in the landward wind, our faces angled up, up to the watery sun.

We open our eyes, looking along the near-finished causeway to small, humped, and almost perfectly round Ferris Island. We see the old lighthouse and cluster of ruined outhouses. Farther away, beyond the salty grasses and black rock, is the North Sea. Then nothing until Norway.

We smile.

We lift and take flight. We speed low across shimmering water for hundreds of miles, down to a pristine beach with pretty little blue and red boats pulled high on the sand. Granny C. has been here before, a springtime trip in a pocket cruiser to the land at the end of the latitude …

The rising wind brought me back to myself. A warmth. I liked April, the blowsy relief of better weather.

"You're doing well, Patti, not far to go now."

I had fifteen metres of the causeway to rebuild before I reached the short, ragged spur extending from Ferris Island. Based on my pace of work, I could have figured out how long it should take. That was the thing, though, those end points. I always had trouble with them.

"We're getting there, Granny, we're getting there," I said, then noticed Spider-Girl had crept up on me again.

"You're caught!"

"Curse you, Spider-Girl." I threw up my arms, a surrender that made no odds. Although she was only five and had moved into Shore House with her mum and dad just three months ago, Spider-Girl knew not to trust me.

She dropped into a pose and threw an arm straight out, making a whooshing noise as the web flew out from her wrist and snared me. Triumphant in victory, she put both hands on her hips, then scampered away, up the shore, picking up the stuffed panda that witnessed all her victories. Outside the Shore House gate, she pulled off her mask and looked back.

She would call for me now—*c'mon Patti, c'mon Patti*—sure she would, the two of us running and laughing, holdings hands, up the path and into the flag-stoned kitchen, then the living room, collapsing onto the sofa, where her family now stared at the television, where I sometimes watched them through the window, the living room that was once my own.

The *fusssh* of distant surf on the western rocks of Ferris Island turned my gaze back to the sea.

The tide was low, the causeway its full height above the seabed. I walked the length, along the flat granite stones—setts, which I once thought were called cobblestones. At the end of the twenty-five metres I had finished, I looked down at the wet sand, the stones I still had to lift and reset.

Many were half-buried, others buried altogether. I'd have to dig more out. I had a recurring dream where I was up to my waist in the sea, the tide rising appallingly swiftly, peering down through foamy green waves, trying desperately to find the very last stone before I went under.

The Letham Causeway.

At least my father was long dead when I started rebuilding it.

I thought how reconciliation was itself a kind of submerging as I turned a slow three-sixty, surveying the Old Empire built by my grandfather's spectacular success with the family business, Dalriadan Stoneware, quarries and construction, then a branching into higher-end ceramics. Ferris Island and a hundred mainland acres centred on Shore House were purchased, along with Little Cottage—servant quarters "back in the day," we said, with a trace of nostalgia for times that weren't better then. All this was "the family seat," as my father said.

Less seat these days than once sat.

Empires fell.

And empires left some baffling legacies. There was me, bunkered in Little Cottage, bequeathed to me and me alone. Neither me nor my twin brothers understood that particular shake of my mother's tail. It was they who had swallowed not only the hook of parental loyalty to the Letham mythology but also the line and sinker, the whole damn trawler in fact.

We had lived in Shore House as children, my grandparents in Little Cottage, where they would end their days. The two houses were separated by a low dyke built when I was much older, when Shore House was sold to cover the nursing home bills of my father and then my mother. The old man didn't live to see his empire collapse. He'd have found it unthinkable that all that was left was Little Cottage, a place of so little value to the asset portfolio that he allowed it to become a kind of frat house for my teenage brothers and their feral friends.

Friends such as Hector.

I turned landwards.

I'd half hoped he would have buggered off by now, but when had Hector been moved by hope? He was still waiting, leaning against the high wall that ran along the Shore House and Little Cottage gardens.

I walked back along the causeway to the shore, trying not to look as if I was hurrying, taking a long diagonal to the gate of Little Cottage. There was no point in looking back; I knew he would be following, the long loping gait of the man with all the time in the world.

"See that causeway?"

Hector calling out to me as he strolled across the garden to where I stood in the open kitchen doorway.

"You'll fall and hit your head one day. Be swept out …"

He came up the steps. We were almost nose to nose. The Gaze That Never Wavered was always mocking.

"We might not find you for days, *weeks*."

"You know me. I'm indestructible."

"Isn't that the truth. Permission to come aboard, Cap'n?"

I hesitated for a moment, then stepped back. A theatrical bow to camouflage another little defeat.

Hector had been in the same class as Keith and Raymond, my brothers. He knew the rooms of Little Cottage and he would remember them intimately. It was why I only ever let him into the kitchen.

"What was the progress today then? Six inches, a foot? Doesn't look like you've done much since I was last here."

"What do you want, Hector?"

He smiled the white dazzle and sat down.

"I'm interested, interested and concerned is all. What's the story over there then? Spider-Man and—'

"Spider-*Girl*."

"Her mum and dad. You met them? What do they do?"

That familiar probing look. I had a flash of primary school. The boys running about playing cops and robbers, Hector always the cop and always so very serious about it, one arm in the air, *woooo*, *woooo*, rotating his forefinger like the blue light Starsky and Hutch slapped on the roof of their car.

"You're paranoid, Hector. Something else being hidden, eh, something dark? Do you not get tired of it?"

"What can I say, I'm a professional. Curse of the job 'n' that."

"Look, it's been a long day. I just want to—"

"Frank."

"What about him?"

"He's just out of the hospital. Something in the lung they were concerned about. I'm worried about him."

"That right?"

"Yeah, that's right."

The concern had never sat right with me, Frank always the punchline to the joke and Hector the cruellest of all, the Alpha Bro if two years younger. I stuck a hand in memory's selection box. Lookee here, another school day, Hector's dragging Frank into the nettles behind the climbing frame. Later, Frank takes out his humiliation on a younger kid, pushing him into the nettles again and again. Each time, the boy tries to escape and screams until a teacher comes running. Hector watches it all with the same smile he watched me with now.

"I know you like to know how he's doing. I'm nice that way, no need to thank me."

"Thanks."

"Guess I better leave you in peace."

"Guess so."

He pushed his chair back, gaze lingering on the door to the hallway. I imagined him breaking in when I wasn't home. Peering in my cupboards and lying on my bed, taking off all his clothes and getting under the sheets, rubbing himself like an animal marking its territory, a faint tang of something I couldn't quite place when I went to sleep, enough for exhausting dreams.

I waited awhile but not long enough. I walked down to the gate, peering round. Hector was past Shore House but hadn't turned the corner up to the car park. He looked back and saw me. As I ducked away, there was a sudden gust of wind, laughter in it that I decided was just a gull.

I went back inside the cottage. Do you remember that time? I was thinking. That's the problem, there's always a time. Fuckin' Hector. This time I had just turned fifteen and Granny C. was still alive.

Hector was over at Shore House with my brothers. Frank, too, for some reason. They all traipsed into the living room, Hector leering and sing-songing, "Look who's here to *seeee* you, Patt-*eeee*." My gaze locked onto blushing Frank. We'd never talked much. All through school he'd been the boy who wasn't there. That gaze was like seeing him for the first time.

"Frank."

"Hello, Patti."

A faltering, submissive smile that triggered another burst of laughter from my brothers and Hector.

The Three Amigos and Gentle Frank, the butt of a thousand laughed-off jokes. My own adolescent cruelty was so discreet it couldn't really be cruelty at all. Men were from Mars, women from Venus, right? It used to be easier to think that was true, to believe in essential differences.

Granny C:

"Would that it was so simple, pet …"

There was nothing simple about rebuilding her causeway, either, laying the same stones that she had, all those decades back, listening to a different set of whispers about "why, why, what's she up to?" The intrusiveness was innate, a function of time and tired familiarity.

I made myself a cup of coffee and wandered into the back room. The same brown carpet we all once stood on.

Christ on a bike, had it really degenerated to nostalgia for a carpet?

"Don't you mean a shag pile," I heard Hector reply, once more the leer, Frank with the quick blush. Then my brothers, faces wrinkling with disgust. Awww, they must have been confused, all those reminders coming their way ever more frequently that their big sister was just another girl classified and reclassified as slut or frigid based on some ever-shifting set of criteria based on rumour, bullshit, and, more than anything, the frustration of never being the interest of any.

I looked around the room. My brothers had a party here once. That time, again.

Do you remember that time …?

If anyone talked to me these days, that's what we'd talk about, sat in The Four Judges on a Friday night.

"Do you remember that time Alan O'Donnell got blootered? That was your party, wasn't it?" The venerable head boy, bumbling into walls, woozy with the first-time booze, the whole class gleeful he'd finally let his guard down as we watched him puke, the goodiest of two shoes deconstructed like the component parts of chicken Kyiv, chips, and peas sprayed at his feet.

I had laughed as well, even Gentle Frank had, and he was Gentle Frank for a long time, because how could a pushover like Frank ever be a bully? The Frank who shoved the head boy's face into his puke, who pushed that young kid into the nettles and held him in there, who once broke a boy's nose for wolf whistling at me? Well, that Frank was just having a laugh, too, right?

The light slipped. Slipped and swelled. Like shadows, like pictures. We were all standing on the threadbare carpet. The two sets of brothers and I. Like the five on a die, me in the middle.

Somewhere in the multiverse that party was still going on.

What a depressing thought.

I rolled the dice. Up came me and Hector. "What *happened* to us?" he asked, but he was grinning.

I rolled again. Just me now, alone at the window. I stared at the morose greys, sky and sea becoming one expanse as I scrunched my eyes, curving back as if I were trapped inside a paperweight, one of my mother's collection, marbling colours like spreading irises, me where the pupil should be, a figure of glass within glass, looking out at Hector peering in.

That day I fell off my bike.

How different would the world have been if Hector and not his brother Frank had helped me up?

Even now, a thought to flip the stomach.

I went back to the kitchen. Pondered the cupboards, the fridge. I was getting hungry; these seedy thoughts needed something mucky. Gotta be a Chinese. The Chinese that just happened to be along the road from The Pines. My evening had unfolded as soon as Hector had said Frank's name.

I left the cottage. Into a colder wind. I studied the palsied sea and the darkening skies, a brief flaring as the sun dipped below the ridge behind Shore House, the water a momentary silvered dapple.

The lighthouse always cheered me up. A great big middle finger to my father, who loathed it. He would have had it demolished pronto if it hadn't been listed. I remembered him gathering me and my twin brothers at the living room window of Shore House, arm thrust lighthouse-wards.

"Imagine it being torn down, boys, the JCBs moving across at low tide, like an army, eh, tanks, imagine the noise!"

He was gleeful, savage, my whipped-up brothers bouncing up and down as I imagined a stormy day, the island vague in spray and spindrift. There was Granny C., shouting defiance as the lighthouse fell, tumbling from the lantern room where I sat for hours as she painted her seascapes, her brushes and canvases showering down with the mortar and stone.

"You cannot believe how close it got to none of us being here at all. None of us. All because of that bloody lighthouse."

Then the story heard so many times.

September 1944.

Granny C. had been painting. Losing track of time in the lantern room as a storm swept in. I was told she worked and reworked the canvas started that day. "As if in penance," my mother once said.

That painting hung in the Shore House living room for decades. My father took it down the day after Granny C. died. Bubbling seas and lurid green-purple sky spirals, a psychedelic rendering of the guilt and panic she felt that evening in the lighthouse. Because it was only when the fading light took her attention from the canvas that she noticed the roughness of the sea and the strength of the wind. Then the flashing torch from the mainland telling her something was wrong, but the sea a ferocious roiling, the channel now impossible to row back across, forcing her to spend hours on the island until the storm slackened. She made it back, eventually, to find that her son, my father, was sick. The appendicitis that almost killed him. He was eleven and never forgave her for not being there.

"That bloody lighthouse."

As a young girl, I dreamed about living there. I was fifty-two now; I didn't have the same dreams.

I walked on.

There was Spider-Girl, up at a Shore House window.

Not my old bedroom, that would have been too much, with every nook and cranny so clearly remembered, the pop star posters, the trinkets and the board games, the ghosts of childhood friends, Beth always obsessed with something, sad-eyed Avril so reluctant to go home, hang-dog in the half-light as I looked down from the window, watching her climb onto her bike.

Spider-Girl was waving.

I waved back.

She turned, and a moment later, her father was at the window, seeing me but not acknowledging me.

No, poor Spider-Girl had my twin brothers' old room, with a more troubling collection of memories soaked into the walls, the lines of toy cars like an Asperger's diagnosis, the ghost-screams of their vicious fights. A pair of animals, I expected them to turn on me like they turned on my favourite Sindy doll, beheading her in the shed with a hatchet. I found her body clamped in the steel vice, the head on the floor. My father only laughed when he was told. But no one titters at childhood weirdness when the serial killer is finally arrested.

Keith and Raymond got some token punishment, me the promise of a new doll, but "only if I stopped crying." This didn't stop me taking my brothers' collection of Matchbox cars, emptying them into the rowing boat and tying off the tiller. I led them down to the sea, their excited little faces turning to panic as I pointed at the cars in the bottom of the boat and gunned the outboard, watching them hop up and down as the boat headed straight for the Ferris Island rocks.

My father was impressed by my ingenuity, I think, but still took away all my dolls as a punishment. Apart from one, returned to me that night with a "don't ever do that again' and a tousle of my hair, an affection borne out of a respect for my anger that perplexed me even then.

At the car park beyond Shore House, I got into the old Corsa. I drove up the single-track to the main-road junction and took a right, townwards. I pictured Hector sitting beside me. That crooked smirk:

"You're so, so predictable, Patti. Just drive on, drive on to The Pines, you're pining for them, geddit?"

I pulled into a lay-by and turned back the way I had come.

I sat in the car for a long time. After a while, another vehicle came down the access road. A big 4x4, driven by the mysterious woman of Shore House. She parked along from me and hurried down the slope. Halfway down, she glanced round, likely sensing me. She had a plastic bag in each hand. I resisted the temptation to wind the window and shout "is that a Chinese?"

Fucking Hector.

I hadn't wanted to go to The Pines.

Then again, I never wanted to go. But not to have gone now felt like a defeat, and I didn't want to go home.

In the distance, a figure in a red jacket stood at the end of the causeway. An admirer, per-*chance*, of my works? Well, it was Granny C. who blazed the trail, folks, another penance for the night my father nearly died. Had it been there already, the heavy sea would have prevented her crossing anyway. Years after she died, her stones were scattered by another storm.

I found all kinds of meaning in that.

The causeway angered my father even more than the lighthouse. Ever the son with the embarrassing mother, ever the held grudge, the mother who wasn't there the night he flatlined but came through, like a miracle, a *miracle*. Lookee there, the martinet on another kitchen strut: "I don't like saying it at *all*, but she made a mockery of the Lethams," my mother all "mmhmms' and "yesses' as he a-pointed and a-declaimed about his father, the legendary businessman who had made the name, the name, the family name that his *own mother* had mocked.

Then the storm broke up her causeway, and the man so aware of his local standing had no problem ignoring the clamour to have it rebuilt. When I took on the task, years later, the reaction was muted, shall we say, my reputation somewhat less esteemed than dear Granny C."s.

I smiled to myself in the dark of the car.

Darker still in the east as I looked through the side window, up towards the cemetery on the promontory.

My parents:

"Ah, Patti."

"Patti, Patti, Patti."

"The way they all look at you in different ways, dear."

"None of them good."

I smiled, moving my gaze back towards the causeway. The

figure in the red jacket was still standing at the end of the causeway. Likely a dog walker. People and dogs, they all came here, waiting with self-aware sighs for human and canine profundities to emerge from the impassive sea.

Empathy Is My Middle Name

I had always been a starer.

A snoop, I supposed.

It unnerved people. There was one time at school, a low drone I eventually realised was the teacher:

"Earth to Miss *Letham*." When I looked up, she said, "Pray tell the class what is so fascinating about William." As the room exploded, I realised how long I'd been staring. "It's not him," I wanted to say. "It's his weird ear, it's like one of those shrimp sweeties, the foam ones." Part of me wanted to lean over and have a little nibble, you know, just to check.

If I hadn't been staring, I would have missed the return of the red jacket. A few days later, almost exactly the same time as before. The same coal-dust skies. I was standing at my bedroom window, surveying the shore with binoculars. A dot of colour caught my eye.

The figure at the end of the causeway could have been male or female. Their hood was up. Suddenly, as if becoming aware of the rising tide, they hurried back along the causeway to the shore. I watched them cross the jumble of stones, heading eastwards at speed, into the gloom.

I lowered the binoculars.

I felt certain that the person would return. I would make sure I was at the window at exactly the same time the next night. I didn't want to get there early and watch them arriving. That seemed inauspicious, somehow. When I raised the binoculars, I wanted the person to already be there. In place at the end of the causeway. As if they had always been there.

For the next two evenings, they weren't.

On the third, they were.

As before, the figure stood very still and stared at the sea, then turned to hurry away just as the water began to lap at the causeway. Again, the darkness was too deep, the face fuzzy.

I tracked the fading red smudge as it headed east along the shore. Then I was rushing downstairs. Sometimes it wasn't enough to stare. Sometimes you had to lean over and have a little nibble.

I hurried along the shore path, parallel to the figure but a bit behind, then took a diagonal straight towards them. They were either unaware of my approach in the rush of surf or unconcerned. All good busybodies carried a mini Maglite, and when I was two metres away, I snapped it on.

The person stopped. I kept the light steady. The jacket was dirty, browny scuff-streaks as if it had been dragged through mud. The shoulders moved up and down, a sigh seen but not heard.

"Are you okay?"

I moved alongside, angling the beam so I could see the face but not dazzle the eyes.

A girl.

She was in her mid-teens, I would have said, a thin and drawn face, pale despite the unnatural light.

"They have hurt him this time. Really, really hurt him."

A foreign accent I couldn't place.

We walked until the rocks and pools thinned out into a short stretch of gritty beach. I swung the beam towards the top of the shore, picking up the upturned rowing boat on the high-tide line.

She took a cue from the light and followed the beam, leaving the shore, taking me into the low dunes and gorse. She knew her way through the maze of bushes, not missing a step, as I did, stumbling despite the torch into a sudden dip. She stopped me falling with a surprising strength.

Then a wooden hut.

She stopped at the door and stared at me for a moment before stepping aside; here was a space being offered, it wasn't mine to take. I went in and immediately saw a man lying unmoving on top of a sleeping bag, a waxen pallor to a face made ageless by the light of a gas lantern that gave a luminescence to the sodden redness on the white dressing taped to his head.

I thought he was dead, but the mouth suddenly opened into a teeth-clenched rictus. An unnerving, high-pitched keening sound froze me in place as the girl crossed to him. She moved so leisurely, as if this whole situation was something she hadn't quite committed herself to. She dawdled to a bench and poured water from a plastic bottle into a metal bowl.

"For god's sake!"

I shoved her out of the way, picking up the bowl and an unopened dressing, hurrying over to the man on the sleeping bag.

Again that keening as I removed the bloody dressing, revealing a deep, oozing gash, viscous yellow at the edges. The infection explained his heat and sudden sweat, the face still waxen but now shiny, a hard dancing glitter in the eyes.

"You need to go to hospital."

"No hospital."

"You *need* to."

"No hospital. No police."

The hand on my forearm was tightening, painful.

Emine was the girl's name. Luca. That was his. Other than their names and that they were father and daughter, these were the only things I learned from her as we half dragged, half walked Luca back to Little Cottage. Upstairs in the spare bedroom, he slipped into fever sleep.

I tried again when he woke. "You're very sick and—'

"No hospital. No police."

"You have to listen to what—'

"*Please.*"

I'd go in to check on him and hear it again.

"*Please.*"

Again and again as he tossed and turned. I was worried. How to explain Dead Luca and the Girl in the Hood to Hector? She didn't say a word. She stared at me as if I were a talking vegetable.

"What *happened*? How long has he been like this?"

She frowned and shook her head but I knew she understood. I had a flash of my mother, that way she looked at me, as if I'd been beamed down from somewhere far, far away. Only teenagers could make you feel that it wasn't an arm's length between you but light years, whole *kalpas*, ten Buddhas come and gone.

She just sat on the living room sofa, beatific almost, leaving it to me to check on her father. He slept fitfully, the mouth a thin, tight line. I put a hand on his forehead and worried he was going to die as soon as I left the room. The only dead body I'd seen was my grandfather's, who, in an early example of the questionable decision-making that has dogged my dainty plod through this most merry of existences, I had insisted on seeing just after he died.

I was ten. I gripped Granny C."s hand as she took me into the death room that was now my bedroom at Little Cottage. Her hand tightened and my stomach felt hollow. He had a duvet sheet with faded oriental lettering pulled to his neck. I was instantly spooked by the tight pull of his cheeks and the jut of his jaw that forced his lower dentures slightly out of his mouth. I had a fleeting inclination to push them back in, imagining a resistance and a slight plop as they settled back into place, loosening the tightness of his face, returning him to a semblance of something, if unlikely to be reassuring, then at least familiar.

Three times I fell asleep in the chair beside Luca's bed and woke up with a start. Three times he didn't die.

Emine was sitting in the kitchen when I came down the next morning. Still the jacket and hood.

"Don't you want to take your coat off?"

A quick and crestfallen look, something muttered in another language. The sudden welling of tears.

"It's okay, it's okay. Don't worry."

"Can I watch television?"

"Of course you can watch *taylayveeshon!*"

My attempt at humour fell flat. She thought I was making fun of her. She ran back to the living room and buried herself under the blanket on the sofa, where she'd spent the night. She spent most of the next forty-eight hours in the same place, watching repeats of *Home Video Bloopers*, only once following me upstairs, standing in the doorway as I checked on her father.

"Don't worry. He'll live."

She nodded, a picture of nonchalance.

My irritation surprised me. I hurried down the stairs after her, switching off the TV.

"A wee thank you might've been nice?"

The tiniest of smiles crept to the corner of her mouth.

"You think this is funny?"

Because daft old Patti sensed a dawning, shaking her head as she stared at the Girl in the Hood. I felt as if I were coming across myself again, hands on hips in the middle of my own living room, starting to wonder, *What the hell am I doing, who are these people I've taken into my house?*

"What happened to your father? *Tell* me."

I took a step and she raised a hand to her neck, grasping the hood, as if she thought I was going to rip it off.

"Why are you living in that shack?"

With dismay that pissed me off even more, my ghost mother

drifted into view again, that time she found the underwear I'd bought with my seventeenth birthday money. She seemed almost alarmed, holding it at arm's length between finger and thumb, as if proximity to a pair of frilly knickers might swell her lonesome clitoris into a pulsing Belisha Beacon for every horny fisherman in the neighbourhood. "Just you wait until your father gets home," the same strident tone I now heard flowing from me as I stood over Emine:

"How old are you anyway? And why the hood? Take the damn thing down."

She was anxious, leaning back into the sofa, away from me, her eyes wider as she looked over my shoulder.

"Stop it. Please stop."

I turned to Luca in the doorway. A new dressing on his head that he must have changed himself. Ashen faced but the beginnings of colour, a red spot on each cheek, like rouge, a hungover clown getting ready for his performance. A circus was exactly what this felt like.

"What about you then? Luca, that's your name, right? Are you going to tell me … I dunno, anything?"

He looked at me. Looked down.

"You're very welcome, too, by the way."

I did an exaggerated curtsy.

"You've got until I get back. The first of May. That's when I'll be back. I'd like you not to be here, okay?"

I woke in the middle of the night but earlier than was usual. Two a.m.-ish instead of the usual three. The bovine emptiness of my insomnia was tinged with regret, as in the aftermath of drunken disgrace not quite remembered. I got out of bed. Stood on the landing outside the spare room.

Granny C:

"You shouldn't have been so hard on them, Patti."

Then outside. An uncertain breeze, cold then warm, a half-moon behind ragged clouds. I walked the criss-crossed Caithness slab and then the causeway, those low-tide cobble-squares dimly lit, a thousand holes to stumble into, shifting and moving, trying to catch me out. I stood at the end and looked back at Little Cottage. I thought of Luca sleeping. Then I went home and back to bed, lying in some half-state until my mobile buzzed a 5 a.m. text.

Here's Bazzie!

He was waiting for me in El Greco, the Land Rover so named for reasons inexplicable. In the back, offering his usual haunted acknowledgment, sat Maurice John, full-time stoner and part-time painter and decorator making a bit on the side. A.k.a Mojo, he had lost it a long time ago.

We were heading north-west. Five-day job. I got up front without a word. It was ten miles or so down the road before it dawned on me that I had left two total strangers alone in my home.

"Something up?"

"Forget it."

"I knew it! C'mon now, spill. My interest is all a-pique."

"I'm tired, Baz, gonna button it?"

"Indeed."

"Indeed what?"

"Indeed, you will spill, I know you. Haven't you figured that out by now?"

"Whatever you say … What's the job anyway?"

"Seven in five. Sector J, 248 quadrant."

"Uh huh?"

"Uh huh."

'Twas a source of now-faux disappointment to Baz that I never asked what the hell these descriptions meant. Then, with perfect timing, we passed the gates to the cemetery where lay those I had disappointed the most. I felt that frigid darkness and gave an appropriate shudder. There they were, discussing me with the time-honoured incredulity of yet another let down:

"She's still at the pylon painting then?"

"I know, she's fifty-two!"

"I feel in some way that she's been punishing us all these years."

"We did our best."

"It's all we ever did, pet."

"All we could ever do …"

Pylon painter, less a job than a self-parody. Years back, when I returned from Glasgow, I had no intention of finding any job, not after the last debacle. Bazzie's offer was made almost apologetically, but I accepted with relief the work that took me elsewhere. Baz had stood by the Notorious Patti Letham and still did, happy to offer me the pylon shifts, happy with yea or nay. I had known him since school, ever-sympathetic to the name he'd been saddled with.

Balthasar.

Why not dress him in pantaloons and a ruffle shirt? An instant target, he responded not by finding his own victims but by becoming a comrade to his fellow oppressed, stepping in to stop fights and inevitably getting his own arse kicked. I'd always been struck by the essential decency of this sweet man. There was something off-grid and indefinable about him; it was almost alluring sometimes. Baz made me want to tell him things, and I did.

***

Sector J, 248 quadrant was a swine. Peat hags so rarely traipsed I expected to come across another Tollund Man. High on a pylon beside Baz, Mojo muttering to himself as per, I told him:

"I found a guy in the dunes—he was really badly hurt."

"I knew it!"

"What?"

"That you'd spill."

"Well, aren't you the—'

"Tarry not, lassie. Tell the tale."

"I never even knew there was a shack back there."

"What do you mean a shack?"

"They were living in it."

"A shack?"

"That's what I said."

"Did you call the police?"

"He didn't want me to."

"You know Hector. He'll find out, sure as shit sticks to curtains."

"There's a girl too. A teenager."

"Where are they now?

"Still there, I suppose."

"In the shack?"

"In the cottage."

"What? You just left them there."

"What can I say, empathy is my middle name. He's okay now, he was fine when I left."

"No, no, I mean you just left them in your *house*?"

"I've told them to be gone when I get back."

"That and all your stuff!"

"They're not like that."

"How the hell do you know?"

"I got angry with them, Bazzie. I don't think they deserved that."

"Okay. Okay. Fair enough. But just to *recap*, you're saying you've left two strangers, one half dead—'

"He's not half dead—'

"In your house?"

"Yes. That's what I'm saying."

He was silent for a few moments, then suddenly smiled.

"Well, why the bloody hell *not*. I mean, look there, see the way the pylons disappear into the mist?"

I looked at them.

"There's nothing, in the end. No consequences and no conclusions."

Bazzie's wisdom. As I said, it was almost alluring.

Whole days passed like that, bursts of conversation and hours of silence. I'd look up, startled, when Baz shouted for break time, down the pylon and back into those time-lapse skies, the *shuush* of bristle on steel might be the only sound in the universe, very occasionally a shouted "hello' to a passing hiker, spooked as they looked up to see three paint-splattered creatures perched in the sky, grinning and waving with a strange but friendly choreography.

Dreams had nothing on these trips. Perhaps that was why I stuck with it. There in the sky, the glass cleared. Time folded back, a concertina, follow the drone of the topmost wire, get as high as possible to go as far back as possible, all the way back to Granny C., arms out waiting, those compassionate eyes full of reassurance. She, too, would have taken in Luca and Emine.

They would have gone back to their shack by now. I'd wander down to the dunes with my guilty, silver-speckled face to check on them when I got home, the journey four days later, which took forever, rain and low mist, fogged-up windows covered in Mojo's mysterious spirals.

Bazzie:

"You want me to come with you?"

"Thanks, Baz. I'll be fine."

"Day or night, ma'am."

"Until the next time then, pardner."

"The next time."

"You think we're too old to be climbing pylons?"

He grinned. "Course we bloody well are!" And Bazzie was gone, El Greco struggling back up the single-track.

I swung on my backpack and headed down the slope, looking across the shore. Two people were sitting at the end of the causeway, one wearing a red jacket. I heard the Land Rover behind me, the revs lifting and falling like the sea, no ambiguity there no matter how hard I looked.

I felt an undeniable pang of relief.

Spider-Girl was standing at the gate of Shore House when I passed. She said, "Look at this." I watched her do an awkward handstand on the lawn, then clamber to her feet and stick out a wrist, firing the web.

"You got me, Spider-Girl." I threw up my hands in surrender, ignoring the "get back here, Green Goblin' when I turned towards the causeway. The click of the gate told me she was following. I glanced back to see her leaping from rock to rock, whooshing noises as she fired her webs.

I was almost at the end of the causeway when they turned, looking uncomfortable and expectant. Meaningful moments tended to distort on my watch, the universe intervening in some strange way. This time it was a shout of "grenaaade!" and a stuffed panda, the soft toy sailing over my head as Luca scrambled to his feet to catch it before it landed in the water.

"A panda," said Emine.

"*My* panda," replied Spider-Girl.

Luca took a step, looked at the toy, then held it out as if it was a sombre offering. "Your panda."

The four of us stared at the panda. It might have been the most important thing we had ever seen. Then Spider-Girl was running shorewards to her father, who was hurrying down from the house and beckoning her home, a lingering look my way as he slammed the gate.

I sat down at the end of the causeway. A few moments later, Luca sat down beside me. Then Emine beside him. I looked at the scatter of granite stones in the watery sand I had yet to collect.

"We're still here," he said.

I leaned away from him—a hand on my hips and a roll of my eyes. "Really?"

"We are fruit pickers. The farm on the other side of the town. I was in a fight with some men. They had …" He glanced at Emine.

"They attacked me. Called me names. I wanted to wait for you. To tell you. To say thank you for being so kind. For—' He pointed at the dressing on the left side of his head. "Making me better."

"Does it hurt?"

He laughed. "Not as much as before."

"That's good. You're a quick healer."

"Well, that is something. It is good to be good at something. So we say thank you again … Patti. We will go now."

"Okay then."

No one moved. We just sat, three little gnomes looking out at Ferris Island, the lighthouse, the blank sea.

"Do you know what day it is, Luca?"

He turned. "May the first. The worker's day."

"Exactly. My grandmother was a socialist. A proper one, none of your reformist nonsense. ""Never be a dilettante, my dear, be true."' I always cook a big meal. Like she used to. You know the Spanish Civil War? She raised money for the Republic." I stood up. "Join me if you want."

He nodded, vaguely. Looked at Emine.

Half an hour later, after a shower, I watched them from my bedroom. They were still out on the causeway. I had the feeling they'd be there all night, trying to figure out what to do. I went down to the garden gate and shouted for them to come back up to the bloody house for crying out loud.

I cooked pasta and we ate outside. Luca and Emine said polite, thankful things and not much else. I tried to outlast the silence but surrendered in the end. Loosened by Rioja, I talked about Granny C. Not a synopsis either, we're talking *detail*. They tried to keep up with the torrent:

"She wanted to go to Spain to fight Franco. With the POUM, the Trotskyists, George Orwell's lot, you know him, the famous writer, *1984, Animal Farm*? The reason she couldn't was my dad, he was only three in 1936. That was a *huge* regret when she got older, especially when he turned out so different, politically, emotionally, everything. He never understood why his mum and dad were together. The big capitalista factory owner and the shop-floor socialist? The hell was *that* about? They met at the summer fete. Whizz, bang, whatchagonnado?

"People thought it was her doing when he brought union reps onto the board, but I'm not so sure. He had a big patrician streak, my grandfather, like his own father. A meeting of minds? Maybe, close enough anyway, when the hormones started to wear off. You should have been here back then, Luca, you should—every year we'd head over to Shore House for the May Day meal. Always a big Spanish stew and a toast to the Republicans. My father, wow, he *hated* it, but he had to go along with it because his father did. That was how tradition worked, right, *authority*. Christ, I can just see him in a Falange uniform, looking over his shoulder, worried he's gonna be fragged, you know fragged? Shot by his own soldiers?"

I lifted my glass. Emine was looking elsewhere, but Luca was expectant, politely waiting for whatever was coming.

"To Granny C."

"To Granny C."

"To Spain."

"To Spain."

"You know something else?"

"What?"

"Come here, come here," beckoning them as I stood up and hurried across the garden. Only Luca followed.

I pointed over the gate, towards the near-finished causeway. "She built that too."

"The sea path?"

"Causeway."

"Causeway."

"By herself, Luca. By *herself.*"

"Wow. That is ..."

"I know. I know, *isn't* it? She only had a team at the start. I've seen the pictures, a human chain passing the stones from the back of a truck down to the shore. Then it was just her."

I closed my eyes.

I saw Granny C., her hand shielding her eyes, picturing the line the causeway would take:

A smooth grey-brown spur of Caithness slab runs across the stony jumble of the shore. The causeway will start where it dips down into the miscellany of boulders and rock pools, then cross the forty-metre-wide channel to Ferris Island. I let a familiar time-lapse begin, Granny C. bending and laying the granite stones, the causeway emerging, a gentle curve. The images slow to normal speed. She stands on the island shore and lays the final stone.

When I opened my eyes, Luca wasn't there, nor Emine. As I

walked back to the garden table, Luca appeared at the door with a serious look, an unlabelled bottle of spirit in his hand.

"I hope you will accept this offering for the feast, Patti. For your beautiful grandmother C."

He actually said that.

So sombre.

I uncorked the bottle and sniffed it.

I heard the sea, and I heard my granny. She once called me a generous soul. That in itself always seemed generous.

"So, are you going to tell me about yourself then? What's it all about, Luca? Where are you from?"

He looked at me. He looked beyond me. He was making up his mind. He closed his mouth, opened it again.

"Albania."

Albania.

"How *exotic*," say the nurses, the Two Fishwives, in sarky unison.

This hospital.

The strangest life I've ever known.

Who said that?

Al-bayn-ee-ah.

Like one of these doctors might say.

Say *ah*.

Al-bayn-ee-*aaaaaah*.

As they peer into my mouth with a little torch, then push it shut again.

What are they looking for?

I have been sleeping. I think I was sleeping. The Red Army is parading in Red Square. Old men in fur hats.

Granny C. says "salud' and shoots her son.

Luca smiles.

Starts to sing.

Singing like Katie Nurse.

In my ear, trilling about the Two Fishwives. "Never you mind about those two, never you mind…"

The pipe!
Someone shouted, "The pipe!"
So close.
A *boooom* of a voice, like God's voice? No, Patti, don't start with that. You're waking, remember, not dying, dem pipes are bringing you up, *back*, the oxygen pipe, the food pipe …
Up there, the days are sluggish, vaporous. Up there, I can't remember where Luca told me he was from. Up there, water is being dabbed against my lips that will be dry again in no time at all.
Down here, though, I am warmer, warmer and clearer and—

Is Katie Nurse talking to me?
Let me talk to you instead.
How Luca told me all about Albania and was amazed and vaguely perplexed, Katie Nurse, that I had my *own* tale about his land of angry goats, paranoid dictators, and deep love for Norman Wisdom. We had a family holiday in Corfu in the 1970s, see. I was six and had a blow-up dinghy. Out I floated beyond the pier, bobbing Tirana-wards before my father noticed. Thus was I saved from a medieval exile in some mountaintop inn, a heaving dirndl and three strings of garlic round my neck, ladling turnip and potato stew to gummy old men.
Nothing wrong with turnips and potatoes, though, no, *no*, NO. If we ate seasonally, that's all we'd be eating, October to March. Sugar snap peas, aubergines, and asparagus what? Eat peasant, save the planet! We have more in common with these people than you can ever imagine.
Similar taste for strong drink too.
Rakia.
We drank it, Luca and I, yes? I say we did, and these here technicolour exaggerations are mine, all mine, and memory, too, is full of mines ready to explode underfoot, and there's me and Luca, drinking the rakia, rewiring our rationality centres with wistful melancholy that leads to an inevitable sing-along. I belt out "Ye Banks and Braes," Luca with some Balkan dirge about a man whose wife was taken by a bear or a wolf, maybe a goat.

Ah, sentiment, the cheap glue that so quickly dries out. You'll brush away the last flakes soon enough.
Here's another:

Frank's proposal, so endearing at the time. We're on the shore of Magnuson's Bay. He steps into a rock pool as he goes down on one knee, dropping the bloody ring. No *way*, you say, but *yes* way, I mean, would I *reaaaally* make this up? Anyhoo, my inevitable reply was delayed, along with Frank's "what's a woman like you doing with a man like me." I thought he was being ironic, but I'm not sure now, not sure at all, not that it matters, not that it matters.

A melancholy man.

A melancholy man I needed, then.

How much time has passed?

I feel it as a slow, endless drift through water, voices like muffled currents, some propel me down and some push me up, up, getting clearer, like Katie Nurse. She tells me about herself and strokes my brow, says things I know are important but instantly fragment, skirling round me like leaves in the rain, disorienting me as I jump and clutch, jump and—

My eyelids are yanked back.

First the mouth and now the eyes.

There is a tremor in the consultant's hand.

Dr Luke.

Cool Hands Luke.

The smell of last night's cabernet. One too many glasses. Cool Hands Luke has a little problem, but *shhh*, I won't tell if you won't tell, Katie Nurse, just stop with the lights, that savage brightness on then off. Then more words I can't make out. A new voice as I slip under. In a flash, I see my whole life has been one long investigation, people poking, testing my reactions.

I am waking.

I am waking but I can't tell them.

It's hard not to feel like an object.

An animal.

A cow. What can be done when even my name sounds like pulverised meat? It all comes back to that cow. I never even apologised after I shot it. It wasn't even my gun but my brothers.'

A .177 Gat air pistol.

I tell myself I remember it, pride of place in the fly-strewn window display of the World's Shittiest Sports Shop at the arse end of the High Street. My brothers coveted it for months. My father finally gave in but made them share, "right, you have to *share*," and lo they complied, taking psychopathic turns to shoot corks at each other, then little feathered darts that made them scream and flee. Amazingly, despite my mother's dire warnings, an eye was not taken out, the only damage the pepper of puncture marks on skinny limbs.

And then there is me:

Seventeen-year-old Patti getting ready for school. I see the pistol on the kitchen table. I stand at the window and feel its weight as I look across the broken causeway to the lighthouse.

I put it in my schoolbag. I wait for the bus at the top of Shore Road. I take the gun out. I walk across to the field and decide on a hefty Friesian about eighty metres away. I raise the gun like Cagney or Lacey. I point and fire with only vague thoughts of wind speed and parabola.

Out pops the plastic barrel and one-two-three seconds later, the poor cow leaps from the ground with an outraged *moooo* at what it likely thinks is a mutant horsefly and not a teenage girl with a lucky shot. It had to be. I mean, who in their right mind would shoot a cow?

All this talk of cows.

Steaks.

Stew.

Down here, I am so incredibly hungry.

Beef chow *mein*! Yes, a Chinese is definitely what I need. And Cookies takeaway is legendary.

Remember the sore finger!

That night when Frank, two tins of Export and a quarter bottle having unhinged his usual shyness, asked for a bag of chips with salt and vinegar that he pronounced "sore finger." Oh, the speed of Cookie, vaulting the counter and chasing Frank down the street, twisting his fingers and screaming "are they sore now, fucker?" Frank avoided Cookies for months and refused to order egg fried rice ever again in case a slip of the tongue rolled an *R* into an *L*.

No more the food tube! Gimme a menu. I want what Frank always had, dammit, chicken noodle soup!

I hear other footsteps.

I am being shunted into another position.

The Two Fishwives, they ponder as they manhandle, "Why

isn't she awake?" "C'mon, she is awake, she's playing us."

But Cool Hands Luke says it can take a while and we just have to wait. Never any patience in this town for the big reveal. Private hauntings are so mundane; I see everything in the faces of the Two Fishwives as they see everything in mine, a TV soap on the endless mindless …

The hands leave me, but the nurses linger.

Saying nothing.

By my fruits do they know me, but they can't agree on which. An apple is too innocent, *"It ain't Snow White lying there all demure!"* A grapefruit is bitter enough but just too yellow, too bright and frivolous, a strawberry too sensual and a banana too sexual. *"I mean, she's not had a man in years." "That's not what I heard." "Oooh, pray tell."* This place runs on sexual disgrace.

Just a plum then.

Generic variety. Hard as flint until you turn your back and it's suddenly sludge. That's you, eh, Patti? Sludge in a bed, a stone where your heart used to be. You think we don't know that you shot a poor cow? You think we've forgotten that you tried to kill Frank one time before?

THE PATTI AND FRANK SHOW

I woke the morning after the May Day feast with Luca and Emine to a hangover I instantly knew was going to desolate the next forty-eight hours. Something was tapping at the window. My eyes were gummed shut and I had no intention of opening them. If I kept them closed, I wasn't really there.

The night before, ah, here we go. Memory bombs, whether bell-clear or blurred, that exploded with a universal cringe. I forced a change of perspective, opening my gravelled eyes to the topmost branches of the apple tree tapping the window with gleeful persistence.

I realised I had taken off my top and bra but was fully clothed from the waist down, wellie boots included. It was distressingly bright, and I slunk to the window to make the light go away.

Then two more detonations. First, an astonishing headache. Next, as I stood there with the wooze and the wince, an irrational anger. The tide was out and there was a figure in the distance, hunched over on the watery sand. Luca. I watched him dig up a stone and place it on the causeway.

I grabbed a top and hurried downstairs. Emine was sitting in the kitchen eating cereal. She didn't have her hood up. For a startled moment I paused, then grabbed a coat and stepped into a pitiless wind.

Luca watched me coming. Grinning sheepishly as he stood beside the pile of stones and waited for me.

"What the hell do you think you're doing?"

The grin vanished. "I don't understand."

"This. *This.*"

With one hand, I gestured vaguely and with the other, I squeezed my fingers against my temples. "If I want your help, I'll ask, right?"

"But I—'

"Maybe this isn't such a good idea." I had no idea what idea I was talking about.

"You asked him to help."

I turned to see Emine a few steps behind me, face scrunched up against the wind. The hood was up again.

"Last night? Don't you remember?"

"Obviously not."

"You said he had to dig the stones. "Help out an old lady." You said it over and over. "Help out an old lady.""

This said in an attempt at mimicking my voice, a pointing finger as she grinned.

I frowned at Luca. "Did I say that?"

He gave an exaggerated shrug, and I sat down beside him.

"I have a sore head."

"You are not used to the plum."

"What?"

"The rakia. The plum."

I burst out laughing. "You're right. I am indeed not used to the plum."

Luca smiled as he looked across to Ferris Island. "I like lighthouses."

"Yes! We talked about lighthouses. You said you'd never seen a lighthouse until you came here."

"Did I?"

"You did," said Emine. "You said there were only seven lighthouses in Albania, but how do you even *know* that?"

I turned to Emine. I decided that these were the most words I'd heard her utter. She, too, smiled, then threw her head back, staring up into the beautiful, frozen blue. She started humming a tune.

We worked off our hangovers across the rest of the morning. Dug the granite setts from the sand. Stacked them. Booze had been letting me down ever since that first time down by the bridge over the old railway. Twelve years old, two bottles of strong cider and down came the shutters. The problem was they never stayed shut, up they rolled the next day, slow and gleeful.

"Hey, Luca?"

He plonked a stone down and squinted up.

"Did we come down here last night?" I had this vague recollection. *Let's go down to the sea, the sea …*

"What, you don't remember that either?"

"I'm guessing not."

"We did. You were very … excited. You made me close my eyes and then held my hand. You led me out onto the causeway. Not far, a few metres. Then you told me to open my eyes. It was like we were standing in the middle of the sea. Then I slipped and you stopped me falling in."

I didn't remember this at all. It seemed unreal, as unlikely as the conclusion that Luca now came to.

"I think you are someone to trust."

The red of embarrassment made the bruises on his forehead more livid, green-yellow shapes swimming in my hangover like jellyfish. I looked away. To Emine, wandering the shore. There was something knowing about the way she looked at me. Everything was so instantly poignant.

I watched as Luca started digging again.

Those wellies I had wakened up wearing, dear god, I was shameless. What if he'd helped me to bed? My gaze moved up to the cemetery on the promontory. I let it fall again, towards the inevitable:

"She always was a reckless little thing."

"The boys were never like that."

"They had their moments, dear."

"Undoubtedly, undoubtedly. But moments do not a person define."

My father who wanted only boys. I realised this at age seven, a red-letter delivery to the temporal lobe: "You know I'm here for you too." That "too," making me an addendum to my brothers. My father loved having twin boys. Here was the uber-male from his head down to his spermatozoa, so potent he created two sprogs when most only got one. My poor mother, serious complications giving birth to me but knocked up again for the sake of my father's need for a "male heir." Twins, *twins*, are you kidding me? It must have seemed like a cruel cosmic joke as she toiled like an animal to push the two of them out, nearly dying in the doing.

And they called me reckless.

Not that I sought any equivalency that frozen morn, not even sentimentally weakened by a hangover. I had never been, as they say, *my mother*, besieged by appearances and doing the done thing, terrified at the thought of the wrong thing. No wonder she sought the diazepam, the pills she hid at the back of her knicker drawer. No, no, no. Granny C. was who I wanted to be, she who put the lassie in laissez-faire, open to the possibility, at least, of waking up half naked in a pair of wellies. Who knows, maybe she had.

I heard a *screk*.

A *screk* from the island, drawing my eyes. It was always the looking up that brought me down.

A seagull.

A seagull circling and a man called Luca.

I dragged that fellow back from death's door, you know. Except he hadn't been close to death at all. The Girl in the Hood knew that all along. It explained her nonchalance as I fussed around him.

I was Emine's age when Granny C. died. Fifteen. I was so angry. Her death was like finding out there were flaws in the most perfect of things. For the next few years, I felt somehow inverted. I did well enough at school; it was more my "fuck the world and all who sail in her' attitude. Maybe subconsciously I wanted my mother and not Granny C. to be dead. The inversion brought Frank too. Had Granny C. lived, I was convinced there would have been no Frank.

Imagine no Frank?

My laughter startled a gull into flight. I blew kisses at the cemetery and made a little bow. I straightened up to see Emine a few yards away, looking at me with condescension that called for a "bravo!"

Yet she chose that moment to ask if she could help.

"Really?"

"If you don't want me—'

"Of course, of course you can!"

We formed a small chain. We said very little. Luca dug the setts from the sand and passed them to Emine, who handed them to me to stack on the causeway. I called a halt when the tide started to turn.

"We'll set them tomorrow."

"Can I ask you something?"

"Fire away, Mr Luca."

"Why did you start all this?"

"Building the causeway? You sure I didn't tell you all about this last night?"

"Maybe. I, too, drank the plum."

"I'll tell you if you tell me."

"About what?"

"About you."

He looked away, out to the sea. A few moments and then a nod. "Okay."

"Right. The causeway. My granny built it a long time ago. It got broken up in a storm. I decided to rebuild it."

He was looking back at me. "So, you built it in memory of her?"

"If you like."
"It is a celebration, too, I think. What a beautiful thing to do."

***

Luca didn't keep his side of the bargain. We worked the stones for the next few days, and he gave nothing away. They were from Albania and were here illegally. That was about it. "No papers." It made me think of war films. Most of my other questions were batted away with mono-details or silence, wistful seawards glances that became affected and then irritating.

Yet I was enjoying the company, though I didn't tell him this. And into his silences I rolled out soliloquys that he may or may not have wanted to hear, embellishments he had no idea about.

I liked to talk. Old Patti here never had any trouble talking. All those tiresome notions about me that had built up across the years, kept simmering by those whose memories hung like broken cobwebs, drifting strands of "she hasn't changed a bit' … "who does she think she is?" … "here comes the ice maiden," yet I was actually a gregarious person; I could even be *effusive*.

Not that any of this mattered, I figured, to Luca and Emine, because I expected them to soon move on.

Except they didn't. They stayed and my questions stopped. Luca worked the causeway, the garden, and even the logs one morning, as if earning a keep by chopping unnecessary logs. He had taken off his top. I saw Emine watching me. "Sweaty work," I said with such unintended suggestiveness that I could have said it in Klingon and she'd still have looked at me with disgust.

She wandered off to the bottom of the garden.

"Ah, don't fancy yer dad," I said to myself, then remembered a better line: *There is no attraction. Just blue eyes that might have looked, once. There is no attraction but blue eyes on a summer morning.*

I found the poem years ago in one of Granny C."s notebooks, dated 25 May 1944. I remembered it as clearly now as I remembered her telling me, "You have lovely eyes, your grampa's eyes." Yet mine were brown, so the instant question was, whose were blue? I would find her blue-eyed boy, of course. I would find my own, in time. And I would not have found him without Frank.

I went back inside. I sat at the table and listened to Luca's axe, rising and falling in the dark of the shed, each thump a jump cut taking me further and further back, back to Frank, always back.

We were seventeen when we got together. A first date in the Copper Pot. I remembered the gleeful stares; half of my year group must have turned to gawk as we walked in. Someone wolf whistled. "We should just go," I said. "Nope. We're staying," said Frank. I heard a few days later that he had sought out the happy whistler and broken his nose. And though unsettled by the violence, my reluctant attraction became something a bit more interesting.

Just a bit more.

That was always the problem. Enough to mean consequences that never felt overly consequential, a sense of something missing that was more retrospective, never critical enough to bring to bear in the moment. The ratings were fine for *The Patti and Frank Show*. Steady, never gaudy.

Emine appeared at the door.

I wondered who she would find when she started looking. Part of me hoped she wouldn't bother.

"What's up? Are you bored?"

Her merest of shrugs was the strongest of agreements. She walked off. To stand at the gate and stare at the sea, to lie on the grass with her arms spread wide, to quietly sit at the garden table.

Always in my line of sight.

Little Cottage acted like a magnet to both of them. They kept to a large triangle, from the slope to the car park, out to the causeway, then east, just before the curve of the shore took the cottage out of view. When I asked if they wanted to visit Ferris Island, Luca looked at me with genuine unease.

"You can get trapped on an island."

"You're joking, right?"

I wondered what had happened to corrupt a summer walk on a little island in the middle of nowhere. I put it with all the other unasked questions that circled in ever more claustrophobic orbits until I insisted we *went* somewhere, "anywhere;' it would have felt somehow negligent if I hadn't, Mother Patti dragging her kids out, insisting on a trip to the supermarket for god's sake, which suddenly had the siren appeal of Disneyland to an eight-year-old.

We piled into the car. Saturday morning but already traffic. High season was almost on us, the tourists who came for the neat rows of multicoloured fishermen's cottages that hadn't seen a sou'wester in decades. Transformed instead into art galleries full of mundane watercolours inspired by the sea, which first made the town, then left it to bleach on the high-tide line.

"This is a very special place."

I glanced at Luca but didn't detect any sarcasm. I clocked a brown sign for what was now called the "Heritage Coast," the route calibrated to avoid the High Street with its metastasising charity shops and tattered fisherman's mission, the whitewash and the shutters, the disconsolate pubs where even the most oblivious Ray-Ban knew it was best not to ask for a Mocha Frappuccino.

The supermarket was almost as vast as its near-empty car park. The fishermen had become shelf-men, stacking the goods they'd later choose from the same aisles. I worked to my usual rule. Fifteen minutes. In and out. Synchronise watches … I was heading for the tills when Luca rushed up.

"Emine is missing."

"You can't go missing in a supermarket."

"You don't understand."

I watched him hurry away into the aisles. The cashier was looking at me. She was around Emine's age.

"What's your favourite place in a supermarket?"

She didn't take her eyes off me, just paused a moment before pointing a finger towards the exit.

I left the trolley by the newspapers and wandered into the aisles, finding Emine in the clothes section. She was standing in front of a mirror holding a multicoloured summer dress against herself.

"Do you want it?"

She instantly went to put it back on the rack.

"It suits you. The colours."

She hesitated.

"Try it on, try it on!"

She looked down at the dress and then back to me. A little smile.

I half expected her to emerge from the dressing room with her red jacket on, the hood still up. But she stepped out transformed. She walked to the mirror, a tentative turn to the left, the right.

"You've got a very nice figure."

She blushed. So sweetly. She had a beautiful smile. Then her gaze moved past me, and her face instantly changed.

I turned to a staring store worker, looking hard at Emine as she hurried back inside the changing room. Nondescript male. Shaved bullet head. Ruddy cheeked. Could have been thirty or fifty.

"Got a problem?"

The body relaxed. The insincere smile of a man whose name badge told me was "Charlie, Service Lead."

"Sorry, madam, I don't know what you mean."

"Don't call me madam."

"I'm sorry."

"You know they say the customer is always right."

"Yes, I do, of course I do."

"Then gonna fuck off, Charlie." I smiled, as insincerely as Charlie, whose own smile hadn't wavered. Nor the eyes. Hard, piggy eyes.

Then Luca was beside me. Staring at Charlie with the same anxiety as Emine. Then anger as he looked at me.

"I didn't want to come here. I didn't want to. I told you this."

He pushed past me towards the changing room. Emine had just re-emerged and he hurried her away.

"We leave. Now. *Okay?*"

"Okay then."

Emine was a frigid silence on the drive home, Luca quietly furious. I asked him about it anyway.

"How do you know that man? Charlie."

"We don't."

"C'mon, Luca. I'm not an idiot."

He was staring out of one window, Emine another.

"What happened? Was he the one who attacked you, Luca?"

"No."

"So what happened?"

"Nothing."

And inevitably, as if offering his services to deftly extract the something that so clearly had happened, Hector was sitting at the garden table when we got back. He heard us but didn't move. Face to the sun and a pair of aviators. That familiar, intense self-awareness, and the oddest of feelings that he'd somehow scripted all of this, even what I was about to say.

"I've been hearing things," he said.

"Haven't you always been a good listener."

"That I have."

The smile widened. The dazzle of too many teeth. He pushed his sunglasses up to his forehead. Brushed something invisible from the shoulder of a powder-blue bespoke suit to bring our attention to how good he looked in it; skinny fit, white shirt with the top two buttons undone. That California detective he was born to be. He'd been there once, a pilgrimage with Frank in their late teens, just before he went off to police college. Came back with a tan he never lost, as if three weeks in Santa Monica had triggered some kind of genetic mutation.

"That, I most surely … *have.*"

The "have' emphasised as his gaze came to a rest on Luca. The head inclined slightly, appraising.

"Hello. And you are?"

Luca mumbled "hello," and he and Emine hurried up the path, Hector's smile tracking them, even after they'd disappeared inside, as if he could still see them. Maybe he could.

"Curious and curiouser."

"What's that supposed to mean?"

"You tell me." He nodded towards the cottage.

"Not much to say."

"Not much is still something."

"All this sniffing around like a dog. I'll get you a bowl of water."

"I'd prefer a coffee."

"Would you now?"

"You fancy one?"

"Nope."

"A beer it is. The sun is shining, so why—'

"Sorry, Hector, I only drink before midday."

He opened his mouth and a gull scrawked, laughing for him.

"So, what have the good townspeople been saying about me now?"

"I know, I know. Sneeze around here and someone turns up at your door with a tissue. Who's your friends, Miss Letham? Not from roun' these here parts. I gets all a-concerned, you understand."

"You're all heart, Sheriff."

"That I am … Well?" He was smiling again. Just not the eyes.

"Does it not get boring, Hector? Having to know everything.

You've got a problem, but you know that."

"So does Mickey Anderson."

"Who?" Every conversation with Hector was a maths problem where you had to show your working.

"Mickey Anderson. Dad runs the poly farms out west. Don't you read the papers? His problem is three broken ribs and a fractured skull. Found in his back garden a few weeks back. He's just wakened up."

"It's good to know you're on the case, Hector."

"That I am. So who's your friends?"

"Family friends. Long-lost cousins. Hitchhikers. All of the above. A clear-and-present stranger danger."

"Let me call the SWAT boys."

"You'll need them. You see Emine there, some say she's a mutant. Powers like you wouldn't believe."

"She's found her mentor then, eh? *Emine*. Nice name." He drummed his fingers on the table and stood up, looking towards the cottage as I berated myself for having let Emine's name slip out.

Then:

"You know the funny thing about Mickey's injuries? They're just like Frank's, down to the last hairline fracture. Pretty strange. Must be something in the air. Let's hope it doesn't turn out the same way."

"Let's hope."

"Cause no one deserves that, right?"

He resettled the aviators and walked down the path, looking around, soaking in the situational vibes, man. His brother Frank missed out on the Californian epiphany. All Frank came back with was sunburn, an American flattop, and a penchant for muscle vests over a torso that refused to comply, a combination so defiant in its misconception, it made me like him even more.

"It *is* unusual, that name," Hector said at the gate. "Emine. I wonder where it's from?"

"Be seeing you, Señor."

His farewell smile aimed for devastating and just missed. He wanted to vanish in the souped-up roar of a red Corvette. Instead, it was tired, sluggish waves and the eggy smell of low tide.

I watched him go. Hector's most generous of parting gifts was always guilt. I waited for today's dot to dot to materialise, then reluctantly joined them up. Look! It's Frank with his Zimmer,

Hector sitting beside him. He's telling him the Mickey Anderson story, and Frank's got a dilemma, pop pickers, his malicious hope that farmer dude ends up just like him is struggling against the insistence that his own suffering remains unique and therefore worse (actually *better*) than Mickey's. I remembered this self-pity all too well. Poor Frank, break out the tiny violins. I could hear my mother's derision snorting down from the headland cemetery. But come now, mummy-dear, your own husband infuriated you as much as mine; let's savour that one connection shall we, call it a harmony of acrimony.

"Who was that?"

Luca was beside me. I hadn't heard him coming. A pensive look on his face, as if he, too, could see Frank's outline hanging in the air. Behind him, Emine watched from the kitchen door.

"Hector. Just your friendly neighbourhood policeman."

"A policeman?"

"You sure you don't want to tell him what happened to you?"

"No good can come of that."

"Is there anything I should know, Luca?"

"Was he asking questions?"

"Of course he was asking questions. He's got a little birthmark behind his ear shaped like a question mark."

"Really?"

"No. Look, he's a cop but I've known him for years."

"We always think we know someone. Until we don't."

"Isn't that the truth."

***

They were still watching TV when I left the cottage just after 10 p.m. I should have reassured them I wasn't going to town to denounce them to Hector. I wondered if they'd be there when I got back.

I bought a coffee at the petrol station. Danny behind the counter. Faded Iron Maiden T-shirt. He'd worked there for years, that shifty look, you knew if you looked over the counter you'd see something disturbing.

"Long time no see."

"I was here yesterday."

"Yeah …? Oh *yeah*. Where you headed then?"

"Town."

"Town."

He looked almost wistful, town a place he remembered but couldn't quite place. "What's up in town?"

"Not so much."

"There's always something up."

His look was so piercing I had a sudden flash of Hector:

"We need to keep our eyes open, Danny boy …"

I took the top road into town. Groups of men outside the Pier Street pubs staring as the car passed, a brittle feeling that they knew where I was going. Then Ship Wynd, the twist of streets that came out at The Pines Sheltered Housing and Nursing Home. I parked down from the entrance.

A sky like old coal.

I walked into the park, silent teenagers on the swings, cigarette ends flaring. I followed the path until it curved sharply and veered into the swathe of cypress. On the other side of the trees, a high fence marked the grounds, The Pines beyond, a liminal place sad with fabrication, from the chocolate-box exaggerations of its over-manicured copses, ponds, and rose gardens to the dozens of downsized residents; a sense of lives become counterfeit.

I found my upturned log and sipped my coffee.

Frank's ground-floor apartment was in a block directly opposite, sixty yards away across a lawn. The light was on, the sliding patio doors closed but the curtains open. Other than the subdued glow of the emergency exit signs, only two other windows were illuminated.

I didn't come here all that often, but yes, I realised that was still too often. What can I say,"twas an unbidden thing. I'd been walking in the park some years back and passed a man with a Zimmer, a nurse holding his arm. A double-take confirmed it was indeed Frankie boy. I followed them to the security gate that led into the grounds of The Pines, then watched her help him along the path to an apartment that, turned out, faced these here dark woods.

I knew that Frank was a resident at The Pines, but until that afternoon, I hadn't really thought about it. I had to come back; it was the simple fact of seeing him, I guess. What can I say, we all have our pied pipers. And if going back there was already loaded with weirdness, what did it matter if I started taking along a pair of binoculars and sometimes a tasty little picnic. Usually, he'd just be sitting quietly in his apartment, the curtains open and no need to close them. Sometimes, like tonight, he'd open the door and come onto the patio.

Frank stared across at the trees. I raised the binoculars to that familiar sense of exposure.

I studied the face.

Although the man was surely Frank, I was always struck by such a sense of absence that I doubted I had ever known him. Perhaps that was why I came back time and again. To try and remember.

Then the seediness. Deep in the gut. As if he knew I was out there and I knew he wasn't blind at all. Which he was, of course. No doubting that. I didn't feel shame for thinking this. Guilt perhaps, guilt is easier. I put the binoculars down, and Frank leapt away. I made my fingers into a square around him, like a miniature TV screen, and settled down for another classic from *The Patti and Frank Show*. Back then it had been an, ahem, *huge hit*.

Remember "The One with the Six Iron"?

I thought of Mickey the farmer, half dead in hospital. Had the crack of his bones sounded like Frank's? How about that spongy scrunch as the side of his skull caved in? How much nuance could there be? Perhaps levels of body fat, tissue depth, and thickness of hair came into it. Undoubtedly, there was someone out there who had experienced the eureka moment when the universe told them to specialise in the sound differentials of traumatic bone injury.

I drove home. Past the Pier Street boys who'd been standing there forever, sniggering as the latest couple walked by on the journey towards inevitability. Maybe those dickheads knew something.

It wasn't that my parents thought I was too young to get married. Had it been Hector, they'd have been delighted. But it was Frank. My father's arm in mine down the aisle felt like localised rigor mortis, my mother enduring the day with a smile as tight as an emergency sphincter. Frank radiated such emphatic happiness during our first dance, I almost had a panic attack.

Then Hector, the best man, taking my arm. "We could've been so much better, Patti, we blew it." A look that shifted with every surprisingly elegant turn he took me through, desolation to mockery.

My mother said I only married to spite her. I was amazed she credited me with such imagination. She figured she knew me, yet never appreciated that understanding a family was like pin-boning a fish, you picked everything apart so carefully, but something always got stuck in the throat.

Because Frank was all about me; Frank, as reassuring as the sea but not as restless, never wanted to do anything but stay put. Slow and steady and that was good, I told myself. Frank who revealed an appealing self-confidence when his brother went off to cop school. I wanted to see where that might lead, but not so far that Frank knocked me off the pedestal he'd stuck me on. I liked the view, until I started asking myself who the fuck was perched up there.

Luca was sitting by himself in the kitchen when I got in. They hadn't fled after Hector's visit after all.

"The man in the supermarket."

For a moment I didn't have a clue what he was talking about.

"Today. The one who was looking at Emine."

"What about him?"

"He attacked her. He wanted to … You can guess. She got away. There were two of them. He was lucky I found the other one first."

He looked down at his hands. Couldn't figure out what to do with them. Spread the fingers wide.

"Mickey Anderson."

"I would do it again. You can tell your policeman friend that if you want."

I saw a golf club being swung. I saw it striking Frank's head. Once, twice. The third one caused all the problems.

You Can Get Trapped on an Island

June did its usual, couldn't decide if it was winter. I left Luca and Emine and headed off on a paint job with Bazzie.

Another drowned landscape in the north-west, peat hag and quartz, lochans like Rorschach blots that I stared into for too long, something unquiet in myself. One morning I found a hiking boot wrapped inside a red scarf and placed in a car tyre in the exact centre of the square formed by the stanchions of a pylon. We stared at this disorienting offering in the middle of nowhere, the overhead lines humming an *ommmm*. Then Baz was buzzed by a raven. It seemed so inauspicious, until Mojo broke the spell by declaring, "Jesus was a sacred mushroom."

Later, in the deserted lounge bar of a sombre hotel, as the rain hammered down and the barwoman eyed us warily, Mojo presented a watertight case. Baz beamed, bowed, and declaimed about Sutherland's animist soul. Limestone seams like frowns. Noses and ears in every rock. "Every face known and still to be." We huddled and speculated. We were outside normal things.

With the familiar but anomalous mix of relief and reluctance, I reinserted myself back into those normal things when I returned home. I closed my eyes against the sun as Bazzie drove away, and when I re-opened them, the trip might never have happened. I looked towards the shore and the causeway, glimpsing someone at the end, as if they'd seen me and ducked out of sight.

A moment later Luca reappeared. He looked across and saw me, waved as I walked down to the shore.

"I have collected more stones."
"Thank you."
"I hope you don't mind."
"Why would I mind?"
"Well, I … Maybe you …»
He looked away, west to the sun, and back to me, waiting for me to say something to release us both.

The light faded, swiftly brightened, and faded again, like a wink.

***

Granny Causeway. Did she have a Luca to help her? A Luca so eager to help, who passed the granite for me to set, as little by little the gap further narrowed between causeway and Ferris Island.

I imagined Granny C. refusing my Grampa Don's help. He's standing at the big windows of the Shore House lounge, back from golf with two cronies. They roll their eyes in amusement as Don's wife, in a yellow oilskin, works her stones in the teeming rain. Red Deborah Fraser, they're thinking, who insisted on keeping her job on the packing line after she married the CEO—she still has Don smitten.

"Your granny's a wild one," my father once said.

"I know, isn't it great!"

I was ten. I wanted to be wild too. This wasn't the desired response. I wiped the smile away as my mother backed up my father. The paintings and the causeway were "a bit odd," apparently. The way she made the men at the fisherman's mission where she volunteered hoot with laughter was "indecorous," whatever that meant, maybe something to do with changing the wallpaper. It didn't take me long to see her freedom as such a thrilling contrast to my mother's conformity, whose life with my father struck me as the marital equivalent of locked-in syndrome. Yet I was pretty sure my mother didn't feel even the briefest squeeze of envy.

Grampa Don never lost his love, even after Granny's blue-eyed boy. There it remained in old photos, the hand on her shoulder, the soft glance. There, too, in film, footage of a community fundraiser I found in the museum archive. They're dancing. The way he looks at her.

There, too, in my own memories:

"Debs, darling, can you pass me the potatoes?"

My jaw almost hit the Sunday dinner table. I mean, a woman who could make my very proper grampa say "Debs"?

No, Granny C. would not have needed a Luca, nor the heavy monitoring presence of his teenage daughter.

Emine, who came and went and scowled, collecting things from the shore that she arranged on the windowsill of the spare room. Pebbles and shells placed in a web of bone-thin slivers of driftwood and dried seaweed, a dusting of sand, intricate with a meaning only she could figure.

I had a dream where Luca and I were kneeling in front of Emine's enigmatic display. An electricity pylon stood huge and incandescent beyond the window, a red scarf, incredibly long, curling round and up towards a slowly spinning lighthouse lantern that it wrapped around, extinguishing the light. In the darkness, Luca took my hand and whispered "thank you' over and over, the words still on loop when I woke and went downstairs.

"Good morning," he said.
"Good morning."
"Did you sleep well?"
"I did."
"Did you?"
"I did."
I made a coffee and sat down opposite.
I smiled.
He smiled back and went back to the days-old newspaper he was reading. "What does this word mean?"
I followed his finger. "Massacre. When someone shoots a lot of people."
"I see."
The headline said "Californian High School Tragedy." An obligatory helicopter shot of the school and a close-up of a muscled cop in wraparound shades, assault weapon and flak vest.
Inevitably, I thought of Hector:
"I wasn't going to tell him, you know?"
Luca glanced up.
"The policeman who came here? The last thing I would do is tell him a thing, about you or anyone else."
There was a pause as Luca located what I was on about. It had been days since Hector had made his visit.
"Right … Thank you."
Once more, I felt a pressing sense of expectation. I angled my head, my eyes asking "aaaand?" Luca seemed about to say something else but didn't, going back to studying the newspaper.
"Oh, for crying out …" My exasperation was as swift as my exit. I strode to the door and tried to yank it open. It was locked. When I'd finally got the damn thing open, I hurried down to the end of the garden. *Bustling*, that's what I was doing, bustling like some old matron, aware and annoyed that I was bustling. I knew Luca was watching me, and when I turned, there he was. One foot in the kitchen, one on the step; half-in, half-out, perfectly irritating circumspection.

I was annoyed all over again. "You have to bloody *tell* me."

"What?"

"Everything. Who attacked you? What happened to Emine? Mickey Anderson. All the things you're not telling me."

He looked away.

"You need to *tell* me. If you're going to stay here. Have you got that?" I was pointing as I said this, index finger marking the beat. Have-you-got-*that*. Luca raised his hands. Flustered and palms up, as if ready to fend me off. His eyes were wide. Emine appeared behind him.

"You can get trapped on an island," Luca had said. He didn't have a choice when I again suggested we go to Ferris Island. He was trying to placate me, of course. Still, I took his agreement as the resetting of a hierarchy. I was nothing if not an intellectual mercenary, what can I say.

We crossed at high tide. Luca struggled with the oars of the boat he had insisted on rowing. That male certainty that they can do it better.

"Let me."

He protested but was relieved, I think, as he lumbered to the stern. The sea added its own stillborn silence to the one between us, the steady slap of the oars magnifying it, lending things a significance and making an awkwardness of two people trying to avoid each other's gaze.

At the bow, Emine faced away from both of us, almost a silhouette, a black and silvered corona around her head.

On the island, I slipped into tour-guide mode, arms windmilling in my peculiar way. St. Columba's Lighthouse had been built in 1888 by the John Miller company of Grangemouth. The keeper's cottages came some twenty years later. Seven hundred and forty-five blocks of stone and 650,000 bricks. It was built on the remains of an eleventh-century monastic chapel. The monks had kept a lantern on the tower to warn passing ships of the rocks. Later, it was a paraffin lamp, the lighthouse not electrified until 1977. Then, eleven years later, the lighthouse was decommissioned, on the very day the first brick had been laid one hundred years previously.

"The very day?"

"The very day. It's the sea, Luca. It does sentimental things to you."

"And now?"

"The lighthouse? It's been abandoned ever since."

We walked the patchwork expanse of black rock and green salt grass on the landward-facing western side, colours so vivid in the hard sun they seemed painted on. We continued around the rest of the island, the lighthouse and its forlorn, peeling whitewash revolving around us, closing a half circle in the east, where Ferris Island tapered to a bow-like, grassy point. Nothing between us and Norway but hundreds of miles of sea.

We ate a quiet picnic as the wind began to rise, a quick darkening in the north. Luca from the forests asked if we should go back to the mainland. That concern again. Trapped on an island.

"We'll be fine."

And like an uncertain invocation, a watery rainbow flared, then vanished, a squall of wind and hard rain quickly upon us, Luca and Emine hurrying after me towards the lighthouse compound, the sea a quickening roil of heavying waves, the three of us soaked now, hurrying through the rotten wooden gate towards the lighthouse itself, a grin on my face, dawning realisation across Luca's as we pressed into the doorway and he saw the key in my hand.

"I found a key years after we had to sell the island. They never did change the locks. Why would they?"

Darkness. Fusty. I found the shelf with the torch and held it under my chin before switching it on. "Boo!" Emine flashed a smile, which, swiftly deleted as it was, she couldn't take back.

I led them through the lighthouse keeper's den.

Bare floorboards and dust. The tracks of little creatures. Up the spiralling echo of the iron staircase to the first floor, the wind muffled and odd sounding, almost thudding, a nearly imperceptible sway of the lighthouse. We reached the first window, a rectangular slit spilling eighteen inches of military grey, a view of nothing but sea and sky that might be sea. "They slept in here, you know. We could do that if you want?" But Emine was already halfway up the ladder to the lantern room, the trapdoor open, letting in more of that ancient light.

We walked slowly around the empty lantern stanchion, two or three times, delight in Emine's eyes that she forgot to hide, considering the three-sixty before deciding which direction to face. We chose east; already the sky was lightening, the squall with a farewell shatter of rain against the dirt-mottled windows. Then weak sun and another brief, ambiguous rainbow.

I was telling them how Granny C. used to paint up here when Luca said something I had to ask him to repeat.

"My wife. She has disappeared."

My first thought, *Really, this was the melodrama you needed, an abandoned lighthouse in a North Sea storm?* My second was guilt about my insistence, how I'd dragged this out of him.

"Her name is Daniela."

"Yes. I see."

He looked uneasy. As if he'd said too much. He waited for me to speak, and I waited for something to say.

The black-purple storm heads moved north. Half an hour later the sea was settling, the wind a lazier skirl, leftover drizzle. I rowed back to the mainland. Luca sat facing me in the stern, arms folded.

We dragged the boat up the shore and I made dinner, glad of the rattle of pots and plates. After, we drank tea outside, dusk emptying the day of the last of its colour, a decanting that showed us how.

"I do not know why this is so difficult," he said.

"How do you mean?"

"I think that talking about it makes it real. If it's real, then it happened. I don't want it to have happened."

I just nodded, even Patti of the Big Mouth knew when to keep it shut. I glanced at Emine. She was looking at her father carefully. As he spoke, I had the impression she'd never heard any of this.

I don't think I saw Luca so animated again. The way he talked about her. Them. His hands and fingers adding detail and nuance. It made me think of a puppet show, Luca and Daniela, his dancing dolls. They met at high school. He was messing about and stumbled into her bench, scattering her books. They both smiled as they picked them up, a starting-gun smile.

With tiresome inevitability, I thought of Frank's goofy grin as he peered down at me in the ditch after I fell off my bike. Didn't we all use someone else's stories as a way back to our own? Luca didn't realise that the ghost dolls of Frank and Patti also worked his stage, parallel lives and different stories: a drab block in outskirt Tirana and our two-bed terrace on the moor's edge, their search for jobs and ours more easily found, workaday Frank and Patti and disheartened Luca and Daniela, running to stand still, who thought about leaving and finally did. The siren call of Western Europe, the flimsiest of hope still hope, even in fume-filled lorries and blacked-out minivans, the terrifying Channel crossing in a leaky dinghy.

"You cannot imagine …"

He was right. My empathy began to feel bogus. I let the Patti and Frank dolls slip into the wings.

"We watched the dawn. All around us were green fields. Then another van. Still north, there is so much north!"

I made no movement. Just an averted gaze. In the distance, the lighthouse, there in the dark, not there.

"It's such a beautiful night."

The gentleness in his voice closed my eyes, briefly. There was Frank and I. Another soft summer night. We're sitting on the patio he built in the back garden. We're arguing. He is very drunk.

Then Luca was standing. Hurrying up the path, into the kitchen. Running water and the clatter of plates.

Across the table, Emine hadn't moved. Then she, too, stood up and went inside. I heard them talking. Albanian mystery words. I looked up to ash grey and the flit of bats, wondering about Daniela. Then Emine. In all that Luca said, he hadn't once mentioned his daughter. I walked up to the cottage and stood at the door, watching him at the dishes. I heard Emine on the stairs.

"It must have been so hard for you both. With Emine, I mean. Taking a young girl all the way across Europe."

He'd stopped scrubbing when I said her name, his face vaguely reflected in the kitchen window.

"It was. It was hard for all of us."

Back to his doleful scrubbings. I walked across to Luca and put my hand on his arm, said something else I wasn't sure I believed. Was it only me who connected more freely with melancholy?

"There's always another side," I said. "You come out on it eventually."

Luca glanced up at the kitchen window. My reflection as indistinct to him as his to me. "Do you really believe that?"

I didn't reply, and we didn't say much else after that. Luca and Emine went to bed, and I went back to Frank and the gulf between things chosen and those we simply let impose.

It was startling how quickly Frank made himself, the two of

us, irrevocable. I'd look out towards the sea, feeling the giant undertow pulling me back towards those black rocks and towering cliffs of convention and anticipated milestones, all the expectations of how to live that had been so repelling while growing up with Granny C. I started talking about getting out of Dodge before we got stuck here forever. Frank was bemused, then offended. I could see the years pass and so could he. But there was a bitter difference in how we felt about that. I started to feel claustrophobic. I glimpsed more often his anger that had always been there.

***

Summer changed its mind again, squalls from the north-east. We couldn't do much on the causeway. Luca clammed up again. I had so many questions I wanted to ask, and I sensed he wanted me to. Yet I didn't. There wasn't anything holding me back, I just didn't and didn't know why.

If I stood there long enough, maybe this woman in my position would lift out of my body, spread like a stain on the ceiling and slowly evaporate, the vaguest of water lines left behind. Then I could finally sigh as Luca sighed, as if the universe had taken a breath, the real deal, none of your angsty sighs in teenage classrooms: "That's it, gie yersel a rest, ya bampot," says the gallus Absolute, "mind the pull aw thae pylons, higher 'n higher, an wan day ye'll finally leave yersel behind an glory be to *me*, folks, if she hasnae jist stepped *beyond ego!*"

Somewhere, Hector laughed:

"Patti does comedy, eh? Beyond ego, that's a good one. Remember that psych-profile and weep. It just isn't in you."

"It isn't?"

"It really isn't."

SIGH

"You're sighing?"

"Well, what is a sigh but a taking of time to … reflect."

Golly gee, I sound so melancholy, but I'm really not. Such heinous allegations have long stalked me. A report card at high school actually said "Patti is prone to melancholy," a young English teacher who decided to see in me a delicate young woman stepped from Brontë to wander these desolate northern shores. A dreamer, though, now that I can agree with. This was noted earlier. Primary school. Another report: "Patti is an inveterate daydreamer," which stumped me for a while because we'd been studying insects and I was pretty sure I had a backbone.

"Nothing wrong with dreaming, don't you ever stop doing that," Granny Causeway said when she read that report. I remembered her ruffling my hair. What a contrast to my frown of a father.

Even before my post-Granny spinout, he was on my back. Ever the pressure of the Disappointed Dad, now the insistence that I "bloody well knuckle down." First, this made me think about gorillas; second, it made me smirk. That sting as he slapped me. My mother was unmoved, sad with the disappointment of what I'd made my father do. She walked it off on another of her endless rambles along the shore. She was never out of my eyeline. I wondered if she was inviting me in or keeping an eye on my empathy the better to run a mile from it.

I wanted to talk to Emine about Mickey Anderson because my mother never would have. I'd looked on the website of last week's *Northern Chronicle* and found the story: "Local man recovering."

Mickey was on solids again. Mickey was a lucky boy. Hector was quoted, hardboiled banalities. "There's always a giveaway … The perp's on notice." And a photo, there was always a photo, the quid pro no quote without a pic. Hector is crouched in Mickey's garden. One hand is *feeling* the grass. He's looking away from the camera, serious.

Mickey Anderson could go fuck himself.

Luca's pause when he told me what nearly happened to Emine. "He wanted to … You can guess." There was a lifetime in that pause. I filled it with troubling details; I couldn't stop myself.

Yet I didn't ask Emine anything, or Luca. *Pry not, Patteeee, let people come to thee.* Not bad self-advice. These aphorisms of mine were ten a penny. Yonder came another. *Under my roof, one will not be aloof.* One to please my mother, that. She wouldn't have held back the snoop. Imagine poor Luca, sat in the kitchen's hard Gestapo light as she fired question after question.

Her need to know was almost pathological. All those lurid "you'll never guesses' and "would you believe its' picked from the soirees of the local business set, sex scandals without the shocking word being uttered. She'd pour details like cheap wine when we, the children whose ears must not hear, were in bed. I'd listen from the stairs, my mother relaying her findings to my father, who'd feign distaste but listen with his own greed, the inversion of their roles creating a strange charge, which was—when I understood such things—*erotic*; she now the authoritative one, the voice oddly deeper, my father with brief interventions that sought salacious details. It explained the cautious bedsprings I sometimes heard later.

So, I wouldn't pry. Luca and I worked when we could, and Emine would watch. We'd have bijou chatettes about the weather and step around the elephants of Daniela and Mickey Anderson. Things happened when they did, Baz said, and they did, which was also down to Baz.

I got a text message:

Bring fish to fry and booze to quaff, between us all we'll have a laff …

Then another:

It's BDHD Time again! Friday night. Sorry, meant to send this msg first.

BDHD. Bazzie's Dad Has Disappeared. This meant his feral father had been shipped to some lucky nursing home for two weeks of respite care. Baz always celebrated with a party. All he wanted was to live in peace, and all he'd got for the last ten years was the task of looking after his sociopath of a father, whose sleazy awfulness I witnessed firsthand one morning when Baz had to drive home to collect something forgotten. His father threw open the door when we arrived, a decrepit scarecrow in a stained white dressing gown open to the naked waist. "Four times married, boy, *four*," he was screaming. "They *loved* a bit of Arthur in them." Then, leering at me, "Even now, even *now*, I *tell* you." For a moment, I believed him.

* * *

Balthasar "Bazzie' Henderson. I loved the man. Thirty-one years (he was proud of this) *zazen* under his extra-large belt and far and away the happiest person I knew, as delighted by the most breathtaking sunset as peeling the cling film from a cheese and pickle sandwich.

"He is so very gentle," his school report card would have said. The gentlest of all are those who stay that way.

And a man of the fringes!

From the frizz-bobbed hair he was always pushing out of his glittery eyes to the house he lived in, the last on a long terrace at the top of the town, perched on the edge of Harrier's Hill, which fell away to the north. When I went to his bathroom, I always looked out the window, a trick of perspective making it seem that I was peering straight down, as if from a high tower, Rapunzel of the sweeping gaze, looking out across the rain-dark roofs, out to sea.

Bazzie greeted Luca and me at the door.

He was wearing army surplus combat trousers and a tight black turtleneck. A Volkswagen badge à la Beastie Boys, 1987, hung from his neck. The combination was so perverse that an outside observer could only have concluded it was deliberate. Yet I had long decided that such outfits somehow *chose* Bazzie, not that this made the effect any less odd, exacerbated tonight by the turtleneck. He looked like a renegade Cluedo character, Mr Implausible.

There was a bear hug for both of us.

"Welcome, welcome, *bienvenue*, come on in!"

Luca grinned, all teeth and uncertainty. Five minutes into the journey over, he'd asked me to turn back. "I'm worried about Emine."

"Emine will be fine," I said, but wasn't completely sure. She'd locked the door when we left. When I looked back, every light had been turned off.

"How're you doing then?" added Baz.

"Good," said Luca.

"Good is good."

"*Mirë se vjen.*"

"What's that then?"

"*Mirë se vjen.* How you say welcome in Albanian."

"Aha!"

And Baz meted out another bear hug, for Luca only this time.

"Mirrysayven."

"*Mirë*—'

"MirrysayVEN!"

Things tended to happen to me at parties. Always that little expectation. Always the stomach churn as I entered a crowded space. Those faces with their instant-recall judgment and expectation of something. Maybe my own anticipation was actually the expectation of theirs, a puzzling logic that I followed tonight down the rabbit hole of "hellos' and "long time no sees."

Most people were outside, standing around the firepit or sitting on Bazzie's mismatched deck chairs. He introduced Luca to a small group beside the picnic table, which offered a gourmet selection of supermarket dips, budget crisps, and an actual cauldron filled with an unknown punch.

He took me aside. "No need to fret, pet. They're AWH."

"They're what?"

""All Welcome Here." The group set up after the flag-shaggers picketed the fish factory? Remember those cunts, "send them home, send them home"? All those Portugeezers and Eastern Euros, they must wonder why the fuck they bothered."

"They probably still do."

"Your boy, by the way. He reminds me of someone."

"He's not my boy."

Baz winked and we re-joined Luca, who was looking bemused in the face of the flailings of an elaborately bearded young man talking about the manufacture of consent. All I could focus on was the glob of taramasalata on the left handlebar of his moustache. He lapsed into a sudden silence that Luca was supposed to fill; he glanced at me with a hint of panic until someone threw him a lifebelt by asking what football team he supported.

"Dinamo! Dinamo Tirana."

"Luca's quite the hit," whispered Baz. "Esteem is *flooowing* your way. But haven't you always made an impression at parties?"

"Shut up."

He was right, though.

Sip the drink, dip the memory stick. That party when Frank and I got together. Granny C. had died a few months previously. I'd been bunking off school. I was very drunk. I told everyone how Frank had rescued me from a ditch, rewarding him with a near-pornographic public snog as Hector looked on with a regret that I decided, in time, was not for his own missed opportunity but a projection of what I would one day feel for what I'd just set in motion.

Then Luca's hand on my shoulder. "Thank you for making me come tonight."

"I didn't make you do anything."

"There are good people here. Good people."

He nodded towards the AWH posse. I wondered if there was a collective noun for a group of activists.

"Do you want to dance?" he asked.

"Dance?"

"Yes, dance."

"Well—'

"Don't think about it too hard. That's what you said to me."

"Well, okay then. Brace yourself."

Had I danced back then, that night with Frank? Maybe I had, as Luca and I now did, a shuffly waltz to Neil Young, "Harvest Moon," Bazzie a big fan, the quintessential music for the pylon lands.

"Will you help me find her?"

He was staring at me very intently. It took me a moment to tune back in.

"My wife. Daniela."

"Yes. I know … Of course."

"Thank you."

He was delighted.

He kissed me quickly on the cheek. My eyes swept the party. Still that teenage urge to see who was looking.

"So where exactly will we be looking then?"

"Glasgow."

A thump in my chest. "You're joking, right?"

"Why would I be joking?"

"Sorry. Ignore me."

"Are you okay?"

"Fine, fine."

"Another?"

He waved his beer bottle and pointed at my empty glass.

"Sure, Mr Luca, another would be dandy."

"Sorry, I—'

"Good! Another would be good!"

He almost skipped away. My eyes shifted, someone staring at me momentarily, then away. The reel switched. Another party. No Frank. Patti is there all by her lonesome and three sheets ahead of the wind. There's Jamie, the blue-eyed boy, across the customary crowded room. Things were falling apart by then anyway, the laboured ascent of a short marriage.

The freefall.

Frank:

"The world. That's what's broken us."

So plaintive.

So bloody irritating.

Yet maybe I once believed it, too, that my shortness of tone, my ever-deepening weariness, were the products not of something truly felt but external circumstance. Maybe Frank's first morning drink and all the others that followed in an unremitting flow were poured not by him but someone he had been compelled to become, the Doppelgänger who told me one night that I'd always been such a "high and mighty bitch," who took the wine glass from my hand another time, when we were sitting on the couch, suddenly bending to kiss me as I pulled away in surprise, the evening I properly noticed the ugliness there all along, from the day at primary school when he pushed the boy into the nettles to the time he punched out that kid for wolf whistling me to the hand now being thrust hard under my skirt and the anger on his face as I jumped up. "Relax, for once just fuckin *relax*."

But it's *hard* to relax, Frank.

Down here.

There's levels on levels below the hospital that have nothing whatsoever to do with the hospital.

Down here, I feel your fingers.

Groping.

Still groping all these years later.

Yet it wasn't painful.

It would not have compared to your pain. I like to think about what you felt. Did unconsciousness reach you before the pain? I really hope it found you anyway. Things will always find you."Twas ever thus.

Now, I feel another pain returning. They are dialling the drugs back. One last heave to bring me up.

I kick my legs.

I am not sure this was an *active* choice.

I sink.

I resist but lift.

The beginnings of a return?

That's not what worries me.

Katie Nurse shrugs.

Endings are what you make them.

But infamy, infamy, everyone's got it infamy!

And those histrionic nostrils of Kenneth Williams are just so appropriate for the paranoia of lying here immobile in a hospital bed. The Fishwife whisper-slander, *"She's a weirdo, a vicious fuckin' bitch,"* it comes across as a prelude to a lynching, a pillow over the face, my little tootsies wiggling a furious farewell, forgive me for not painting my toenails for the trip.

Another wee *comic aside* there, Katie Nurse, get ye out there and spread the word, spread the *word*, invalidate the idea, long-written in dusty local scripture, that Patti Letham was never the light-hearted type, wouldn't know a joke if the punchline came in the mail, etcetera.

A total travesty!

I decided many fools' moons ago that it would be a waste of time to correct the stereotype."Tis a historical given that no one learns a damn thing from history. Antisemitism, Islamophobia, homophobia, sort out one prejudice and there's another, another, then back comes the first, it's like Whac-a-Mole, a man in skin-tight Lurex and boa saying "don't be so gauche," *whack*, a hook-nosed man astride the world dancing puppets on a string, *whack*.

The Two Fishwives are all a-bluster. *"Hark at the delusionist! To see her experience as akin to antisemitism!"*

Well, I'm truly sorry, be Gentile with me. See, more jokes! Well, you can't please all the fuckers all the time, one woman's guffaw is another's chutzpah. Another, *boom*! I wish only to emphasise that I care *not* what is thought of me, attitudes in these parts being essentially unchangeable despite any façades of forgiveness that may have periodically been erected and—

Hands!

Hands under me.

The world lurches and I feel an instant nausea, the strangest sense of falling away on both sides.

I think I have been sat up in bed. Yet nothing else seems to be happening. Nothing and no one is touching me. They're still *there*. I'm certain, I think I'm certain. I can sense proximity.

They're here to peer at the freak.

Can I forgive them?

Can anyone?

Here's another case study:

My brother Raymond. Bullied at secondary school by one Derek Gibson, a yokel from some back-country village. As a persecuted minority, Derek responded in classic fashion by becoming an arsehole all of his own. Poor Raymond endured the head flush, the dead arms and, a new one for the *Oxford English Dictionary*, the *Johnny Eggy* (n): the vicious rap of knuckles on top of someone's unsuspecting head. As in, *He gave him a proper few Johnny Eggies, like.*

All this for *five years*, twelve to sixteen, when Derek left school to fulfil his destiny on the fish lines at the local processing plant. Raymond was left with relief and shame, a bitterness that faded in time but didn't altogether disappear, the memories still sneering at him now and then.

Then, years later, Raymond found himself on a near-deserted railway platform with one other person. Derek. Instantly, Raymond was twelve again and ready to flee, but Derek was already on his way over and Raymond braced for the dead leg that instead became a heartfelt, "I'm so sorry for being such a bully at school, can you forgive me?" "It was a long time ago," replied Raymond, "of course I do." But when they got on the train, he went straight to the toilet and burst into tears, silently screaming *Fuck you, Derek,* over and over into the mirror.

Forgiveness?

Maybe some indeed have that elusive little New Testament gene. I fear that most prefer the more savage assurances of the previous edition. It's easier to be a vengeful psycho, and way more entertaining. Two millennia may have passed, but the ink's still wet on the Good Book, I imagine it running down my face as the Two Fishwives take turns to batter me with it.

See how *she* likes it.

But my vengeance was never biblical, although it was just as much of a blunt instrument.

I wake violently.

As if someone has just shoved me.

The slow fade of something that sounds like *axe, axe, axe, axe* …

My fists are gripping the sheet, and I try to move them to my crotch. To protect myself from Frank?

I try to pull away again.

There are tiles on the ceiling.

One is cracked at the corner.

Is that where they peer down from? My eyes close, I see a flash of light, someone lighting a cigarette.

Then darkness.

This darkness.

It is oddly small.

Tiny planets drifting, bubble-faces of Frank, my mum, Granny C., too often it is Hector, winking as he passes, always that treacherous burst of lust I have long given up making excuses for. He feels it, too, *bien sur*, but Hector is too arrogant to apologise for anything he feels.

Then there's Jamie. He, too, is always orbiting.

I think about him.

About them.

Thinking and therefore not asleep. There have been whole periods of my life when sleep or consciousness would have made no difference to my essential functioning. All of this feels so familiar.

Life is what happens when you're busy making other plans? Not really, Mr Lennon, life is what happens when you're busy doing fuck all. Yet my soundtrack is not the Beatles. My soundtrack is these beeping machines, like dissonant electronica. Makes me feel cold, cold and getting colder, maybe I'm not waking at all, these lucid flashes not awakenings but closings.

Y'know, death …

I shall, I shall, I *shall* make one final effort to speak. I shall roll out the deathbed line of a thousand films.

I feel so cold.

I'm laughing. I can't stop myself. Maybe I'll die of laughter.

It's hurting my ears.

I feel like I'm twitching.

Maybe the Two Fishwives have clocked it, maybe they're standing open-mouthed, peering down at my smile, big 'n' cheesy as a half-Camembert as they wrongly decide that she's waking, Patti Letham is waking, racing to tell Hector, who stalks in wearing the robes of a King's Counsel, eyes up and down my body, gaze lingering shamelessly in the places they always have.

Then the briefest of soft lips on my ear. I can't help a smile, and he says, *"By thine actions will thee be known,"* swiftly taking a picture on his mobile phone and standing quickly up and away.

He's wearing a wig! But courtroom wigs are a ludicrous English affectation, not Scottish! He's decided this supplies more *gravitas*, which may have succeeded if it weren't too small, perched on his bonce like a kippa. He speaks:

"I, Hector Ruthven, will present clear evidence, dear jurors, of Ms. Letham's toddler-like lack of remorse for her psychological, yes, but more critically, her physical assaults. For verily and thoroughly must we always remember, that is, see, my poor ... blind ... brother. These, the myriad inflictions of Letham, will remorselessly be laid bare as a baboon's bum cheeks."

Hector pirouettes dramatically, his wig flying off like a frisbee to land on the lap of a gleeful old woman, who strokes it with the remembrance of penis's past, Hector generously trailing a finger along her papery hand as he retrieves it, tossing the wig high and landing it back on his head, shouting, *"Extraordinary, I know, I know, yet not as extraordinary as Letham here, for who, whoooo would smirk in her situation yet smirk she did, the evidence here, here, a photograph on my own phone, damning evidence of the skulking psychopath."*

He pauses:

"Are you shocked, my good cheese-burghers?"

"Shocked by what she is."

"She who roamed elsewhere for lusts that were here all along, but clearly she was far too good for them."

Dear god, this death thing.
Who'd have thought it could be so bloody funny?
It takes the blues away.

Luca, Emine, and me in my beat-up Corsa. The Big Road south. The A9. How many years since I'd driven it?

Instead of telling me, if Luca had asked me to guess where his wife Daniela might be, I could only have said Glasgow. Before Glasgow there had been a *crack*. That's how the light gets in, Leonard Cohen sang. But cracks let in other things too. Yes, it could only have been Glasgow. That was how the world turned, ever-decreasing circles to where you'd always been.

Jamie Wright.

Instead of Luca, I pictured my blue-eyed ghost boy in the passenger seat. I didn't let him stay.

I had to work my way back there.

That *crack*.

I had to stop calling it that. One was *not* a melodramatic type, one was *sophisticado*, right? Time had softened the sound anyway. Now it was less Zorro's whip than the tired snap of something brittle.

Luca stared ahead, Emine out the side window, be-hooded in the rearview mirror. I turned on the radio. The Beach Boys. Luca turned with a weak smile, as if the tension I had to break with music was his fault. I tried my own. I tried not to think of Jamie Wright.

Outside, a train moved along the rail track running parallel to the road. A mile or so of glancing faces, a waving child. Then it edged ahead and was gone. If only everything vanished in silver.

Luca, again the same question:

"Are you really sure you want to do this?"

"Stop asking! Of course I do. I'm beginning to wonder if you want me to."

"I do."

"Really?"

"I do."

Luca's eyes that said no, that said yes, that went back to fixed contemplation of the road ahead.

"You haven't told me how long it's been since Daniela, you know …"

"Disappeared? Just over a year. Fourteen months. I wonder if there is any point."

"Of course there is … right?"

Emine said something in Albanian. Luca tensed and ignored her. She repeated the words *very slowly*, and I didn't need to know the language to understand the sarcasm. He muttered something in reply. It had been like this for days, a mutually simmering resentment.

They both slumped moodily, mad Brian Wilson was singing, and wouldn't it be nice to know what the issue was as we zipped past another sign pointing south, *south*, SOUTH. I was fifteen again, a four-hour bus journey and a bottle of Mad Dog 20/20, strawberry, of course. That first trip to the Big Smoke, I remembered my excitement but let it segue into another journey and an altogether different kind of suspense, a memory long prone to uncertainty. Were we ever in Jamie's BMW? Was that hand ever on my knee, moving under my skirt?

When I glanced in the rearview, Emine was looking at me with curiosity. *Why Patti?* the deep brown eyes were asking. Why Patti who took us in, and not one of the local worthies? Right on! They deserved the solidarity of homemade chicken soup and not my budget tins. They deserved compassion unnuanced, goddammit, the camaraderie of a WhatsApp group, no hour in the day left unsupported. They deserved people who knew how to be normal.

We came off the motorway and headed up Great Western Road. Sandstone streetscapes in the afternoon gloom. My memory kicked in like rows of lights being switched on in a vast, dark room.

The holy melancholy of remembrance, stasis and flux under a sky that was always a little too close in Glasgow, a heavy grey that started just beyond the tenement roofs and made those occasional, blue summer days so giddy, the city reaching out into the relief of open space.

The Parkside Hotel looked like it existed on a host of memories that had been misplaced a long time ago. Part of a Victorian terrace, it was half hidden behind a line of plane trees and a low wall, the façade tired and the flower beds unkempt. I had stayed here twice before, that being the reason I booked the hotel this time, a mistaken indulgence.

A sad-eyed, scarlet-lipped young woman named Alicja checked us in. She looked through me as I thanked her, pointing to the stairs with such profound gloom that I wondered what was waiting up there. It turned out to be a faded tourist board poster on the grubby landing wall.

The familiar Mr Happy and his slogan: "Glasgow's Miles Better!"

"What do you reckon, Emine, miles better than it used to be, or miles better than anywhere else in the world?"

She shrugged. "Cities play tricks. They all pretend to be different, but in the end, they are just the same."

She was too young for that kind of cynicism; I remembered how thrilling it was, leaving home and arriving in a new city, the anticipation. Then I thought about small boats and the freezing, terrifying blackness of the English Channel, journeys made through compulsion rather than choice. She stopped at a door and said, bluntly, "Our room." I had been dismissed.

The hotel didn't encourage you to hang around. We dumped our bags. I took them across to Kelvingrove Park and past the university onto Byres Road. Down a lane, rain sent us into a café-bar and a surge of memory. I'd been here, I thought, a drink before my brothers' graduation.

Luca:

"It's nice round here. Lots of green."

"It's the "Dear Green Place," Mr Luca. Where did you live when you were here?"

"Southside. Govanhill."

"Said like a local. How do we do this, Luca?"

"Do what?"

"Daniela. How do we start? I'm guessing we don't just walk round asking random people questions?"

"No, no. We drive. We drive around. To see what we can see. Emine cannot come. She stays in the hotel."

"Okay then. Tomorrow we … go looking."

The blue-eyed ghost nudged me. I went looking for him, too, once. I picked up my wine and washed him down.

"What were the colour of her eyes?"

"Daniela? You mean what *are* the colour of her eyes?"

"Of course. I'm sorry."

"Blue."

"Why are you smiling?"

"I knew they'd be blue."

"They were more bluey-green," said Emine. "Like the sea. When I think about Daniela, I think about the sea."

When she went to the bathroom, Luca leaned over:

"There is no green in her eyes. None at all. They are blue. *Blue*. These details, they are important."

"Okay, okay, but come on, what are you *really* trying to say, Luca, out with it. That her eyes are what … *blue*?"

"Yes, why is that—'

"I'm joking."

"Fine."

"But you're sure, yeah? About the blue I mean?"

"Yes!"

I saw Granny C. in the lighthouse, writing her poem: *There is no attraction. Just blue eyes that might have looked, once.*

Luca sipped his beer. Three quick sips, a pause, three more. He stared into space, frowning to some internal movie. Emine returned, bent to the table and slurped her Coke through the straw. I wondered if she was thinking about her mother, her mother she had called Daniela.

I never called my mother Janine. Or my father Lachlan. Granny C., on the other hand, told me to call her Deborah, Debbie, whatever I wanted. Just to annoy my parents, I was sure. "There's no need to stand on ceremony, my dear, we are all equals here." And a quick wink.

So occasionally, which was enough to infuriate my father, I called her Debbie, a brazen error of convention he corrected on the day of her funeral. It may have been my first, but fifteen-year-old Patti knew a dismal eulogy when she heard it, the oh-so-bleak whittling to the banal of an offbeat firecracker of a woman, my father staring at me as he emphasised, "The *grandmother* adored by her grandchildren." I knew she was dying but was unprepared for the haemorrhage of vitality that followed. The light never seemed quite as bright again.

I looked at Luca and thought about the difference between a vanishing you saw coming and one you didn't.

* * *

The next morning, we headed to the Southside. Rolls and square sausage in the overheated car. Pouring summer rain.

Luca directed as I drove. Street to street and back again,

rain-streaked pavements, mobile phone shops and shady money transfer places, bakeries, board-ups, and vape emporiums, Zainab's Fashions and a pound shop selling "necessities and novelties," *"Roll up for your rainbow lightbulbs and barking door knobs,"* an austere Halal butcher next door to Milan's Mini-Market, the windows full of overly colourful posters of so many Slovak salamis. There were few people: some pram-mums and the inevitable old woman with the scarf and trolley; a group of sombre, bored teenagers smoking outside the Magazin Traditional Romanesc; the striking unexpectedness of a beautiful man in an immaculate, electric-blue kurta under the awning of Lahore Travel, a questioning hand outstretched for the cold rain.

"There. That's it."

As I slowed, Luca told me to "speed up, speed up," looking back over his shoulder, then saying "stop here."

"What are we looking at?"

"Back there. Flat four, second floor. We could smell the shisha from the restaurant downstairs."

"That's where you stayed?"

"When we got here, it was the middle of the night. We were exhausted. Three hours later, they took us to the factory. At night they took us back. Over and over, shisha and shisha. Apples and strawberries. I wanted to go down there, just us. A wonderful meal. Daniela would be laughing, the smoke making her dizzy. We would go back to the flat and there would only be us."

"How many were in there with you?"

"Too many."

He turned to me. "I can remember the way from here."

I pulled out. Still the rain. The backland commercial units and edgeland no-goes, fenced-off "To Lets," grassed-over acres of forgotten hardstanding. The phantom factories of sad-eyed industrial Glasgow; car hire places and drab funeral parlours; low-slung, one-storey pubs all brick and no windows, the stunted old men smoking outside, never seen in the days before the ban, ever-leathered in more ways than one, staring forever in the city of the stare.

"The van took us this way every morning. We left at five in the morning, back at seven at night."

"Every day?"

"You think there was time off?"

"None at all?"

"Once every few weeks. Nothing regular. We wanted to come to Scotland, and we saw nothing but these streets. We couldn't go anywhere. We wanted mountains, you know, whisky, men in skirts."

"Whatever floats your boat."

"It's what you hear about! It's what we wanted. You tell me."

"Tell you what?"

"Tell me what you think about when you think of Albania."

"If I tell you, does it mean I want it?"

"Just tell—'

"Okay then, goats."

"Goats?

"Yup."

"Anything else?"

"Gangsters in bad tracksuits."

Luca started to laugh. Making me laugh too.

"You know what? My grandmother did have goats. A little farm in our mountain village. Maybe I, too, think of goats when I think of Albania. When I told the man in Tirana where I came from, he said I will love Scotland, they have mountains as well. But he didn't have a tracksuit. Stop here!"

I pulled to the kerb. Luca leaned across, a finger pointing out the window. "That place. There."

I looked across the road. More hardstanding, a scruffy red-brick building behind it like an oversized, abandoned petrol station, pumps removed from the forecourt. A series of lowered black-metalled shutters ran along the façade. The sign on the low roof said "Supreme Meats."

"Look. Isn't it a place of such *hope*?"

I turned to Luca's sarcastic amazement, his wide and rolling eyes, a shaking of his head. "Isn't it *beautiful*, Patti? That's the luxury hotel we paid six thousand Euros to come and work at. Can you imagine?"

I couldn't. Although I was desperate to escape my own hometown, it was never going to end in dead meat. My horizon that approached from the Citylink coach worked a straight line, not Luca's Euro zigzag. Nothing forced me onto that bus, it wasn't the back of a lorry with thirty strangers trying not to think about those stories of people suffocating, who swayed against each other in the dark like the carcasses on hooks they didn't know were waiting for them.

"It was six in the morning. That first day. They took us out, ten of us. Then they split us up. This way for women, this way for men. I only saw Daniela when we got back in the van in the evening."

"What about Emine?"

"Emine?" He hesitated. "I think she was too young to work. They waited. They kept her in the flat."

"All day?"

"Of course! All day. *Every* day. Then there was one day. Daniela wasn't there when we got back in the van."

"She wasn't at the flat?"

"No."

"Was that the last time you saw her?"

He looked straight at me. I saw the troubling. He looked away.

Back at the hotel, Emine was sitting cross-legged on her bed, staring at a muted TV. She hadn't left the room. She had put the Do Not Disturb sign on the door, but the cleaner, an "ancient woman," came in anyway. She had made the cleaner a cup of tea. Tea and a bit of the room's complimentary shortbread. They watched a show about antiques and the woman called her "hen."

"Do I look like a hen?"

Luca was confused. He had a plastic bag in each hand full of chocolate, crisps, and sundry treats bought for Emine on the way back that he slowly raised, shrugging, almost to shoulder level.

The afternoon took us to Kelvingrove Art Gallery. I stared at Dalí's *Christ of Saint John of the Cross* but imagined Luca's bags hanging from the hands. A saviour indeed, Cost Saver, two budget supermarket bags full of two for ones on instant noodles, who wants bread and fishes these days.

"That is a terrible, terrible sin, Patti!" Luca was wagging a finger.

"What is?"

"Laughing at Jesus. My grandmother with the goat? She would tie you to a stake, throw stones at you."

"Not just your grandmother. Listen? Do you hear that?"

"What?"

"That whirring noise. It's my mother in her grave. I've heard her get up to forty spins a minute."

"My grandmother could make fifty."

We headed to the café. Drank Ethiopian coffee and ate homemade cakes, surrounded by all those things that never happened; a battered people carrier outside a meat processing plant, a husband ordered one way and a wife the other, a daughter locked in a flat. Under these chandeliers, in refined hubbub, we convinced ourselves that beauty still existed. Here, it was safe. Here, Luca passed me a photo. Daniela was smiling. Medium close-up. Long brunette hair in a breeze. The background was split diagonally from top right to bottom left. Blue sky and green hillside. She wore a yellow shirt and long silver earrings.

"She's beautiful."

Emine sniffed and got up.

I watched her. She walked only on the blue tiles of the patterned floor, zigzagging her way towards the galleries on the other side of the central hall. I realised she was copying a much younger child, who then noticed with delight that Emine was doing what she was. For a brief, beautiful moment, you could see the transference, each the other, happy.

"She must miss her mother."

Again, Luca's hesitation. Every time I mentioned Emine and Daniela. "She does. We both do."

He took the photo and put it back in his pocket.

We walked back through Kelvingrove Park, towards Great Western Road, but none of us ready for the hotel.

I suggested a pub, The Doublet.

Emine went exploring instead, my twenty pounds accepted with delight. I took the drinks to a nook at the far side of the bar. I asked Luca about Daniela so I could think about someone else.

We drank some more.

We drank to the ongoing possibility of Daniela. He started talking about her eyes again. "It was the way they …" He seemed to come across himself. The flush became more of an embarrassed red. He picked up his drink. Three quick sips. "It was the way they … You know what I mean?"

"I do. I *do*." I nodded, emphasising my agreement. For Patti had guzzled three drinks and everything was becoming definitive. She existed, I wanted Luca to say, her blue eyes and how they shone, but only for you and everyone knew it. "It is *not* ridiculous to talk about eyes, Luca."

We lapsed into jukebox silence.

The Pogues "Fairytale of New York' in mid-June, someone at another table reliving another broken something. So many private, mid-distance matinees when you started to look: to the right a puce-faced, middle-aged man as out of time as his suit; over there an elderly woman, face so overly made-up I doubted she would recognise herself in a mirror. Maybe that was the point.

I hit the sweet point of drunkenness. I knew *exactly* why Jukebox Man's second choice was "Chance' by Big Country. Then a thump on the table as Luca slammed down a piece of paper, a flyer. He was in the process of sitting down, but I hadn't noticed him get up in the first place.

"Parkgrove Sauna and Massage?"

"It was at the bar. Beside the newspapers. I used to collect these. You'd be surprised how many there are."

"That day I got into the van after the factory. When Daniela wasn't there and wasn't at the flat. They said we owed money. She was pretty, she could make money. They said, "Don't you understand?"'

"My god, Luca."

"When you start to look, you see these everywhere. But you never see anyone pick them up. It is strange, Patti. I used to wait. We could sit here *forever* and not one of them will be picked up. I wanted to see who did, what they looked like. I wanted to follow them. I wanted to see their lives."

"I'm … I don't know what to say."

He shrugged. "What's to say? That's the way it is. They said that. "That's the way it is, so don't look for her, Luca, no peekaboo. It would be bad for her." But they fucked up. They moved us from the factory to a car wash. The police came and got everyone except me. Even the boss man. Everyone but me."

The "me' emphasised by driving his fist into his hand. Like a *crack*.

I flinched.

That *crack* that came before Jamie Wright.

I was instantly there again:

Frank is pacing up and down the patio, his anger discolouring an ethereal, pale-pink sunset. "That fear you might be trapped? You were right, you were fuckin' right, thanks so much for that, Patti."

I see everything very, very distinctly. Frank's right arm pulls back to the shoulder. His right hand has become a fist. At the same time, his left arm drops down, slightly out from his side, balancing the weight of the other side of his body. He looks surprised, as if he can't quite believe the motions his own body is going through. I notice the lower half of the thumbnail on his right fist is discoloured. Then he makes up his mind, accepting the significance of whatever justification has drawn his arm back in the first place. The fist drives forward, smacking my left cheek with that gunshot *crack*, and I drop to the patio, now feeling him pummel the top of my head, his fists swinging in and out, epic parabolas that will inexorably lead to Glasgow, to a taxi and Jamie and me, pressed together, my hand moving to his thigh, a question and an insistence, the taxi that dropped us off at this very pub.

And now:

Luca was still staring into the mid-distance.

Painted Lady and Jukebox Man still quietly sat. I felt such a crushing sadness. My breaking heart.

I put my hand on top of Luca's. "I just want you to know …"

I hit the brakes before skidding into the bullshit. Luca's expectant face demanded more than the leaden empathy I was about to offer. And I couldn't help wondering about *his* capabilities, all those things you never think about until you're watching a stranger and swallowing hard. Just ask Mickey Anderson. A father would do anything for his daughter, right?

I used to imagine what my father would have done had I told him what Frank did. I even decided on a setting for the revelation: the Shore House dining table, Sunday lunchtime. Nothing was more suitable; that weekly ritual of mutual resentment was very important to us.

"How was your week, Mr Letham?"

"Just fine, Frank, yours?"

"Oh, you know, you know."

"But I don't, son."

"Sorry, sir. Fine. It was fine."

"And fine is good. Fine is consistent. How about you, dear Patti?"

"Well, Frank beat the shit out of me."

A pregnant pause, likely quadruplets in there.

"What!"

Expectant, *eager*, we all turn to my father as he slowly stands. His eyes fix on a shrinking Frank. My father wants to speak but can't. For the moment, he can only chew the roast beef my mother always overcooks; he's annoyed he can't swallow and starts chewing faster, red in the face, the moment's wasting! But by some herculean act of mastication, he forces it down. He reaches for his wine and takes a slug before sombrely raising the glass.

"To you, Frankie my boy. To the cojones I never knew you had."

We scramble to our feet, glasses in the air, even me, as bashful Frank beams, lands a playful fist on my chin.

* * *

Luca had a list of parlours. He'd checked them out a year back. Waited outside for hours to see if she appeared, and eventually went inside all of them, where, frantic, he asked too many questions and was swiftly ejected. The next day, we drove round them again. Some were boarded up, some vape shops or bookies, sex the big seller that kept moving, one step ahead of the police. A couple of places remained. We parked outside. Waited for the miracle of Daniela.

I watched a young man in a baseball cap and white jeans go inside one place. A skip up the steps, he'd been there before, *"Seventy for whatever you want, son."* He's out in less than twenty, an appetite now, Istanbul Kebab across the street does a crackin' chicken shish … I pictured Daniela sitting quietly inside. All those men, maybe he's one who keeps coming back. He likes her, tells her this because he thinks it makes it better when he does things to her.

Luca shook his head. Leaned back and closed his eyes. Leaned forward and peered out the windscreen. "Look at all these windows. She could be up there, or there. What's the point sitting here?"

"You said there were other places."

"That's the problem. All the other places we'll find and won't find. We're wasting our time."

"We're bloody *not!*"

I was surprised by my vehemence.

"You know what the problem is, Luca? It's normal. There's nothing fucked-up about normal. It's like going to the dentist. Can you imagine it? Hearing them come in, sitting in a waiting room for their turn. Then *knock, knock.* Here's a fucker, here's another, all the fuckers in all the world."

He opened the passenger door and got out. I thought he was going to march over to the massage place, but he just strode down the street. No jacket, striding into the rain. I shuffled across and opened the window, shouting at him to come back. He slowed. Then stopped in the middle of the pavement with his face to the sky, people sidestepping him, staring …

He walked back to the car and bent to the open window. "I looked for her. All winter. Night and day, all these streets. I saw her on every single one. Now I see her again." And again he strode away.

I let him go without a word.

I got the futility of what we were doing. His hope. Coming back was hearing Daniela's steps around that corner, seeing her in a shop trailing her fingers along a rack of clothes, a face in a taxi and the familiarity in a stranger's walk, the downy hair on the back of a neck.

I made a three-point turn and drove down the street he'd turned into. I saw him up ahead and slowed to his speed. When he stopped, I stopped. He bent back down to the window.

"Sorry."

"There's no need for sorry, Luca."

"There is one more place I need to go. Is that okay?"

He directed me farther west. Rain was still drowning the city. Streets heavy with traffic. A bleak, spilling light.

He told me left, then right, straight on, no-nonsense. I imagined him following a hundred different sets of directions from a hundred different starting points to reach the same destination. He stared out the windscreen. Now and then, he'd turn to look back at something just passed, something remembered or something triggered, a private agitation.

"Here. Just coming up. Stop in front of that car."

I did as I was told and killed the engine. I looked at him looking along a line of cheerless tenements.

"That one. Two doors up."

His left hand was gesticulating. It stayed in the air, still pointing at the tenement as he turned to me. "That was the last place I saw her."

"Here?"

"Yes. Right here."

I looked at the black mouth of the close. Up to dirty net

curtains. Bitten-away sandstone windowsills.

"I was told there was a place. I came day after day, and one day I saw her, can you believe it? At a window. That one there, you see? I came back the next day. I was going to wait for her to come out. All day. If she didn't come out, I was going to go in and get her. I had a hammer. In my pocket! Can you imagine that? Luca the Big Man ready to take on the gangsters! But when I walked up the street, I saw tape across the door. The tape that police use. "Do not cross."'

He peered back at the tenement. "I'm sure I saw her." Then again, a few moments later:

"I'm sure."

I was glad that I held back from saying what I could have, what I wanted to, how spectacularly ill-chosen it would have been to tell him about my blue-eyed boy, to suggest any kind of equivalency.

Static Between Tracks

We headed north from Glasgow. Squalls in the mountain lands, sombre as a Béla Tarr movie, the odd, tantalising sky-pastel, there and gone. I glanced at Luca. I wondered about things extinguished.

Our mid-afternoon return came with an unexpected warmth, a quietude that made a refinement of things. I stood in the garden, gazing into deep-focus compositions, the shifting, elegant sea. A fragile affinity for this place stirred, a rare sense of well-being waiting for the deflation.

"Long time no speak, sis! Hope all's well."
I had rejected the call and waited for the message. My brother Raymond. A call from one of my brothers would be followed up with one from the other an hour or so later. The pattern was long-established and coordinated. I let the second also go to a message:
"Pick up, Patti, we're worried."
I was two when they appeared. I couldn't remember their arrival but told myself I did, one on each of my delighted father's arms. *"Say hello to your little brothers!"* One of these creatures was bad enough, two seemed like a personal attack. As I gazed upon the identikit humpty-dumpties, my little face must have puckered. It did, after all, become my default expression whenever they were around, as if I'd just funnelled fifty grams of sherbet into my gob.
Years later, I learned my mother had spent three months recovering in hospital, an exhausted heifer on the barn floor, coming home with hip pain that she bore stoically for the rest of her life, never one to complain. This absurd generational fortitude infuriated me when I was old enough to properly think about it. I wanted her to fling her fury at the two boys whose intelligence and physical qualities would have instantly doubled had there been only one of them. Not that I lacked sibling warmth. They just made it so hard, like when they were hauled in front of the headmaster for papering the classroom door of their physics teacher with sticky wrappers from those liquorice sweeties, Blackjacks. Naturally, the first thing Mr Fry did was make everyone line up and open their mouths. The image often

came to mind when I thought about them: two sweaty faces, two lolling black tongues.

I put the phone down.

Luca was expectant. "Everything okay?"

My face must have been doing the sherbet pucker thing. Did they have gurning competitions in Albania?

"My brothers."

"I didn't know you had brothers! I have no brothers. Or sisters. I always wanted them. It is a shame."

"Is it?"

"Isn't it?"

They were coming. Ray and Keith. Fannies in their Armanis. The question was why, and Hector the answer:

"There's someone staying with your sister, boys."

Cookies Chinese did deliveries. High-speed drop-offs by an amphetamine-thin young guy in shades, more souped-up than his yellow Golf. When I heard the distant, pounding bass, I knew he'd reached the car park, and I set the table. Moments later, he was twitching and grinning on the doorstep.

Emine ate in the living room, watching her blooper shows, me and Luca in the garden. Sunset skies. Shades of honey and lemon. Washed-out watercolour blues becoming darker. It made you nostalgic, indulgent. Sweet and sour chicken the perfect accompaniment. Memories steeped in monosodium glutamate. Moreish, keeping you awake too long.

"Thank you for helping me," he said. "You didn't need to do that."

"There's still a chance, you know."

He looked at me hard, then relaxed. "You're right, you're absolutely right." But he didn't mean it.

"Can I ask you something?"

"Sure."

"After the police raid, when they arrested everyone at the car wash, how did you get Emine out of the flat?"

For a moment he looked as if he didn't know what I was talking about.

"I went back and waited awhile, to see. But there was no one there. Just Emine. The place was empty."

"Where did you go?"

"We slept out a few nights and then I found people that could help us. A charity. They had a flat we stayed at."

"That must have been such a relief."

"It was like a gift."

"I can imagine." Luca was a terrible liar. I hated myself for picturing Hector: *"Look for what's not being said."* Maybe I was too old to care about being lied to. Or maybe that was just what I expected. He gazed seawards. He'd attempt to shift the perspective, but he knew I knew.

"Tomorrow will be a good day to work on the stones," he said. "High pressure, reasonably settled weather."

"What, you're a weatherman now?"

"The TV man told me. Perhaps you could show me how to fix them. The stones. With the stuff?"

"The mortar? I could do that."

"Really."

"Of course."

I went with it, his delight and my own. I pressed fast-forward and ten years flew by, the causeway long complete, but who's *that* still sitting there, well if it ain't old Luca, a thousand evenings of beef in black bean sauce come and gone, the same two grains of rice on his stubbly chin.

"Did someone teach you?"

"Teach me what?"

"To build the causeway. How did you know what to do?"

"I had some people to help me at the start. They taught me the basics and I got better as I went along."

"I'm impressed."

"Just don't look too close at the stones closest to the shore."

Inside the house the phone began to ring. Luca glanced round, but I just gave a dismissive wave.

"Just my brothers."

"How do you know?"

"I know."

"Are you not going to answer?" He started to gather up the plates and the empty trays of food.

"Nope."

He tutted and walked back up to the cottage. "You should be grateful, Patti."

"You haven't met my brothers!"

I went outside. The midsummer dark. In the lull of wind,

Emine's raised voice and a slamming door. Luca appeared at the door briefly. A light came on in Spider-Girl's room in Shore House. I closed my eyes, the surf a whisper. I saw Ray and Keith playing their computer games.

Frank would join in.

Frank who became my brothers' Big Influence when Hector left town. Frank who loved that role. Frank who wanted it to continue after the twins left for university, the intrepids who flew the nest but were back most weekends, their contempt growing both for Frank—who wanted to play the same shoot-'em-ups— and me, Big Sis stuck there in the old hometown. "You and Frank, you'll never change."

The superiority remained, in every phone message urging me to call back or the periodic, tiresome inevitability of them turning up in their flash cars to "check I was doing okay." I never reminded them I, too, could have left. I wouldn't have been able to stand their pity.

So Ray and Keith got the scholastic robes. On graduation day, we raised our glasses as high as we could to a miracle that almost faltered getting them into university in the first place but spluttered through *six academic years* before collapsing at the feet of third-class business degrees.

What intellectual prowess!

My parents had never been so proud. Frank was there too. It was two months after "that night," as he called it.

His attention was oppressive. I flinched at his touch, but he kept saying he didn't mean it, he was so sorry and I knew it'd never happen again, right? And I hadn't left, so that meant I'd stay, right, "We'll find a way past that night, won't we?" Perhaps he was right. I started calling it "that night' too. Maybe it was the aberration "that night' made it. The thing is, I did leave, every night. I lay in bed and planned it. I made so many plans. I made new ones after I was introduced to Jamie Wright during post-ceremony drinks in the university cloisters.

A handshake for Frank and me both.

The eyes only for me.

"*Finally*. Nice to meet you, Patti. I've heard so much about you. Here's to your brothers. Here's to you too." Our champagne flutes met with a clink so profound it could have been called a tinkle.

That "finally."

I decided it was the equal and opposite reaction to what Frank had done. I knew I liked him because I instantly decided not to. That way he was good-looking and funny? The Neptune-blue eyes? Yet there was an ease to him, a disarming grace, such a contrast to Frank, the reluctant attendee, skulking moodily behind endless re-fizz and bacon-wrapped figs.

"You know I've got an internship with your dad? I'm coming north, you'll have to show me all the sights."

"I'm sure that can be arranged. When are you moving?"

"Couple of months."

It felt like the premonition of something significant, a slow train arriving that I hadn't realised I'd been waiting for. Those premonitions. I used to wish for them, once. To be able to see what was coming down the line! But you found whatever you wanted if you decided to look, angel or demon, trauma or delight, whatever significance you decided you deserved.

A gull screamed.

I started to shiver. I looked back up at Spider-Girl's bedroom, the light now off. A distant dog barked, and the wind started to pick up. I wanted to be back in Glasgow. To sit in those pubs and fully remember. To be as Luca was when I went back inside. That haunted nobility.

***

Luca's weatherman was right. The next day was a good day for the stones. He was up before me, a plate of scrambled eggs set down as soon as I appeared in the kitchen. A determined lightness.

"I went to the garage for eggs. Oh, and these." Hurrying into the hall and coming back with a bunch of flowers.

"You shouldn't have."

"You don't want them?"

"No, of course I do. Thank you."

He sat down opposite me. Watched me as I ate, then realised he was watching me and looked away.

"We can go back to Glasgow. Anytime you want, Luca. There's no telling—'

"There's no point."

"There's always a point, it's just a matter—'

His lightness shattered.

"*Patti!*"

I felt bad for my breezy insistence on hope.

"I'm sorry. I didn't mean to upset you."

"I know what you're saying, okay? She has to be somewhere, right? Maybe she's still there. But for now …" He swung an arm round, taking in me, the kitchen, the shapeshifting clouds on limitless blue beyond the window and beyond even that, taking it all in, the whole world that kept turning and insisting, moving on, keeping him one step ahead of the sadness I'd brought right back.

Cue the parents, up on the promontory in their grubby urns. The impeccable timing of their merry slander:

"Never could help herself, our Patti."

"That she couldn't."

"Always something contrary about her, they'd have had her on the Witch's stool three hundred years back."

"Her granny's doing."

"You mean your mother?"

"Don't start!"

Two squabbling genies, pity the archaeologist of a thousand years hence who rubs off the dirt. Yet there was an irrefutable something in it. My unfailing ability to say the wrong thing, or the right thing at the wrong time. It's a *talent*, Daddy, you should be quite the boneyard boaster.

Emine appeared at the door.

Looked at her father and looked at me. They spoke in Albanian and she shrugged, took her cereal elsewhere.

Luca rolled his eyes. "Girls."

"I'm a girl!"

I flung a piece of toast at him.

We headed down to the causeway. Along the path, Spider-Girl came sprinting out of the Shore House gate, her father just behind. She waved enthusiastically, followed, after a slight delay, by her dad.

I waved and walked on. I had the sudden certainty that Hector had visited; a jaunty knock and a dazzling smile, a few easy pleasantries before the main feature: *"Let me tell you the whole sordid Patti Letham Story. You're new here. You're her neighbour. You have a right to know."*

I knew what else was coming.

One morning, I'd look out my bedroom window and down on

the causeway would be Hector and Luca.

Hector was insidious, he made you want to tell him things. Back then, I almost told him what Frank had done to me, but I couldn't shake the suspicion that he already knew. I hated him for that, but I hated myself even more for my own silence that I made so many excuses for.

Luca had reached the end of the causeway and now turned to face me, arms folded, businesslike.

"Six hours!"

"Until what?"

"I thought you were the expert. Until the tide turns. Five hours, forty-five minutes to be precise. I looked it up."

"Okay, boss."

"So, where's the mortar? Didn't you take the bucket?"

"I thought you were taking the bucket? You always take the bucket."

"Not today."

"I'm not a mind reader."

"Okay, *okay*. I'll get it."

"Forget it—it's fine."

"I don't—'

"It's *fine*."

I curtseyed and turned shorewards.

Emine was leaning against the gate to Little Cottage, Red Riding Hood readying for another day on the terminal shore. She moved away before I reached her, heading east to where the shore curved away, a corner never turned, keeping the cottage— and me—always in sight. It somehow made her even more inaccessible than if she'd disappeared for days at a time.

"What about school?" I asked Luca later.

"I know. I think about that. The friends she should have. But we can't do that, can we? Send her to school."

"I don't know … Maybe there's a way."

"Yes. There is." He spoke carefully. "He will come, eventually, your policeman friend. And we will be sent back. Back to Albania. Emine will go to school. School for a few years, then work. But nothing she wants, then back into vans and lorries she goes. Germany, France, maybe back here again."

He put a hand to his brow, shielding his eyes from the sun and looking across to Ferris Island.

"Who do you think you will see?" he asked.

"What do you mean?"

"At the end of the causeway. When you have put down the last stone."

The next evening he told me they had stayed too long. Emine stood beside him, subdued. Again, he thanked me, and I said there was no need to leave, they could stay as long as they wished. His eyes filled. Emine suddenly threw her arms around me, a wrong-footing, unexpected tenderness.

I saw myself in her, all too obviously: the skirmishes with Luca that needed no translation, the flouncing while barely moving, the profound sighs as she sat rigid on the settee. She, too, had a scornful face, not best made for connection. I infuriated my own father in exactly the same way.

"Don't smirk, Patti."

"It's a smile, Daddy. A smile is not a smirk."

"Don't smile then."

"What? So now we're not allowed to smile?"

"That's not what I meant!"

"That's just so sad, Daddy. Are you sad?"

"That's enough!"

The art of disdain, Emine, too, had it down pat. The tiniest twitch of an eyebrow, the cut-glass looks. And the startling, indiscriminate volatility that slammed doors and stamped up the stairs.

I followed her after one of these outbursts. She was genuinely upset at something Luca had, or had not, said. She gave a strangled "yes' when I knocked at her bedroom door, stopped wiping her eyes the instant I came in. Straightaway, it was my teenage self at the window.

I took a risk and put my hand on her shoulder. Yet she immediately pulled me to her and hugged me. I was taken aback by the strength of her embrace. I said, "It's okay, it's okay, pet."

After a while, she stopped crying. We listened to the rain. Then she pulled back and wiped her eyes, turning to her collection of windowsill tide-wrack, absent-mindedly moving things about. I suddenly remembered Betty Dubh. "Oh *yes*," I said, squeezing her shoulder. She turned with an expectant but bashful smile, uncertain what to do with our newfound intimacy.

"I'm going to take you somewhere that I think you will like."

"O-*kaay?*"

She gave me a different kind of smile. Unencumbered. Just a smile. A little girl's smile.

***

Strange, the places you ended up. I was nineteen when I started at the museum. I'd only been there twice before. Once on a school trip and once for my interview. Miss Jameson and Mr Kirk were their own artefacts: 1970s exemplars, heavy on the wools, twin sets and three-piece suits.

In the museum foyer, I could still picture Mr Kirk sitting behind the desk, patrician aloofness and a clipboard. He instantly deferred when he took me to Miss Jameson's archive domain. She wore her austerity as a disguise, a giveaway compassion in those sparkling eyes.

Mr Kirk acquired the Betty Dubh Collection when the old woman died at age 96. She'd lived down the north shore, an old fisherman's cottage. For decades she collected, hoarded. Driftwood arranged with arcane care, polished pebbles, deformed shells and old creels, whaling and fishing ephemera, braiding needles and sailcloth, gaffs, rods, and nets, hundreds of sepia photographs of farmers and fishers, wary barefooted children squinting at the camera.

Betty's cottage was open to everyone. No labels, just ask Betty and she'd tell you all about it, tales tall and taller shouted from her little corner, an exhibit all her own on a rickety wooden chair. Mr Kirk presented the collection as an exact recreation of Betty's front room.

We headed straight for the gallery.

Emine was fascinated. Slow-wandering Betty's world. Luca squeezed my hand and nodded downwards.

"This *carpet.*"

I looked down at the dull brownness, the faded yellow and orange diagonal stripes, "What about it?"

"Where did they get it? Stalin's bedroom?"

I smiled. I used to tell myself that I was happy at the museum, and I was, for a while. I was working. Can you not be pleased for me, Mummy and Daddy? All grown up with her man, Frank and I making our own way, Frank who is not Hector, I can do nothing about that.

Emine was nudging me.

"I think I want to be like Betty."

"I know. Me too."

Off she almost skipped to the fossil displays. I followed. I wondered if Miss Jameson could still be alive as I peered into an elegantly lit cabinet, all those ancient, mysterious stones, placed on plinths to be gawked at centuries later. For the oddest few moments, I pictured a tiny netsuke Frank with his Zimmer. And there was me, too, all the rest of the family. Hector as well, Jamie. The caricatures that we'd been all along. Even Granny C.

If it hadn't been for the museum, I'd never have found out about Granny C. and her blue-eyed boy. In Mrs Jameson's archive office one afternoon, I picked up a photo album on her desk.

"Rotary Club—1914 to 1964."

I didn't get past 1941. The montage was captioned "Christmas Troop Fundraiser." The town hall was strung with decorations. In an Auxiliary Territorial Service uniform, Granny Causeway stands in a line of people facing the camera. A handsome man is beside her, also uniformed, almost everyone is. On the facing page, I found the two of them in another photo, side by side at a dining table filled with plates and bottles. He's leaning in and saying something. His lips might be brushing her ear. Her left hand is playing with her hair, her right on the table with the fingers splayed, almost touching his. My grandfather is sitting on the other side of Granny C. He's looking the other way, as if he doesn't want to see.

My appetite for all of that was voracious, once. Now I saw only the one-dimensional reflections in the display case glass, soiled here and there by fingerprints the cleaners had missed.

"What *are* you looking for in there, Patricia Letham?"

I turned to Bazzie. An exaggeration of frowning concern as he looked at me, a netsuke made life-size.

I was confused. "What the hell are you doing here?"

"Hiding."

"Eh?"

"Dad."

"He's back."

"Oh yes, he's back."

Luca hurried over. "Hello. Hello again, Baz. I don't think I said thank you for inviting me to your party."

"A pleasure! Come around anytime, anytime. Except when my

dad's around. Then don't come around."

"Don't come?"

"What I mean is, don't be there when he's there. All that "you wouldn't like me when I'm angry.""

"I hope I don't make you angry."

"No, that was the Hulk."

"The Incredible Hulk?"

"No, no, I was just using the Hulk as … I meant him."

"Who?"

Bazzie was on the verge of panic. He looked from me to Luca to the floor, then landed on a way out.

"What time is it?"

"Just gone four."

"Well now, here's a little something to ponder."

"What?"

"Happy hour at Jesters. Cocktails. First one's on me, Luca. Patti's always liked a bit of Sex on the Beach."

"You know me so well."

"Damn right, girl!"

"Girl?"

I turned to Luca with a shrug. He looked utterly stumped, and I knew how he felt. Across the gallery, Emine stood beside a cabinet, a pair of information headphones on her ears. She looked at us, the most enigmatic of looks, as if some marvellous knowledge was being whispered.

We walked into town in the rain, deeper into afternoon, then an evening that became another outpouring.

"*Mo-hee-TO, mo-hee-to.*"

Bazzie with the chant.

Bazzie on a mission to oblivion. His father was in a mood phase described as "mad manic mental fucker," which included random acts of violence, one involving a poached-egg pan, "Yes, a poached-egg pan, the water was boiling, look at my arm," said arm thrust out indignantly.

We leaned forward to shake our heads, Luca the closest as he tried to catch the flow of Bazzie's words, closer still as the volume in Jesters swelled with as-advertised "cheesy pop classics' and the office-emptyings, a clustered group who glanced and conferred about the Girl in the Hood, who looked away quickly from the white-haired woman staring them down.

"It's not nice to stare."

I didn't tell Bazzie he had a piece of mint stuck to a tooth. From a distance, it looked as if he were missing one.

"It's not nice to talk the hind legs off an Albanian."

"He's a nice guy."

Luca had weaved a way to the loo some time ago.

"And your point is?"

Bazzie grinned.

"Come now, kemo sabe."

He raised his glass with an exaggerated wink. I blushed and blamed it on the booze. Luca reappeared to "Stayin' Alive," a big smile on his face as he strutted over like John Travolta. He stopped in front of us to flick out an imaginary collar, throwing arms and hips into the iconic pose.

We applauded, Emine rolled eyes that were actually delighted. The table beside us cheered, the friends-forever co-workers with a sway to the left, a sway to the right, a half-coordinated hand jive as they burst out laughing. Luca sat down. A brief hand on my knee I tried not to notice.

And so on.

A fogginess of set pieces: Luca talking to a woman called Annie, who I recognised from some time, some place. Emine saying, "I'm fine, you don't need to keep asking," and going back to watching. "You're a watcher like me," I told her, and she smiled graciously, politely declining the connection. And Bazzie's intermittent laughter, Bazzie who was suddenly not there.

Then a taxi.

Homeward bound with the windows down. Singing along to the driver's Eagles CD. Take it *eaaaaasy*. I asked the driver to drop us up on the main road. I led Luca and Emine through the dunes, under the blue slounge of never-dark summer night, ghost clouds in a tumbledown sky.

We stumbled and laughed, Luca's teeth glowing like fluorescent stars on a child's ceiling, Emine lost in her hood and maybe watching us, maybe not, whisper time in the marram, my thoughts as desiccated as the sand, gritty grains I'd find in my bed the next morning.

We left the dunes and took the shore path to Little Cottage, the sea beside us, static between songs on an old LP. I couldn't get the key in the lock. Luca took my hand, helping me guide it in.

A catch of light in his eyes.

I remembered the thrill of beginnings. Another evening in a different pub, Cath and Jo and "well now, see who's coming on over, if it isn't the *looker* just moved up from the Big Smoke." Then a few minutes of loaded chitchat, the "oh aye, Patti," when he wandered off, my "shut up the pair of you' and the "*c'mooon,* Pats, it's fresh *meat.*" In this tired backwater, where demand far outstripped supply, there was no defence against the tyranny of novelty.

"I'll dance if you dance," Jamie said, the next time we met.

The party I had gone to without Frank, who would find out, of course, but I didn't care about that.

"You wanna dance with me?"

"I wanna dance with you."

"Then we must find a place to dance—but it can't be here."

"Then we better find somewhere else."

We slipped out of the party. We thought no one noticed. We wandered the beach in a midnight squall. A comic waltz on the sand. Then the rocks and bare skin, his hands on my hips, my fingers under his T-shirt. Blue-eyed boys, the women in this family and their blue-eyed boys.

Not sky blue like the uniform of Katie Nurse.

Deep blue.

Deeeeeeeeeeeeeep as the depths in here.

I dream of Luca.

I dream of Jamie.

It's weird as *The Wizard of Oz.* No place like home, no place like … I have to look away, look away, hide your …

They're back.

One by one, to peer down on me as I lie in some kind of flowing white nightdress like a Hammer vampire.

Hundreds of them.

"Remind me why we're here?" someone asks.

"Paying our disrespects."

In which case, as the old joke goes, ah must be dead.

I dive down again.

I am standing outside a massage parlour in Glasgow.

Big neons blinking "girls, girls, girls."

There's a line of men along the side of the tenement and

round the corner. I'm shouting, "What is wrong with you fuckers, what is it you're lacking?" They just look amused, brazen with normality, suited or track-suited and chatting about the football as they patiently wait, summer holidays and Netflix, the turnstile clicking, one out and the next one in, the line shuffling forward, the pub afterwards, "you were up the sauna, too, then, sorry, must have missed you," "busy the day eh, *fresh meat*," "did you hear that wumman on the other side of the street shouting the odds, someone needs to do something about that, ah swear ..."

I drift up, up, up.

I'm so brave in these dreams. If you never really know who you are, you can be anyone you want.

Ha!

The nurses aren't buying it. The nurses coming further into focus. A canula is reinserted into my wrist with casual yet unmistakable intent. They know me and therefore think they know me.

So pray tell who I am!

For it is not these alarming smells, sinister beeps, and occasional screams that have alienated me from myself, no, no, such bagatelles have nothing on the deep, unsettling certainty that I am *not me*, not this person drifting up to look down at herself in this coffin bed.

Pick the bones out of that, dear Fishwives, as you sit on the loo, uniforms bunched around your spreading thighs. It'll be quite the intellectual conundrum if you ponder it, which you won't, because Patti has always talked a lot of shite, hasn't she, always so full of herself.

That's what you remember. Though to remember is not to know. I remember blue eyes, a swirl in the iris like ink in water, show me those eyes only and I will recognise him in an instant, recognise him but not know him. If I had truly known Jamie, I'd never have gone looking for him.

Like everyone is a-looking for me.

Even my brothers.

They appeared days after I got here. It's heart-melting, affirming, the speed with which they rushed to my bedside ...

Their voices that swim in and out of a consciousness that the big machine drawing doodles of my tiny brain shows has been swelling slowly stronger, but now beeps in alarm as I fade once more, recoiling from Ray and Keith's routine chunter-burble. The docs should have brought them in to put me under, no more effective a sedative can be known to medicine than the warm twitter of those brotherly voices, the whispers the two plums think I can't hear.

"She looks fuckin' awful."

Another searing insight that makes the Boy Wonders so universally admired. Maybe I just laughed or lashed out before dipping under. I imagine their spook as I settle from violence to silence, the shared glance at the wall sockets and the joint unuttered thought.

To pull or not to pull the plug? That is the question.

That light.

Remember light?

I feel my eyelids lift and open, a seeking of illumination that is less chosen than instinctive.

You *want* to surface.

I do?

The light is bright in the room, daylight.

And how are we today?

A sonic boom in my left ear. Katie Nurse. "I had a good night too," she is saying. "We went out, me and the other half."

A pause.

"A good night … Yes, I do believe it was."

Ah, Katie.

That need to convince yourself, I hear you, I hear you.

All memories are like mine, I know, photographic negatives revealing not what is there but what you want to be. Just as the face on the Turin Shroud is Jesus and *no one else* to those who desperately need it to be despite the carbon-14 evidence. They know it is, they just know.

Know what?

That revelation is always projection, ha!

Stay tuned for more wisdom, folks. I'm full of it, people have been telling me that for years.

Hear me out.

Think of it as the selfless provision of a public service.

In this nether world, all knowledge surrounds me. I reach

an arm into the vegetable darkness and feel everything. It is *all* there for us all, and the tragedy is that it always has been. When we finally realise, we'll be *gods*, Katie. Big J's face on the Turin Shroud will break into a matinee smile, and a thousand calcified nonnas in northern Italy will have simultaneous orgasms.

If only I could let you know, Katie, down here I thrash like a salmon and reel like a Dervish, but up there it registers only as vague fidgets and the tiniest of spikes of the heart-rate monitor. I try and fail to stick out a tongue like Einstein in that famous photo, my tongue that feels like a piece of wood. I'm so bloody thirsty! *Ein Stein* is actually what I need. Ein Stein of beer. Don't be Heidi-bound, strap on the dirndl and bring me one. I'll sup quietly, ponder from this safe distance the raucous Hofbräuhaus, all that Sturm, Drang, and pork knuckle.

Is that your scene, Katie?

It'd be my worst nightmare. So just the beer, puh-leeze; sip, sip, and there we have it, another esoteric mystery solved, bring on the next, the next, I'm on a roll, picking up speed!

It must be the proximity to death, the pressing need to finish, to get things done. I always was a grafter, sure I was, an apostle of labour's nobility. Hi-ho, hi-ho, to the bullshit mine I go, one beady eye on that plug extension unit, the fraying cord running to the socket on the wall.

Have these machines been PAT-tested? I am a woman of particular demands, has it been PATTI-tested? Overload is my one true fear, not my brothers slipping back in during the shift change to flick the switch off, no chance of that, I can hear the clip of those brogues a mile off.

Another sonic boom.

My right ear this time. The rustle of sheets and Katie's hands. The lukewarm water on my thighs that—

"He was here you know."

A near whisper and a pause for a few seconds. As if she's been interrupted, likely the Two Fishwives, arms crossed over by the door, eyebrows raised as they wonder why Katie's so nice to me.

"Hector, the policeman, he was back again. He just stood there looking at you. He took a photo. Told me not to tell the Sister. "It'll be our little secret," he said. I can't decide if he's creepy."

Creepy?

Asking if he's creepy?

That's like asking God for confirmation and ignoring the booming yeeees, yeeees as the building collapses all around you. Standing there silently and taking a picture, what's not creepy about that? What's he going to do with that picture. His motives have always been arcane, this isn't my brothers and the picture they took when they visited; I heard the photo-app shutter noise, likely a selfie, stick it on social media to validate the experience, one last snap with their renegade sister, sixteen likes, ashes to ashes, pixel to pixel, we all know Patti Letham's a vegetab-el. But Hector's photo is for his eyes only, midnight black and PC flicker, zooming in, zooming out, here a Patti, there a Patti. Hector wants more, he always wants more. He'll mosey on back to the hospital to pull the sheets back, slowly open my institutional smock, trail of fingers on my skin as he so gently washes me, an inscrutable little smile, as if he is both immediately present yet observing me from a great distance.

"There you go, Patti, all done." A gentle squeeze of my arm.

Katie's as old-fashioned as tea.

I know she keeps her photos in battered shoeboxes. Looks forward to the delight of coming across them years later. No worries for her when the Cloud dissolves and our digital identities suffer the terminal wipe, not even a murky image on a pixelated shroud left behind.

In fact.

In fact, it is all just …

Emine started borrowing my bike. An irregular and then daily vanishing after weeks of never leaving my eyeshot. It was a tentative discovering, the way she idled along the shore path.

I loved my bike at her age. Everyone was out on bikes back then. Choppers, Grifters, then BMXs. Free 'n easy and the sun always shining, sure, that was the point of nostalgia. Perhaps Emine heard us on her solitary grand tours, the laughter of our ghost pelotons zipping past.

One lunchtime at the work camp, rain-drum on the garden parasol, I asked Luca where she went.

"I have no idea. She cycles. A girl should cycle."

"A *girl* should cycle?"

"Of course."

"Just girls?"

"Boys should cycle too."

"Good."

"You're making something of this … a thing."

"*I'm* making a thing."

"Yes. I think that if there was a world without things, then you would be the first to … make a thing."

"Really."

"Yes. Look at this." He gracefully raised his half-eaten cheese and tomato sandwich, then stuffed the rest into his mouth, chewing frantically until he was able to speak again. "See? Now there are no things. Cycling is good. Daniela and I cycled everywhere. She was a good ride. Is that right?"

"Not quite."

"But you are right … Where does she go?"

That evening, Luca's question was met with a *fabulous* look of contempt, as if he were a talking potato:

"The … *beach*?"

"The Strand," I said. There was only one beach for miles and miles and that was the Strand.

She looked blank.

"Lot of shingle? The beach about as big as a snooker table?"

"Snooker?"

"I mean the beach isn't very big."

A quick shrug.

"Were you there by yourself?" asked Luca.

"No … with Claire."

"Who's Claire?"

"*Claire*."

Like, how can you not know Claire, CLAIRE!?

"I met her on the beach. She has to go back to school next week. Can I go to school?"

"School?"

"Yes."

"Well. I don't … How can we do that, it's not as if we can just—'

"Forget it." She slumped back in her chair, arms folded.

"Emine."

"Just … forget … *it*."

"Maybe we could all go to the beach one day? Your friend too. It would be nice to meet her … Claire."

Emine snorted. An actual snort. "Right!"

"What?"

"Are you two sure you can spare the time? From your *stones*?"

I opened my mouth but decided against saying anything. Luca's helpless glance met mine. I could hear the ghost-cackles of derision from Big Urn and Little Urn up there in the cemetery:

"Ooooh, do you think Patti felt that, dear?"

"Felt what?"

"Think about it."

"Oh yes! She must be able to—'

"Yes?"

"The boot! She must indeed be able to feel that boot being squeezed onto the other foot."

"Ha!"

"Never made it easy for us."

"Never once."

"After all we did for her."

"All we did."

"If only she could have been more like her brothers."

"Ah, the boys."

* * *

We were in the middle of the "Big Push." A determined

attempt to finish the causeway before winter. Day on day a riprap of stones, a rolling meditation. I'd seen the causeway gleam like a mirror in a hundred fairy-tale dawns, emerge from the receding tide a hundred other times, unsure if the stones were rising or the sea falling, the trickster light of this thin and shifting place.

I brought the projections, nothing new, re-runs of episodes sweated out under incongruous sun, trowelled like stubborn mortar in all-season cold, hands slick or frozen, the hands of someone else, Granny C., working through me, the most dependable of illusions.

I stood now and then as she did in the photograph on my mantelpiece, white hair billowing and an inscrutable smile. I'd run my hands down my jeans and feel the rough tweed of her skirt.

"You'll never see the same wave twice, Patti dear. Think about that, the same sea that is always different."

I was happy.

Happy to see Luca appear on the causeway twenty minutes after me. Happy with him being here.

"Look at this!" He held out his hands as he approached. Palms up and a week's beard. "I have blisters. What have you *done* to me?' He shook his head, grinning, a goofy prophet.

I took one of his hands, rubbed a finger along the callouses.

"They hurt."

A softer voice, an older feeling in my stomach. "Vinegar," I said, abruptly dropping his hand.

"Vinegar?"

"Uh huh, steep your hands in vinegar. That'll harden you up, little boy."

"Little boy?"

He wagged a finger, fake outrage and a fast stream of Albanian.

"Well?"

"Well, what?"

"What did you say?"

"You want to know?"

"Yes."

"Really?"

I punched him on the arm.

"Okay then. It means ... it means you will end up as food for chickens."

I leaned back, mouth open. "You … *animal.*"

My gaze moved up the shore. Emine was emerging from the gate with the bike. She wheeled it past Shore House, mounting it at the bottom of the single-track hill that led to the top road.

I saw myself falling off my bike.

I saw Frank looking down at me in the ditch, embarrassed on my behalf, his face red and close as he lifted the bike off me, avoiding my gaze, grey sky and rain, mud in my mouth, the smell of something foul. Oh, the romance, while three thousand miles away, Daniela and Luca cycled through "a forest, sunlight through the trees, like in a fairy tale." This not a Patti projection but words that Luca had actually uttered. "The most beautiful of times."

Those words were flowing now.

Luca had switched off mute. Every day brought a new story. I had the feeling these monologues had been running on an internal loop for a long time, so familiar they came out polished, almost overdone, set down as diligently as the way I had trained him to place the stones.

Who was I to question the arms entwined as they ate each other's ice creams, a little girl laughing at them, or the net curtains billowing in a soft breeze as they lay dozing. Maybe they had indeed been in that ancient, empty bar in the Skanderbeg Mountains, an old piano that Daniela started to play. Over the wind on the causeway, I heard my mother's gusting amusement:

"Come now, Patti, haven't you got your own story that no one would believe?"

"Don't encourage the lassie."

"We've all got stories, dear, even me and you."

"That we have."

"Do you remember my toe?"

"You should never mention the toe!"

"We all have a past, dear."

The toe, the toe, I'd forgotten all about the toe! I told Luca about it. His incredulous reaction:

"This is a made-up story, yes?"

"No, Luca, it isn't."

For my mother had indeed told me, giddy with the sherry one memorable Sunday afternoon when a swashbuckling nine-over par lightened my father's mood from morose to merely sombre.

"It was my toe that did it for us," she told me.

"I beg your pardon."

She blushed and bent down, removing a furry pink house slipper. As I considered her bony, translucent tootsies, wondering if she'd finally lost her marbles, she offered further detail:

"The big one."

And she solemnly pointed at it.

"We were courting," she said. My father-to-be had paid her a call:

I imagine the heavy tick of a clock, oblique Expressionist shadows in a late-winter living room, the two of them poker-straight in high-backed chairs. She smooths her gingham dress, and he moves his feet, the squeak of his brogues making him flush. An entire century passes.

"When your father said he was leaving, I stood up too quickly. One of my pumps somehow flew off my foot."

"Did you say pump?"

"What?"

"Pump?"

"Yes. My pump."

The pump! It arcs through time and space and lands on the hearth. They look at her naked foot. Another century passes before my gallant father goes over and picks up said pump. Then the lightning strike. Placing it at her feet, he inadvertently touches her big toe.

"This one." My mother pointed at it again. "Imagine what would have been said if someone came in?" She looked genuinely alarmed as I bit my lip, trying not to laugh as Luca did:

"My goodness, the scandal."

"That's what I said, "*Mum*, imagine the scandal!" I was being sarcastic, but she said, "Yes, yes, *exactly*.""

My mother, my fearful mother.

I remembered another conversation when I found out about an actual scandal. I glanced up to the promontory, but the parentals were oddly quiet. My mother knew exactly what I was thinking, but even death was refused a licence to rummage in the box of family disgrace.

"I found a photo in the archives. There was a man beside Granny C. at a dance. In a uniform?"

The fall of her face.

Then the almost hissed, "We don't *talk* about that."

If she were Catholic, she'd have crossed herself. Protective embarrassment was a default reaction, the continual defence of the breach between public image and private reality must have been exhausting. She grabbed me as I moved away. "Don't you dare mention this. It could have ruined us, *ruined* us."

"She had an affair then," said blasé Patti. "What's the big deal?"

I swear to god my mother put a hand to her throat, as if grasping for that non-existent crucifix.

Luca and I finished for the day. Homeward bound to stand side by side at the kitchen sink, washing our hands. A touch of hips and the brush of fingers. I thought of the Toe That Changed the World.

"You know people," I said, "who say "if I had my time over, I'd do this or that different"? I never believe them."

"Well, that's it, that's just it ..."

"What is?"

"*It.*" He walked across to the fridge and took out two bottles of beer.

"You'll have to enlighten me."

"We think everything gets better and better. We are fools for progress, for better, *best*. We know more than our parents, our parents knew more than their parents. You know what the problem is?"

He opened the bottles and handed me one.

"What?"

"People. They're too *fucking* fucked-*up*."

He thrust up his arm with a gëzuar—cheers, he had told me—beaming like a holy madman and starting to laugh, setting me off. We'd just calmed down when we saw Emine at the door, staring at us.

***

We did go to the beach to meet her friend Claire. A few days later. It was actually Emine's suggestion. Matter-of-fact, watching TV:

"If you want to meet Claire, we're going to the beach tomorrow."

We were told to meet them there, but Emine appeared alone, strolling across the beach with overdone nonchalance to say Claire had something to do, then continuing past us, down to the water.

Luca watched her:

"Do you think there is a Claire?"

"You think she'd make her up?"

"She's lonely, Patti. We need to look out for her."

I thought about that "we," felt the tiresome blush and looked away. C'mon, Hector, let's hear it. He's leaning back in his chair in his disturbingly neat office, wagging the gleeful finger. *That's always the thing about you, Patti. The extraordinary capacity for betrayal. Yourself, others."*

This beach. The Strand.

I hadn't been here more than a few times since the night of that party. Me and Jamie. The rocks over by the cliffs. It was exactly six months after the *crack*, a symmetry I remembered briefly thinking was auspicious before subordinating myself to more basic considerations.

Hey, you think it was easy to craft an obsession? I worked at it goddammit! Those colours had to be bold, like Granny C."s lurid seascapes or Luca's soft-focus Daniela rewinds. Edges had to be sharpened, the *finest* of edges, the ambiguity of first encounters turned into a Big Top of insistence, the cuckold tinkling in Frank's head transformed into an air raid siren. I handcrafted our uniqueness, *no one* had ever felt the way Jamie and I did.

Luca and I wandered the Strand. Emine in the distance. Beachcomb mode, head down, picking something up to be cast aside or put in her pocket, an instant assessment of worth. If only it were so easy.

"What are you smiling about, Patti?"

"Was I smiling?"

"You were. It's something you do. I've noticed it."

"You have?"

"I have."

"Do I do it a lot?"

"You do. Maybe you have lots of secrets."

"You have no idea. Maybe I'll tell you a few one day."

"Maybe?"

"You could be worth telling. I haven't decided yet."

He looked closely at me, then looked away. That was Patti. A passing curiosity. Something from the Betty Dubh Collection. Then Luca again, nodding with his chin back across the beach.

"Looks like we were wrong."

Emine was hurrying along the sand to a girl who was waving from the top of the shore. They came towards us, Emine stopping to say something to her friend. She looked at us, hiding a smirk, acknowledging Emine's undoubtedly unflattering pocket review of me and Luca.

I playfully shoved him. "*Dad*, why are you so *embarrassing*?"

He just looked confused.

* * *

Claire became a fixture. Friends do at that age. The two of them combed the shore as Luca and I worked the stones. She would stay for dinner, occasional Saturday sleepovers. Never said much. Prefaced every response with a swift glance at Emine, as if checking it was okay.

Luca was unsure too.

The suspicions of the parent. He thought they spent too much time together. I asked if he'd prefer Claire was a boy, or if he'd forgotten the Time of Permanent Erections. His attempts to fathom his teenage daughter were as impressive as my mother's had been deficient, unable to offer empathy without disapproval. Luca at least gave it a shot.

"It's a strange time of life, isn't it?" he said. "A lot of change."

We were in the living room, bursts of laughter from Emine's upstairs room. The long after-silences.

"Sure, you gotta roll with the weirdness."

I reassessed this generosity of judgment one evening when I drove the girls to Claire's house in such a treacle of monosyllables, self-consciousness, and sly, amused glances that I wondered if it was some kind of hermetic language before deciding they were taking the piss.

Claire's mum appeared at the gate as I pulled away. She was waving a hand, wanting me to stop. Nicola wanted to "get to know me," it was clear the first time we met, my brief introduction-cum-explanation that Emine and her father were staying with me for a while. She was one of those people who, despite all defeats, still felt the need to seek connection. "Maybe we could … meet sometime?" Emine and Claire must have been merciless with her.

I pretended not to see her.

By another quirk of the fates that had long ceased to surprise me, Claire and Nicola lived two streets from Frank and Hector's old house. On a whim, if whims existed, I drove by.

Their father died when they were very young, their mother an oblique, provisional presence. The boys sought a way in, ever thwarted by their dead dad. I felt sorry all over again for adding to her sadness as I took in the garden filled not with her eccentricity of asters, azaleas, and roses but the clutter of a faded plastic slide and a sagging trampoline, an overturned trike.

Frank's bedroom. It was so messy, a scatter of books and magazines, a train set tacked to chipboard under his bed. He still played with it as a teenager, driving his InterCity 125 across the hand-painted foam landscapes, overdone greens and browns, dotted with trees, bushes and animals built to seemingly random sizes and scale. His pleasure echoed my father's, years later, as his mind fell away. He, too, had a train set, my mother quietly apologising to the ever more infrequent visitors as the hoots of "choo choo' drifted through from the living room. If only they had seen their connection in the more lucid times.

Then there was Hector's *very* neat room. Sparse, not one poster, a half-empty bookcase and a laden trophy cabinet, Hector the captain of the swimming and the football teams. Only once did I see his bed mussed up, when, like a lost missive finally arrived, Hector and I gave in to each other. Frank and I were together but not yet engaged. As I dressed, Hector told me he loved me. I was less shocked by that than the sight of those mussed-up sheets.

I accelerated away from the old house. I told myself I was going home but went instead to The Pines.

Not directly.
A roundabout way.
To make the point that I hadn't chosen to do this.
I never chose anything, neither that afternoon in Hector's bedroom nor the series of events with Frank still unfolding their consequences decades later. At least, not actively. These happenings just, well, happened. With an unfortunate regularity, leading others to think the cause, the fundamental fault, lay with me and not the capriciousness of circumstance.

If anyone asked about this current circumstance, why I was sitting in the freezing woods staring at my ex-husband's sheltered housing apartment, I'd say one was being stalked by fate. I managed a little laugh but part of me, bigger than it should have been, kind of believed it.

That *crack*. It had never stopped reverberating.

I never called it a punch.

By refusing to consider it as an action, I somehow maintained the significance but diminished Frank. It was both exclamation and farewell, a "fuck you, Frank." There was no Jamie without it, and likely Granny C. and her soldier would have slipped past me as well, no deep need to know if he was the blue-eyed boy in her poem. I wanted Granny C."s story to mirror my own. I wanted to be her, and her to be me. I wanted her to take me beyond Frank Ruthven.

His apartment was in darkness. I put down the binoculars. There was pine sap on my forefinger. I squeezed it against my thumb and pulled it apart, feeling the tackiness. I pictured Frank in the intensive care unit, the ventilator squeeze-boxing to the rhythm of my sticky fingers.

Miss Jameson lit up like a flare when I asked her to help me identify Granny C."s soldier.

She was a huge Agatha Christie fan ("Marple of course, my dear."). She'd find out. There was no lucky invite list inside the album, so Miss Jameson took her magnifying glass to the other photographs from the event. In one, five comrades in stand-down mode, our boy in the middle. They are all holding their caps, the regimental badges obscured apart from one. A military gazetteer in the library identified the Gordon Highlanders. Then came the telephone call and the three-week wait for the 1941 service list to come in the post. The 51st Highland Division. Names and photos, including one Captain Alexander Nicholson.

Medium close-up.

He's looking beyond the photographer. A curl of a smile as if there's someone looking back at him. Miss Jameson ran a finger over the photo. "Well, doesn't *he* look like Gregory Peck?"

Captain Nicholson surely did, I thought, pushing aside the vaguely troubling image of Miss Jameson ripping off her lewdest of hand-knitted bodices. Wartime Gregory. *The Guns of Navarone.* Black peacoat and polo neck. The captain would scale cliffs! Not the limestone of Rhodes rising from impossible Aegean blue, but the rain-stained sandstone looming over the disconsolate North Sea. The gods round these parts were more peelie-wally, but here was Eros redux, appearing over the cliff edge, coiling his rope as he strolled elegantly into the dusk.

I imagined the reaction as I stood up one Shore House Sunday and announced his name. *"Alexander,"* I would say, brandishing the photo. *"Do you think Granny C. called him Sandy or Zander?"*

Those lunches were tense enough without that; my mother eating with such disinterest I was sure I heard a little sigh after each unwilling chew, my father with gravy dribble on his chin, sporadic dialogue like machine gun bursts, loosed off by someone just to break the silence. Then there were the increasingly strange things said by my father. "Murder!" he shouted once, pointing out the window at a couple of crows. "Why is it always bloody murder with crows?' If anyone thought these were the first outriders of dementia, no one said. I didn't, I just ate that little bit faster, wishing I had an MG like Granny C. to escape in. I pictured her and the captain speeding the coast road, accelerating away from all of this.

I sought her out in the long-undisturbed boxes in the Shore House attic. Her photograph albums were all there. She'd taken me through them, now and then, as I cooried beside her with such delight. Now, tears in my eyes in the musty half-light, I found a photo that recorded one such occasion, the colours dulled, the fade of everything towards sepia. We are sitting on a red sofa. I'm wearing white knee socks and a blue pinafore, my arms around her neck. Granny C. is smiling at me, an album on her lap, elegant as ever in a white blouse and black neck scarf. A pencil note on the reverse reads "July 20, 1979."

That made me nine.

Nine years old.

Nine years old, and there beyond The Pines still this same sea that was always diffcrent, as she had told me.

That fuckin' *crack.*

I seldom felt embarrassed about coming to The Pines, whether I sat there dumbly staring or turning everything over again. What I hated was my anger and my occasional, unbidden compassion.

Frank wanted to know why I framed the photo of me and Granny C. and put it on my bedside table. He didn't ask, he couldn't, the *crack* that let so much in had also let so much out. Frank had forfeited the right to know what was going on below and he knew it. All he could communicate was apology. It was exhausting. We'd lie in bed. I'd wait for him to shuffle across.

"I'm so, so sorry."

"I know. Let it go, Frank."

"Do you forgive me?"

"Yes."

I didn't. He knew that too.

His desperation for forgiveness verged on anger. In some distorted way, he saw himself as the victim, as if my indifference had become a justification for what he'd done. He'd stare as I went through the albums, silently screaming, *What the FUCK are you looking for?*

The photos were easy, the letters an imposition. There was a shoebox labelled "Don," short for Donald, my grandfather. Envelopes with brittle string. I kept that box closed. I felt no need to read his letters to Granny C., whether early ones filled with his own love, or later ones responding to another man's. As for Captain Nicholson, there was no sign of him in anything I'd taken from the Shore House attic, still nothing apart from the poem in the ring binder:

"There is no attraction. Just blue eyes that might have looked, once. There is no attraction but blue eyes. Blue eyes on a summer morning."

One morning Frank came into the kitchen at breakfast and slapped down the book that I'd been reading.

"Nice words."

I'd written Granny's poem on a piece of card and was using it as a bookmark.

"They are."

"Who wrote them then?"

This was soon after the party, the beach. I felt an instant flush.

"For Christ's sake, Frank."

I went upstairs. The bedside drawer with the box of letters was slightly open. Frank had been rummaging. Inside was "Don' and only Don. The captain's letters were either long gone or he'd never written to Granny C. in the first place. It seemed right; I couldn't picture her rushing breathlessly to intercept the postman. I idly flicked through Don's letters.

As I did, I noticed something, a change in the pattern of what I was looking at. I went through the letters again, much more slowly. In the middle of the bundle, several were addressed in a different style, each line of the address indented. The handwriting, too, was different. I untied the bundle, and from the shadow of Grampa Donald stepped Captain Alexander Nicholson.

Sandy, rather.

That's what she would have called him, each letter being signed "yours until the end of time, Sandy."

The end of time.

The most beautiful of pipe dreams.

The end.

Frank's apartment in darkness.

I sat back on the log.

I closed my eyes to a mocking wind. I sat there until I might have been asleep. I saw Luca on the Strand, Daniela at his side. I saw Granny C. and Sandy, me and Jamie. There were hundreds of us. We walked with eyes only for each other. As a spectacular sunset dimmed, we started to look round, blinking as if waking, already forgetting the besotted present.

****

I drove home on the top road. The wind picked up and I opened all the windows, letting the salt-tanged cold rush inside. Out on the black sea, the lonesome red running lights of a ship. I let the conceit come as it usually did when I looked at a passing ship, that someone on deck was looking back, wondering about me as I wondered about them. When I reached the car park by Shore House, I felt refreshed. Then instantly exhausted as I noticed a familiar car.

They were sitting in the kitchen. Hector got up with a full-beam smile. "Well now, Ms Letham returns."

Luca seemed relaxed enough, which was concerning. Then Hector's arms were around me. A "long time no see," even though it hadn't been that long, a hand slipping to my waist for a quick, ambiguous squeeze, never a suggestion Hector couldn't help but leave behind.

"Luca here, he said I could come in and wait for you."

"Well, here I am."

"We were having a good old chinwag."

Luca stood up.

"I'll leave you to talk. Nice to meet you, Hector. And thank you again. I'll see you tomorrow, Patti."

I looked at him closely, but again no giveaway anxiety. That was Hector, the Great Seducer. He sat back down at the table as

Luca left the kitchen. Pointed a finger at the door and nodded.

"Interesting fella. I can see myself getting on with him."

"Why did he thank you?"

"For being such a good … *guy*. Never mind me, though, what about *you*, eh? I have to say, it's nice to see, it really is."

"What is?"

"You and your boy, it's sweet."

"He's not my boy."

"Me think she doth protest too much. I like him."

"You like him, do you?"

"I do. He was a bit nervous at first. The cop thing. Thought I might deport him, I suppose."

"Why don't you?"

"You know how many illegals we'd net up at the poly farms if we wanted? That's one major hassle. Who's going to pick all that fruit, Patti, you? I was telling Luca, it's like a sieve round here, sooner or later everything just drips out. If we know each other, we can look out for each other."

"You're all heart."

"I know he beat the shit out of Farmer Mick. I told him."

"Did he tell you why?"

"He did."

"So I'm guessing Mickey Anderson gets lifted for sexual assault as soon as he gets out of hospital?"

"Not as easy as that."

"What's to stop Mickey doing it again?"

"Mickey'll get his, don't you worry. But if he gets collared, so does your boy. I don't want that."

"That's why he thanked you?"

"I told him about something I heard going up at The Pines. Cleaning."

"You're joking, right?"

"Nope."

"Really. How's that going to work then?"

"Davie J. up there, he's been running people off the books for years. A quiet word from somebody and—'

"Gimme a break, Hector, you're gonna turn a blind eye to the *illegal immigrant*? Why would you do that then?"

"C'mon, it's not about a blind eye, I like him, it's about keeping an eye *out*. I mean, how long can one man live on Patti Letham's largesse alone. He's going to have to do something, but he can't just do what he bloody well wants, eh? There's the social contract to think about, right?"

"Thank god you're looking out for us, Hector."

"You're welcome."

"You're a control freak."

"The best way to control a cow is to give it a big field to roam about in. Ask Farmer Boggins up the road there."

"And The Pines? It could only be The Pines?"

He gave it a one-two beat, then deployed the Smile. "Not necessarily. Not at all." He stood and stretched, the shirt tightening across the chest, watching how I watched. "The thing is, it *is* The Pines."

"Fuck off, Hector. There's something wrong with you."

"Bit too late in the day to compare psych profiles, eh? I saw Frank tonight by the way. Took him down to the Ship. We played dominoes, I hate dominoes. You know what I always think about when someone can't go and they start chapping on the table? A coffin, some poor sod buried alive and chap-chap-chapping to get out. It's weird, right? Anyway, Frank wouldn't shut up about you. When I asked why, he said it was your anniversary, so happy anniversary. "All these years," he kept saying it. "All … these … *years*." He still wants the best for you, Christ knows why, and best for Patti is best for her boy. Luca there, he deserves a break."

"I told you he's not—'

"Remember, though, see tomorrow when Luca's sitting there supping his porridge? It'll be like Frank's sitting right beside him. Every … single … *morning*. It's comforting, eh, to end up back where you started?"

He pulled on his jacket and walked to the door.

"How many years is it anyway?"

"Since what?"

"You're right, I never know if you count from the beginning or the end."

I stared at the door for five-ten seconds after he closed it, but when had Hector ever done a curtain call.

I knew it was our anniversary.

That wasn't the reason I'd decided to go to The Pines earlier that night. That was not the reason.

Any Old Iron

People figured they knew me. My state. And that state had been variously described by many people across the years. Vicariously, too. It was quite strange; people who knew me told others, who told others … So many subjective opinions had therefore been brought to bear upon my good and bruised self by both those with direct and indirect experience of Patti here.

The peculiar thing, maybe even troubling, I suppose, had I cared enough to think about it, was the ease with which I, too, could stand outside myself, beside all those others, nudging them as I looked back at myself and said things like "oh aye, I know just what you mean, I heard that too," shaking my head as well, that other me looking back with profound bafflement and no small amount of fury, having been betrayed on some deep existential level that made no sense at all and simply confused the matter even further, there being no essential oil one could dab behind the ears or on the wrists and say "that's it, that's eau de Patti!"

A claustrophobic sense of being both completely known yet totally inscrutable was the inevitable outcome.

Hector, long an authority on my state, knew this. There ye by he also knew that my interpretations of him finding Luca a job where Frank lived, and his motivation for doing so, would run in frustrated circles like a toddler who can't accept that he's not allowed to ride the cat like a horsey.

"Don't make the mistake of trusting him."

"Trust him," said Luca. "Of course I don't trust him, he's a policeman!"

"Then why are you taking the job?"

"He could get me deported now. He could get me deported in three months. But if I leave, where do I go?"

So Luca took the job.

He was nervous the day he started. Savvy Luca. Hector's dubious motives were a-niggling. I'd spent my entire life trying to get a handle on them, swinging across me like Poe's pendulum: now his genuine goodwill, now the seedy certainty of a trap sprung for reasons unknown.

The manager of The Pines didn't reassure me. I had accompanied Luca, and we both now considered the small, crestfallen-looking man with over-large, flaring nostrils. His words were oddly stilted, lines he couldn't quite remember. "You must be Luca. Harry will show you. The ropes."

White-smocked Harry lumbered over, tall and wide as a Marvel supervillain. I saw him leading Luca straight to the car park and into a government meat wagon, on to some immigration dungeon.

Luca seemed to be thinking much the same. "Patti."

"What?"

"You never did tell me what happens when you reach the end of the causeway."

"I'll start again on the other side of Ferris Island. Just keep on going. Into the sea and on and on."

He paused. "Good … *Good*. I will help you."

He smiled with such melancholy before Harry led him away, as if we'd never see each other again.

Yet Luca was all smiles, deee-*lighted*, when I picked him up after his shift. I'd made the mistake of waiting for him in the reception, peered at by the staff who clearly knew all about me and Frank. They seemed primed, ready for the tackle if I suddenly made a run for his apartment.

"Get her, she's here to finish the job!"

They made me think about how I'd do it. In some detail. I couldn't help myself. The different means that could be employed. If I'd burst or sneak in. The implement. The mess that might be made.

Although it wasn't the wisest idea to keep picking Luca up, I kept doing it. Not every day but too often. Sat there in reception. That innate contrariness; I never had quite managed to transcend that inner emotional Pygmy, no offence to the little fellas. All my sophistication was but a painted thing. Yonder comes Patti Letham! Marvel at my bonhomie as the automatic doors of The Pines open with a blast of cauliflower cheese, disinfectant, and death, the receptionist returning my counterfeit smile with her own fake pearler.

And despite The Pines being miles from the cemetery, there it was again, the hoots of the bony old-timers. The receptionist's smile became a frown, maybe she, too, had heard the laughter.

"Never quite figured it out, did she?"

"What life was all about?"

"What life was all ab-OUT!"
"Not like us."
"We made the most of it, sure we did, pet."
"We did."
"We DID."
What lessons my parents did impart!

My father's inner churn, those extraordinarily dense sulks triggered by a tiny something, my mother's faltering dignity and silent retreats, shoulders heaving with silent sobs as I peered through the crack in their bedroom door as she sat in front of the dressing table. She'd appear a few minutes later as if nothing had happened. Not even the tiniest of troubling in the eye contact. It was extraordinary, a masterclass in emotional displacement.

Their happier moments tended to syrupy overcompensation. I inherited the sentimental flaw. The devastation on a child's face when they dropped their ice cream, the dance of the summer swifts, Luca's smile as he finished a shift, all could bring a lump to my throat. Yet sentiment was always self-regarding; I felt estranged by my empathy at the same time:

"Thar she blows again, dear!"
"Can't help herself, always picking at something, like a scab."
"Is it an illness?"
"Don't give her an excuse, man!"
"I know, I know."
"Tragic, really."
"Suck the joy from a child's Christmas that lassie of ours."
I tried not to.

I smiled and I listened as Luca told me about his days. The bodily fluids and foodstuffs cleaned from floors and Formica tables. The chess matches that took a week. His genuine enjoyment.

When Luca asked about my day, I played the ball straight back. I wanted his details, not mine, all the details to hear out about one alone; Frank, had he met Frank, Frank who I also used to pick up from work, Frank who told me about his day with no encouragement, the hermetic world of town planning, the peculiar hierarchies and imperatives of the Office.

It was interesting, for a while.

When I told him about the museum, Frank, too, was interested. Until one day, defeated by the relentlessness of familiarity, neither of us were. I had to choose something else to be interested in.

Jamie moved to the town permanently a month or so after we did the Strand. The internship over, my father offered him a full-time position. He was surprised that Jamie accepted, the topic one Sunday as we gathered at Shore Cottage for the usual lunch. My father:

"The lad's a talent, there's no denying it. He's got that "do anything, go anywhere" thing about him. He wants to stay on, I don't quite get it, but I do believe we've hit a home run, boys!"

My brothers went through the motions of indignation, some low-wattage reply about him not being all that talented, deflecting any attention from the treacherous blush in my cheeks.

I needn't have worried.

My embarrassment slipped by them as unseen as I slipped by Frank when I told him I was going for a walk and instead headed straight round to Jamie's new place. An affair was so banal. We knew that. Like everyone else, we told ourselves that ours was altogether different.

Yet it remained a peerless experience, an outlier but still definitive, one of the few periods in my life that I fully trusted my happiness. I liked the tang of those memories. His living room, red wine in the dark, the expectation and uncertainty of the wait for every rendezvous. Here's the DeLorean, Patti, would you choose to go back? A not insignificant part of me had never left.

His flat was one of the new builds down by the harbour, fish warehouses become luxury flats. After finishing at the museum, I'd head there via a series of detours. I joined a gym so I had a ready excuse. Soon enough, I got bolder. We got bolder. We started meeting in pubs. I stayed out later, and Frank began to notice, a controlled, unnerving anger.

"Patti, *talk* to me. *Fuck* sake!"

I started to wonder about endings. What would Granny C. have done? I had a dream. Her and Sandy in the MG. She's gunning it along the coast road. "Faster, Debs, they're gaining." Granny C. with a blithe "don't worry, Cap'n," continuing straight on as the road takes a bend, dropping into third and accelerating towards the cliff edge. Then out, into space, they're laughing …

A Patti-Jamie suicide pact in my battered old Cavalier, the sagging seats and heater stuck on full?

It lacked poignancy.

Anyway, suicide to maintain a moment?

Operatic melodrama was too exotic round these parts. You

imagined it from sun-dried Spaniards and hair-trigger Sicilians with hot blood feuds handed generation to generation like holy relics. I was Scottish, melancholy was my thang, settled across me like a peat hag.

***

Luca took to cooking dinner when his shifts at The Pines allowed. He was so careful, almost painstaking, the neatest of chopped vegetables on individual plates. I sat at the kitchen table and read, steamed-up windows and late-afternoon dark, Emine coming and going, suspected rather than seen. We chatted and ate as if all of this was normal, and maybe it was.

The Pines. Stories told at dinner or when we worked the causeway. The relieved, quiet elation of someone who had found a place and was determined to hang around. Luca may have been there for years.
"The manager, the man with the big nostrils, guess what we call him? The Mole. The way he *stares*."
Apparently, the Mole liked Sheena, a nursing assistant, the knowledge so common that even his wife knew, according to Harry, Luca and the supervillain now the best of buds. Harry with a dinghy he was going to take Luca fishing in, Harry with a thing for Annie, another nurse, but Annie liked Luca, said Harry, Luca protesting "she didn't, she didn't," Harry with a "don't sweat it, L-Man." Luca liked having a nickname, a cool one like L-Man; no one wants to be the Mole.

Annie. I knew Annie. Luca started to mention her more often. They'd met in Jesters that night with Bazzie. Christmas was on its way, the opportunities of the season. Ah well, let the children run free.
Luca:
"What are you smiling about?"
We were standing at the end of the causeway, another few stones laid, looking out at Ferris Island.
"Nothing. I was thinking about Christmas."
"Think we'll finish before Christmas?"
"Unlikely. Winter's coming and—'
"It's still Autumn! We might get a few decent days."

"Autumn. Ah, Luca."

"What?"

"Luca, Luca, *Luca*, there's only two seasons in Scotland, don't you know the joke?"

"No, what joke?"

I put my hands over my ears and started walking back down the causeway. "What's that? Are you saying something?"

"The joke!"

I glanced over my shoulder. He was hurrying after me.

I took off running.

I could hear him laughing behind me, then shouting something. He caught up with me where the causeway became Caithness slab. I felt his hand on my shoulder. Turning me. A look of expectation, a moment from those "choose your own adventure' books I used to read.

"Spider-Maaaaan!"

He looked as I looked. The little girl from Shore House.

"I'll get you!"

I started running after her, not glancing back. I didn't want to see that Luca wasn't looking my way after all.

I caught her at the Shore House gate. We were giggling when her father appeared. I said, "Hi". He said, "Getting colder now." Our first pleasantries. Luca dawdled but had to eventually reach us.

"Luca. This is Andrew."

"Nice to meet you, Luca."

"You too, Andrew."

"Call me Andy."

"I was telling Luca the joke about there being two seasons in Scotland."

"June and winter!"

"I see." Luca smiled. "Good. Very good."

"What about where you're from, Luca?" said Andy. "Is it jokes about the weather or something else? We make jokes about the Irish. The French make jokes about the Belgians. What about your people?'

"My people?"

"Well, you're not from here, eh? That's not a local accent! Do you mind if I ask where you're from?"

Luca, well he looked away.

"I don't mean to—"

"I am not good with jokes."

"Come on, everyone remembers a good joke!" said Andy.

"You mean everyone remembers a bad joke."

"True, true. There's lots of—'

"When is it Christmas in Albania?" said Luca.

"So, you're from Albania?"

"When is it Christmas in *Albania*?"

"I-I don't know."

"Two days after Christmas in Greece. Ha!"

Andy looked surprised.

"A Greek man says to an Albanian man, "I've just bought this tie for ten pounds." What did the Albanian say?"

"…"

""Idiot! You could have bought the same one just down the street for twenty pounds!'"

And silence.

Gawping, awkward silence. One, two, three beats that stretched into one, two, three centuries.

"I need a poo, Daddy."

Thank the Lord for little girls.

We all looked at her. We started laughing a bit too loud. We used the poo to disperse a little too rapidly, father and daughter to Shore House, Luca and I to Little Cottage.

I sat at the kitchen table. Luca stood at the sink, staring out the window, gripping the worktop.

"You all just have to know. Don't you?"

"What do you mean?"

"Do you know what it feels like?"

He came over to the table and pulled out a chair. Then placed it in the middle of the floor and sat down.

"Like this. Like an interrogation."

"I'm not sure he meant it like that."

"Really?"

"C'mon, he was just being friendly."

""Your people." That's what he said. Do you know what that means? It means you are different, *your* people are not *my* people. And because you are in *my* country, I have the right to *know* about you."

"I wouldn't read it like that."

"No? Okay then. Why don't you tell me how I should?"

The challenge in his eyes. Quiet scorn now, in my absence of reply. He got up and left the kitchen.

Another "choose your own adventure' cliffhanger. There's young Patti, reading by torchlight under her midnight duvet: "At the moment of connection, it becomes clear that you will only ever disappoint people—go back to the start of the book." Estrangement! Read all about it.

It took me right back. Scenes so loaded I expected the shout of "cut." Frank and his hair-trigger presence, my nonchalance. He studied me as I answered his questions, assessing my responses against criteria I wouldn't meet. He kept his hands by his side, as if he didn't trust them.

"We can get it back, you know."

I was standing against the sink with a glass of water in one hand, total disinterest in the other.

"There's still time."

The thought of time horrified me, what it signified. Frank didn't have a clue that he was saying all the wrong things.

"We've got something special."

"That so?"

"Fuck you, fuck *you!*" He stood up quickly, slamming a hand on the table and taking a step forward as I flinched, my heart thumping, instantly returned to "that night' as Frank picked up a tumbler and hurled it against the floor.

I looked at the shatter. I was wearing three-quarter length jeans and a shard of glass had caught my shin. A thin line of blood was trickling towards my foot. I extended the leg towards him. Fuck "that night." I'd never call it "that night' again.

"Can you see that, Frank, can you?"

"I can see it."

"Well?"

"What?"

"Who *are* you, Frank?"

"You're asking me?"

"Fuck you. I'm gone."

"*Patti.*"

"I'll find somewhere. Soon as I can. Sooner. Fuck you."

"Who is he?" shouted as I left the kitchen. Then up the stairs as he followed me.

Frank beat me to it. The next day, I came down to a note. He was giving me some space. He'd booked a bed and breakfast in Edinburgh. We'd talk when he got back. He got it, I "just needed time." I was incensed by his delusion. At my feet, where the tumbler had smashed against the floor tile, was a thin fissure. I pressed my foot against it and pushed until the tile cracked.

Three days after Frank vamoosed, Hector appeared at the museum, Hugo Bossing the Diet Coke look, top buttons of the white shirt undone, clip-clopping his Cuban heels to that Slow and Rangy Cowboy Step™. My colleagues Kate and Carla followed just behind, Etta James on silent loop; *I just wanna make loooove to you*. They were quietly crestfallen when Hector asked to speak to me in private, somewhat uplifted by the parting "I'll see you girls later."

"You seen Frank?"

"Not for a few days."

I was amazed that Frank had lasted that long. That vulnerability, which once pressed those mothering buttons, had long degenerated into a certainty in the exceptionality of his self-pity. Alone in a bed and breakfast? He must have thought he'd ceased to exist.

"You didn't think to say anything?"

"Well, Hector, I guess he's just taken some time to himself. Things haven't been good."

"Haven't been good? Is that what you call it then?"

"What's that supposed to mean?"

Hector smirked, the wide-eyed innocence of a person who knew. "If you hear from him, tell me. We're worried."

We. Wagons being circled. Frank the victim of a crime yet to be confirmed. Something to ponder as I walked to Jamie's that evening by a more circuitous route than usual. Jamie was concerned. He'd been getting funny looks from my brothers in the office. They fuckin' *knew*.

"Don't worry. Lookee here. This is the normal world, right?" I turned the dimmer switch on the lights to full brightness. "And this is my brothers' world." I turned the lights as low as they would go. Jamie laughed, I laughed, and the laughs dried up. We tried to watch a film.

"I should go home. In case Hector comes round."

"Okay fine."

His agreement was too quick. We clocked it instantly. Here was the Big Kahuna Moment, returned to time and again, the realisation we'd been over-extending whatever we had right from the start. We were a pastiche, like the old harbour that his flat overlooked.

Hector did come round. A visit every day. A phone call every evening. "Have you heard anything?"
"Nothing."
"I'm getting worried."
"Really?"
"Yes. Really. I am genuinely worried."
Except he wasn't. The brothers were Rizla-close, the chances of Frank staying incommunicado, zero. Hector knew where Frank was, and he knew that I knew. I tried to persuade myself that he hadn't found out about Jamie, but of course he had. Hector was a damn seer. But so long as he kept up the pretence, so did I, keeping those shrinking few steps ahead of inevitability. The form of that certainty was the big old mystery a-rolling down the track.

A couple of evenings later I arranged to meet Jamie in a pub up the coast. A place we'd been several times. The barman acknowledged me. Handed me a glass of red and a series of more frequent looks as time passed and Jamie didn't show. "Helluva night," the barman said, another shitty night on the quick approach to December. Rain against the windows and a banked fire.
It was still teeming when I left the pub, rain lashing the ground and not a soul about.
They talked of the devil's footprints round here, tracks from nowhere to nowhere mysteriously appearing in the empty streets. The drown of all other sound had me turning my head, a certainty of something following me along these sodden pavements, invisible footsteps coming down hard, splashing, illuminated in the regular cones of dim yellow streetlight, instantly imprinted on the vision but obliterated by the rain before I could be certain.
Helluva night.
Those words in my head, all the way back to Jamie's flat.
I went up the stairs to the second-floor landing. I had a key but the door was slightly open.
I was expecting the end. I wasn't expecting this.

I saw his legs first, lying horizontally across the living room doorway at the end of the entrance corridor. *They're so pale*, I thought, the trousers runkled up to the knees. I walked slowly towards him and peered round the door. He was lying face up. I started to shake. I heard myself cry out, and he flinched, nose bubbling with blood and an awful, animal snuffling.

***

The quietness of a hospital as you approach it. The noise of waiting. Several endless hours. I was told he would be okay, and Jamie managed to reassure me, too, before the adrenaline and opiates took him beyond lucidity into a brief and surreal monologue about birds: flamingos and ravens, storks.

***

A drive I shouldn't have made. Shock and exhaustion and an exaggeration of sound and vision. Occasional cars. Driver silhouettes peering as they passed. Turning skulls. Grinning, gleaming teeth. I heard them laugh and turned on the radio. AM talk radio time. *"Patti Letham has called, she wants to tell us something, she wants us to bear witness. Patti, you're on the air."*

***

I pulled up beside Frank's car in the drive. Frank was back. Frank didn't look up as I walked into the kitchen. He was sitting at the table eating a fried egg roll. I bowed three times to my self-control. Not as acknowledgment, more as farewell. The fried egg roll pushed me over, the self-satisfied way he was eating it, the contempt in the dribble of yolk on his chin.

"You're home early."

"You bastard."

"It's good to see you again too."

"I'm guessing it wasn't just you. Who else then? The usual suspects, eh? You could have killed him."

"Don't be ridiculous."

"That's not what the doctor said."

"Just what the doctor ordered, if you ask me."

I picked up a mug and threw it at him. Amazingly, he reached out and caught it, right in front of his face. He looked as astonished as me. I threw another and it smacked him on the forehead.

He came at me, and I backed into the hallway. I put my arms up as he forced me back against the wall.

He was looking at me but not seeing me, looking through me. I smelled egg. He pressed his face into my neck and I shoved at him, looking at the opposite wall, the montage of photographs I'd put together a few years back, a holiday in Crete, sun and smiles and the tang of retsina became egg in my nostrils, my mouth as he forced his against mine, his tongue pushing a way in as I pushed him away. "Never was good enough for you, was it Patti?" he shouted before lunging again, "never fuckin' good enough," his hands trying to lift my skirt, that awful realisation of his strength, yet none of this happening, none of this really happening, the red phone still on the table, the letterbox, the faces in the photos still smiling as I scrambled into the living room, and he was on me and everything was so quiet, how could it be so quiet? I remembered the thought distinctly, my feet against the carpet, my voice still AWOL even as I felt him, I felt him, even as I crawled away and saw his golf bag lying against the sofa, the clubs he took with him when he left to "give me some space," the six iron he would have swung, swung so viciously, imagining Jamie's head, because Hector had told him, undoubtedly it would have been his brother who told him, the six iron that I now pulled from the bag, backing away, Frank hesitating as I said, very clearly, "Don't, just fuckin don't."

I sat down beside him. I thought about the sound. I felt Frank's fist driving against my face. The six iron was more slounge than *crack*. Less startling. The *crack* had been the moment of absolute change.

This the coda.

He was moving, he was trying to move. A funny kind of twitching. I stroked his head as I called the ambulance. I pulled up his trousers and, taking care not to catch him, closed the zip.

A zip.

A zip to pull together the pieces of this schizophrenic night.

To take me far.

Take me to another night far beyond this hospital.

A tent, a holiday on the West Coast, close the zip before the bloody midges get in, too late, too late!

I am singing, I am swamped by a wave of utter delight. Zip-a-dee-doo-dah, zip-a-dee-ay, my, oh my …

No one to hear me.
They'll be so disappointed.

Someone cries out.
There are hands at my throat.
I dream of pistons and old locomotives, a regular *whump-whump*. I am tied to the track and the train is closing in.
Steampunk nightmare of the ventilator pipe.

A water pipe, filling me and swelling me, but I still want more. I'm gripping the sheets again, the moon, too, is liquid.

Katie Nurse is reading to me. A detective story, I think. Set somewhere icebound. There's a character who stops off at a supermarket on the way home and buys himself a takeaway boiled sheep's head.

You know, to snack on.

I burst out laughing.

Katie looks at me with a concern that seems familiar, as if I do this a lot.

She pats my hand, keeps reading.

I cannot get beyond the sheep's head. I look towards the door and here they come trotting in, sheep after sheep, bleating and jostling. I reach out to touch one, stroke its soft head and want to eat it.

I feel saliva rising.

I force myself to stop thinking about devouring a sheep's head and focus instead on Katie's voice.

It's appealingly breathy.

The jib of many a man could be cut by such a voice. If only the poor girl had the self-confidence to realise this and hadn't settled for the tiresome boyfriend of local tradition whom the Two Fishwives liberally slander when they think I'm sleeping. Though he does sound pretty sketchy … What would happen in the story Katie is reading? She'll start to *suspect something*. She'll find a *computer disk*, no, the key to a *door*, that takes her to a *shed* and a *grisly discovery* that she backs away from before a hand is *clamped over her mouth* …

Katie doesn't deserve that.

Anyway, it's me who's lying here like an overdone plot point. 'Tis me about whom the Two Fishwives will cast ever more fruity speculations. I have failed—marvellously—in my attempt to lead an unobtrusive existence. I have become the back-cover blurb on an airport potboiler.

Inevitably, the word *haunted* will be used. Yet what's an antihero without trauma, some ever-extendable sin?

They watch me when I sit up all sleepy dumb.

Waiting for me to speak.

To explain.

My stores of vanity being so inexhaustible that even here in the sprawling governor's mansion of the Great State of Catatonia, I find myself thinking of atonement, that what I did to Frank was all about making amends, exorcising the nagging feeling that has tracked me since I was a little girl that I'd never amount to much. Cue the shaking heads of my disappointed parents and I know, I know, I'm sorry, I feel such a deep sense of failure, a lump in my—

My goodness.

Katie Nurse. The words like gunshots.

"You're *crying*. What's wrong? There's no need for this, come on, come on."

Then the sound of something hitting the floor. Probably the book. Katie looms over me, she cuddles me.

"You'll get better, you'll get better."

"*A miracle!*" they proclaim. TOOT TOOT! There is no more impressive a feat than a return from death …

I open my eyes, and behind Katie is a semicircle of gawping doctors and cleaners, the Two Fishwives as well. My bed has been moved to the function room in a pub. They're drinking. Someone says, *"Even after all you did to poor old Frankie boy, we forgive you, we forgive you …"*

I wonder how Frank's doing.

I dream that he's just next door. That he's dreaming of me too.

I cannot decide not to dream.

Yet a decision to not make decisions remains a decision. Even down here, I can't escape them.

Katie Nurse!
Bring me ointment to make the decisions go away and prevent reinfection, you know, like athlete's foot cream.

I wake again.
A silent night, full of holes.
I feel an overwhelming immediacy I don't want to have anything to do with.

The pain.
The higher I rise, the more it grows.
I work harder to sink.
I'm not feeling at all well. A fundamental nausea and generalised pain. I dream I am in a stadium, the stands full of fans. I am the only player. The referee's pointing at me, blowing a whistle. The Two Fishwives hurry onto the field. Squeaky-tight shorts that footballers wore in the 1980s. Each carries a bucket with cold sponges that they take turns slathering against my face.
"Wake up, wake up!"
I may as well not be here at all as they talk with wry professional wistfulness about the exits and re-entries they've witnessed over the years, the endings that sprang their tears, the awakenings that they still can't believe. Remember that guy, a flatliner that came through? *McGuffie*, that was the name, blinked awake like fluorescent lights coming on one by one.
Remember what he said:
"Are youse angels?"
Oh, how that made them titter and now how they titter no more, now that it is me being assessed.
The compassion of the Two Fishwives is an occasional rasping sigh dragged from tar-black lungs. The peering others are more professional, Cool Hands Luke and his entourage. The gravity of my situation, someone intoned, and it must be getting on for six atmospheres down here, maybe that slow crush of my organs is the cause of this all-consuming pain.
Thank goodness for Katie Nurse!
When Luke and his quack team of consultants have done the merry conga to the next lucky patient, she bustles and she blethers and sometimes she almost *nuzzles*, breath on my neck, distracting me from the ruthless objectivity with which they have filleted and filed my condition.

"Ongoing fluctuation in brain function."
"Heart still strong."
"Signs of infection in the head wound."
"Still?"
"Still."
"Concerning."
"Concerning."
They say these things? I think they say these things.
Katie says, "Don't you worry about that nonsense." She tucks me in. I have no idea if any of this is happening.

I sleep.
I may not be sleeping.
I am neither one thing nor another.

Most people relent, in time.
Me?
I've always felt an overwhelming urge to maintain. Likely, I'm terrified to catch up with myself and be irrevocably presented with my own mediocrity. I could have been anyone, gone anywhere!
Maybe this is the final chance.
Hector will bend over me as the nurses take the opportunity to study his arse in tight trews, straining to hear the words meant only for me: *Well, you finally did it, Patti. You've made something of yourself! You know how bloody long I've been waiting to update that Wikipedia entry?*
I do indeed have a Wikipedia entry, Katie Nurse. Do not pretend that you have not perused and pondered those paragraphs. Outrageous horseshit, but these bony ole shoulders is broad. All because of Frank. Frank at The Pines. Now Luca at The Pines. A job that was Hector's doing.
My oh my oh my oh …
It's enough to make me laugh again. Or maybe I'm crying, crying as I go, another exit story for the Two Fishwives.

How quickly everything changed.

Luca.

The before and after of the "your people' incident with Spider-Girl's daddy from Shore House. Things that should have been said. Things that were. We danced on the head of a pin.

He went to The Pines, and we worked the stones on his days off. Colder, wintered days, sunlight that would swell and swiftly fade to broken slate, an enthusiasm whose heart wasn't in it anymore.

We retreated.

We talked but didn't talk, every conversation a verbal pasodoble, a dialling back of confidences we had started to share that now became a mutually unspoken regret it might stay that way. I had always been a brooder and found a fellow dweller in Luca, who also couldn't say the something that would clear the air. I waited for that surging north-easterly.

I wondered about telling him about Frank.

Take this olive branch: Frank's crumpled head on a tarnished salver.

No.

Reasons to be cautious, part three, my presumption of his empathy risked an equal and opposite antipathy.

Yet I nearly decided I would, that now was the time, out on the causeway one Saturday. Luca was staring at the sea and spoke without turning, his quietude disarming, momentarily suggestive:

"I could like it here."

"There's worse places to be."

"Worse people we could meet!"

He wasn't wrong.

Some people watched the sea without interest. Others stared as Luca did, the absorption of a convert. Every sense was engaged, the gaze fixed and mouth slightly open as if tasting, an acuteness in the listening, too, a twitch of the head noting a rise in the wind or the *fusssh* of a harder-breaking wave. Luca watched as if time had decelerated, like the slow-motion arcs of spray bursting over the rocks of Ferris Island, or the unhurried swells in the east.

"It's moving! Is it moving?" He was suddenly pointing. "The lighthouse."

"No, you daft sod. It's the clouds that are moving. But they did build lighthouses to move. To sway in the wind."

"Did they?"

"Imagine being at the top in a storm." I saw Granny C. in the lantern room. Singing as she painted. *If you're blue and you don't know where to go to …*

"Do you think you can learn the sea?"

"Learn the sea?"

He gave me an unencumbered smile. The first in days. "Yes. I want to learn the sea. You can teach me!"

"Can I now? What do I get?"

"Mountains. I will teach you mountains."

"The mountains. What do I want with cold and pointy things?"

"Is it a deal?"

"Why not."

He turned away again. "I could like it here."

A softer voice, less a statement than a question he was considering, a "here' where he might choose to remain that encompassed not only the town but Little Cottage, and me. There was no arrangement that he and Emine could stay, but we both knew they could, if they wanted. I didn't know what I thought about that, just as I imagined Luca didn't really know what he thought about building a life a thousand miles from where he came from.

I remembered Shore House Daddy:

"Your people."

I gazed at the jumble of waves between shore and Ferris Island, that effortless interconnection that no one learned from. It was always exiles who tried hardest to belong. I had even tried myself, an aeon or two back, until I realised that belonging meant kowtowing to certain wearisome expectations I was unlikely to live up to and had zero interest in trying to.

Not Luca.

He was a proper tryer.

He brought home those tales of The Pines with the elation of someone who'd found a place and was determined to hang around. He was the L-Man. What was a nickname if not a sign of belonging?

Not that I trusted signs.

Bazzie once told me that he saw a dead frog splayed flat on a pavement and felt, quote, "a deep and certain freeing." I wasn't built for that kind of epiphany. There was a checkpoint into my Land of Wisdom, manned by a foul-smelling Cold War sentry, drunk on voddie since the crushing of the Prague Spring, cackling as he rejected my passport time and again.

***

I watched Christmas come. The Pines night out. Luca bought three new shirts. He wanted to know what I thought.

"The navy one, the Mod design. With black trousers."

"You sure?"

"I like it."

Annie would, too, the three drink rubicon crossed and a hand that touched his arm. Once, twice, and then it was just a thing, no significance, it was only a works do, only a Christmas do.

I went to bed. A dream of dancers, hundreds in a vast aircraft hangar with the doors open, a multicoloured lightning storm scarring the black: neon greens, blues, and reds. Thunder rose in the fall of pounding drum and bass, the dancers moving slowly round in a choreographed circle, edging towards the walls until there was only one couple at the centre, me and Luca in his new shirt. We're close, so tender, but we're looking over each other's shoulders.

Then even louder thunder shattered the images. I woke up, taking a few moments to realise someone was hammering at the back door. I got into my dressing gown and checked the clock: 2:55 a.m.

I opened the back door to a frozen blast of snow, blinking my eyes clear to reveal a grinning Hector in copper's winter gear. A DayGlo-yellow waterproof with silver reflective strips. Black padded trousers and an incongruous non-regulation, bright red, furry hat with ear flaps that made me wonder if he was on duty or not. All the usual ambiguity.

"That hat's as red as your nose."

He jabbed a thumb over his shoulder.

I peered round him at a shape slumped against a garden chair. Maybe a vague muttering behind the wind.

"He was on the harbour wall. Down at the end of the pier. You seen the water tonight? He'd have been singing all the way to Norway."

"Singing?"

"Singing. Christ knows what. Him and Annie Kittle singing away. A bottle of vino. Chianti, dontcha know."

"Annie Kittle?"

"Annie Kittle. You know her?"

"Not really."

He went over and shook Luca by the shoulder, who brushed his hand away violently, then stood up and swayed, grabbing at Hector, who steadied him. He allowed himself to be briefly helped before again throwing off the arm with a burst of Albanian. He frowned for one-two beats at the kitchen door, brain struggling to pinpoint where he was, then careered across to the hallway, where he stopped suddenly, placing a wavering finger against his lips and blowing a "*shhhhh*." Then more Albanian, an expectant pause, and a brusque wave of his hand as if brushing away the words he remembered we couldn't understand.

"She is gone."

Swaying as he looked at us.

"*Her.*"

He rummaged in one pocket and another, finally pulling out his wallet, taking things out and dropping them on the floor before holding up a photo. Another one of him and Daniela. He staggered over and slammed it down on the table. Luca is sitting, perhaps in a bar, Daniela standing behind him with her arms draped around his shoulders. They are laughing.

"She is gone, but tonight I danced. I danced and sang. I *danced.*"

He waited for a response he didn't get before dismissing us with another terse wave. I followed, watched him thump up the stairs. When I came back, Hector was sitting down, holding the photo.

"Make yourself at home."

"It's a helluva night. Have a heart for a poor old plod." He held up the photo. "Wife, girlfriend? Someone back home?"

"You on duty then?"

"Never off. You know the song. A policeman's lot is not a haa-peeee one."

I sat and waited. He always broke the silence. I delighted in these smallest of victories.

"I hear your boy's settling in nicely at The Pines."

"That's getting a bit old, Hector."

"True. True enough. The boy's sure moved on. The way he was chewing the face off that Annie."

"Was he now?"

"A rival for you, pet."

"Don't call me—'

"You think he's met Frank yet? I mean, that would close the circle right up."

I stared at him. Again, that spooky feeling that everything in my life was somehow directed by Hector. The hallway door opened. We turned to Emine. Claire behind her, pale and semi-detached.

"We came down for something to eat."

"It's the middle of the night!"

"We don't need to—'

"*Patti*," said Hector. "C'mon. It's Friday night!"

"Okay. *Fine.*"

And back we went to silence, more awkward now, the girls hurrying to get their snacks and get out pronto.

"Claire, give my regards to your mum and dad."

She nodded at Hector before giving me the briefest of glances as she quickly followed Emine out.

"A happy family indeed—it's nice, Patti, you should enjoy it. I do believe it suits you. Who'd a thunk it?"

"What can I say, people just gravitate towards me."

"Emine, though. She could do with being in school."

"She says that herself."

"Bit of a harder one that. I'll see what I can do."

"You'll see what you can do?"

"I'll see what I can do."

"Why?"

"I'll see what I can *do.*"

"Gimme a break."

"What's your problem, Patti?"

There it was again. The sense of being played. I clattered the empty cups into the sink. "I haven't got a problem. I know my motivation, never any trouble there. Yours, though, that's something else."

"What can I say? One has one's … *reasons.*"

"Go on then. I'll make it easier. Say this is the TV cop show running in your head. What's your motive?"

"Well now … I'd have to put it down to goodness … Pure goodness."

"I'm serious."

"So am I."

"Oh, for—'

"What about you?"

"What about me?"

"All that drama you can't ever shake."

"Can't deny that."

"Thing is though, it's all so …»

"What?"

"Romantic … You're just such a terrible romantic." He was getting up. Settling his woolly hat back on his head.

"That so."

"It's not a bad thing. It just …"

"It just what?"

He was at the door. Opening it to another blast of snow. "It just has that habit of always getting away from you."

"You're full of shit."

"Why are you always so hard on me? I've looked out for you your whole life. I've stuck with you, think about that."

"Fuck off, Hector."

"And a very merry Christmas to you too, m'lady!"

He touched a finger to his hat, smiled the white dazzle, and disappeared into spindrift and sea-buzz.

I stood waiting. Waiting for Hector to rematerialize, the way he'd been rematerializing all my life.

He had this whole town in the palm of his hand. There hadn't been any dramatic ascent; he'd seemed to slowly will himself into what he wanted to be, a kind of cosseting autocrat, all friendly insistence and counsel that may be threat. And all the dolts, relieved, reverted to the default programme and doffed the cap, because that was so much easier than any trust in their own agency. They wanted the strongman on the Manichaean mission, the one still trying so hard after all this time to convince me too. Because wasn't that always the thing about absolutists near and far, old and new, how they were all just so fuckin' needy.

I started to shiver.

In a sudden drop of the wind to near silence, I heard a giggle upstairs, the drone of Luca snoring.

You're a terrible romantic.

Romantics didn't do black-and-white. Romantics did the shambolic. Such as taking in this father and daughter duo. Such as daring to think *family.* I went inside and picked up Luca's photo. Daniela looked like she had grace. I pocketed the photo and thought of grace I didn't have.

Calmness, though. That I always had.

The snoring and giggling strangers I listened to as I went back to bed, my calmness had brought them here.

My "preternatural calmness' a court-appointed psychologist called it. This in reference to my 999 call to get an ambulance for Frank, a recording played during my trial: "I need an ambulance, please," I told the dispatcher. "My husband has been attacked and is unconscious." When the paramedics, whose blue lights brought curious neighbours one by one onto the street, asked their questions about who might have done this to Frank, I felt a similar serenity, or was it euphoria? "I don't know, I've no idea who'd do such a thing."

At that, Frank lifted a hand from the pool of blood on the floor, the hand I continued to hold as the paramedics carried the stretcher out of the house, my other lifting in a reassuring salute to the neighbours now craning and crowding closer, the very image, again, of calmness.

Those memories were as bold as they get. The journey to the hospital. The buffeting of the ambulance and the efficient paramedics. The odd detachment at being an intimate yet unidentified part of both the cause and the effect of the whole situation, a secondary presence, acknowledged by occasional glances of assurance as I watched from a fold-down seat.

I sat in the A&E waiting area.

A distracted nurse hurried away after telling me Frank was in emergency theatre. "I hope he doesn't fluff his lines," I said to the drunk man sitting beside me with a thumb wrapped in bloody tissues. He just frowned like Stan Laurel and went back to staring at his thumb.

I stayed there until ten in the morning. A policeman appeared. I gave the same account as I had to the paramedics. The policeman seemed as distracted as the nurse. He had other questions, but they could wait. Another nurse told me Frank was in intensive care. He was stable. She said go and get some rest, and instead of going home, I went to see Jamie on ward 7b. A smell of old soup.

Not a nurse to be seen. He was awake. He smiled and took my hand.

"You did what?"

He wasn't smiling anymore. He was horrified. He let my hand go. Let it go and never held it again.

"He's stable. First time for everything, eh?"

"You think this is funny?" He was whispering, but no one was listening, only one of the other six beds taken, a super-doped old man with a military-looking breathing contraption strapped to his face.

"You could have killed him."

I looked at the bandage on Jamie's head. I pictured an identical one on Frank.

"Fuck, fuck, *fuck*."

He was starting to annoy me.

"Why did you do that?" repeated as he turned away from me.

"It just happened. Same as it happened to you, or have you forgotten why you're here?"

"For Christ sake, Patti."

"I'll be back."

"No, you fucking well won't."

I leaned down, my arm across him. "I'll be back."

He had started to cry. This annoyed me even more, but I managed the mummy-whispers, it was "going to be fine, just fine," a squeeze of his arm before I headed for the lifts. The two policemen waiting when the taxi dropped me home said I'd have to stay elsewhere.

I had no intention of staying with my parents and phoned the Station Hotel to book a room. The cops accompanied me upstairs, past the living room and the now-darker stains on the carpet. They watched me pack a bag, eyes lingering on the letters I took from Granny C."s box. They said that after I had checked-in, I should come to the station and give a formal statement. I nodded, re-running what happened, and almost told them the whole story.

After they dropped me at the hotel, I asked the receptionist to order a taxi, which took me up the coast to our favourite pub. I took a room with a sea view and thought about Granny C. and Sandy. Their own affair also ended by the sea, at the Applecross Inn. I saw her at the window, the door closing behind her. Sandy's fading steps. There would have been nothing special about the sea and sky she looked out on, just those eternal shades of grey, the same ones I was looking at from my own window when, a day later, the knock came.

I was disappointed it wasn't Hector who arrested me after telling me that Frank was conscious. I was fascinated by that awakening. Frank sits bolt upright, memory flooding out of the morphine haze.

"Paaaaaaaatti!"

As every vase of flowers on the ward explodes, throwing stems of roses and freesias into the air, the patients leaping and shrieking to catch them. A tumbler with the falsies of the old man in the next bed falls to the floor, teeth snapping like one of those clockwork contraptions, Emine and Claire guffawing as the blooper show replayed the scene over and over.

"It was sheeee that did this!"

A *sheeee* that now merged into the rising whine of the wind around Little Cottage. The walls gave a little shudder as I huddled gleefully under the duvet. I always felt a deviant delight when the wind did this, that its steady fury might be maintained forever. But the sudden drop would always come. Like me, like you, roused to a peak but never able to maintain it.

I got up.

I opened the window to black.

The black of Frank's panic when the bandages were removed. The black that didn't go away, a night without end. Tonight's black. No ships. No lights. Things heard but unseen, the overlapping, overlapping of the waves, never one finished before the next was easing in, a jumble of other sounds coming in on the wind, taking form now, becoming words, my parents:

"It took him a couple of years to adjust, the poor bugger."

"Well, it would, wouldn't it!"

"Imagine silence when you are blind."

"Like being struck dumb."

"I'd sing to myself, I think, to keep myself company."

"Don't say that, she doesn't need the encouragement."

"Oh, don't be so—'

"Too bloody late. I told you. She does it to annoy me!"

My singing that drowned out their voices. "That's Amore." My mother the big Frank Sinatra fan, which was why I always chose Dean Martin. "When … the … MOON hits your eye like a bigga pizza pie, that's amore," louder and louder until there was a sudden flaring light behind me.

I turned to Emine's silhouette. She said something, I think, before closing the door, sending me back to black.

I woke to uncertain, gravelly light. A tune was going round and round my head. Not Deano. Some theme from an old children's TV show. I lay in the pensive calm of a day that hadn't figured out what to do with itself, then got up. Silence from Luca's room across the landing. Silence from Emine's.

I made coffee and checked my mobile:

Bazzie.

Patti! Never mind this Yuletide schmaltz. Get thee ready for New Year. Bring red wine and corn snacks!

Bazzie's Hogmanay party.

The second of his two annual jamborees. This one unable to avoid the presence of his awful father. At least the old man got so drunk he was asleep by ten, farting and drooling on the sofa until dawn, a profane yet forgiven centrepiece. Because it was New Year, New *Year*!

I might go.

I wouldn't go. New Year always felt like a mirror I was being forced to look at. If I had to stare at myself, I didn't want half the town drunkenly leering over my shoulder at the same time.

I much preferred Christmas. Christmas was a pair of mottled silver earrings held up to the light, glinting with time and memory. Granny C. liked it too: "Remember. Jesus was a socialist revolutionary!"

We spent long afternoons looking for presents. We loved the tinsel and lights, the music spilling from shops, the church at the top of the wynd, the stained glass all cosy-glowing. I wanted to go inside, but we never did, perhaps the gauntlet of gravestones you had to walk past put Granny C. off in the same way it now deterred me. That promise of rapture seemed as crooked as the slabs. Unlike the cemetery drunks, I couldn't believe in hope so cheaply offered.

I heard slow feet on the stairs.

Then Luca.

"Good morning!" I said.

He silently acknowledged me, glancing sink-wards, as if weighing up if he could make it before puking.

"So how was your evening then?"

"Yes."

He sat down heavily at the table.

"Yes?"

"Yes, it was good."

"Do you know how you got home?"

He put his arms on the table and rested his head on top. "I know, I know. Your friend Hector."

"Seems you and Mizz Kittle put on quite the show down at the harbour."

He closed his eyes with a mortified groan, but he was smiling. "She is a nice lady. A lovely lady."

The eyes opened again, looking up at me, past me. I continued to look at him. The quick flick of disappointment. I thought about Christmas, old rituals. The reassurance of things whose meaning was long-lost.

* * *

A couple of days later I put together the usual backpack. A picnic blanket and two flasks, one for coffee, one for soup, pea and ham. And where there was pea and ham soup, there always had to be corned beef and cheese sandwiches. If you needed to ask why, then you'd never understand.

I drove up to The Pines and headed into the trees."Twas the day of the Christmas party, Luca had told me. I trained the binoculars on the communal lounge, just along from Frank's apartment.

The inmates had been rousted, a semicircle of chairs facing the panorama windows. I had observed this seating arrangement before. It could only have been deliberately, and somewhat disturbingly, planned. From the far left of the circle, the chairs moved through the younger, more compos mentis of individuals to the increasingly slumped and decrepit, reaching those on the extreme right who looked in need of immediate defibrillation. Regularly spaced at intervals behind them were green- and blue-smocked nurses and orderlies. All the staff were smiling, but only the more baffled of residents, the majority sitting with a crestfallen mix of dejection and unease, as if pondering how many chairs further round the semicircle they might be sitting a year or two from now.

In front of the semicircle, their backs to the window, stood half a dozen Brownies, undoubtedly belting out "Away in a Manger,"

"When Santa Got Stuck Up the Chimney," and other classics to put Christmas cheer in the hearts of all, including Luca, who stood ready and waiting for spillages of eggnog or bodily fluid. Annie Kittle was beside him, tired-looking, thin as a whippet.

There was no sign of Frank. I scanned to his apartment, the curtains open but no Frank. I swung back to the lounge. The Brownies were marching out and the audience clapping.

A man with an accordion was next up, his back to the chairs as he composed himself with several deep breaths as if preparing for the Albert Hall. Then he suddenly cracked a smile, holding it while still looking out the window, as if making sure he could trust it when he faced the crowd and launched into his maudlin folk dirges. Give it a few numbers and everyone would be climbing over each other to reach that last chair of the semicircle.

As I watched, Frank appeared in the lounge. My stomach somersaulted. He was in his wheelchair, Emine and Claire pushing, one handle each. They stopped beside Luca and Annie for a few moments, Annie bending down to talk to Frank. Then the girls wheeled him out.

I watched the tableau come together in Frank's apartment. Christmas-cosy, an Advent candle and a few tea lights on the coffee table, the three of them on the sofa, Frank in the middle. The girls took turns reading a book called *Journey into Fear*. Something was going to happen, I knew.

Frank was smiling. Frank was wearing an orange paper hat. Frank put a hand on Emine's knee. She let him leave it there. My heart thumped, an instant dryness in my mouth. The bread I had eaten was a solid mass in my throat. The scene in Frank's apartment started to break apart. I tasted bile coming up. I watched other images spread into my vision.

I watched my arrest all over again.

The silent, dreamlike drive back to town in the squad car. A leaden sea like a painted backdrop in a film, a green tree-shaped air freshener I couldn't take my eyes off, twisting like a body at the end of the rope. The interview and the charge. The ink on the tips of my fingers. That stinking cell. Crouched on the floor and the sickness swift-rising. Rushing to the filthy toilet.

I flushed and it didn't drain. I felt wetness on my knees and smelled piss. I watched the watery mess rise, up and up the sides of the bowl, then over the rim, water and puke pouring over my shoes, across the floor and still rising, across the narrow concrete shelf that was the bed, forcing me to jump onto the mattress as a raft, the cell door suddenly opening and the water gushing out, taking me with it, someone shouting "get back here' as I surfed awaaaaaay …

The water drained with an ugly slounge.

I started to cry hysterically, and the observation hatch rasped open. I knew it would be Hector. I stifled the tears. My snot dripping into the bowl. I heard whispers. Then silence. They were watching me. Curled there in the foetal position. They might have watched me for days.

Then Hector at the hatch:

"It seems you made quite the impression, Patti. I'm not just talking about Frank's *head*. Eh, Orin?"

"Not exactly subpar technique, Hector."

"Ha, exactly! If you wanted to swing, Patti, you just needed to ask. I mean, the drama, a golf club? You should have stuck with acting at school, RADA would have nabbed you. *Be* that psycho. You know what the quacks are saying, pet? That you might have fuckin' *blinded* him."

The hatch slammed, the clip of Orin's and Hector's heavy shoes in the dark. I hadn't spoken. I started to laugh. I hadn't said a damn *word*. I felt the tears come flowing back and was sick again.

I stared down at the mess.

I wondered if I could divine my fate from the tendrils of my puke. I stirred my fingers through it, searching for a revelation I could live with, reassessing and redistributing motive and memory, trying to introduce another me, who was in no way connected to now, yet not succeeding in fully decoupling myself, still that common origin however distant I got from the familiar, further and further until the cell door opened and they took me to court.

The charge was assault to severe injury. I replied, "Not guilty." I swallowed the urge to add "m'lud," contenting myself with a smile I hoped wasn't too deranged. My solicitor and the fiscal argued about bail as I stared out the window. The fiscal lost and the sheriff gave me a curfew, ordering me to make no attempt to contact the injured party and to reside with my parents.

They had been sitting in the gallery throughout the hearing. They were overly solemn, as if overcompensating for the wholly ambiguous impression being given by their daughter, who seemed "distracted," they said afterwards, almost "cheerful," as if I wasn't taking this seriously at all. "What is *wrong* with you, Patti, what were you *looking* at out the window?"

They took me to Shore House. They asked questions asked ever after. My brothers were there, too, jumpy as two ventriloquists' dummies. "Gottle of Geer," I said, and laughed. Everyone looked alarmed, then everyone was shouting. I listened briefly, then realised I didn't have to. My gaze moved to the window. I felt the rest of me follow. I couldn't hear them anymore.

"They burned witches out there," I said. "Shinnery Point."

They stared at me.

"Imagine the flames. Everyone watching. Flames against the darkness. It would have been beautiful."

As beautiful as Emine.

As beautiful as Emine in Frank's apartment. Coming back into focus through the binoculars. The three of them were still sitting on the sofa. Frank grinning like the cat that got the cream.

His hand still on her knee.

Nothing had happened, yet everything had.

I felt suddenly exhausted, as if I had suffered a great defeat, though I had no idea what victory I was fighting for. Emine was so comfortable in Frank's presence, much more than in mine.

Maybe she felt safe. What could a blind man do? Maybe she pitied him. I wanted her to pity him. I wanted to jump the fence and sprint across the grounds to the apartment and yell "she pities you, she pities you," the accordion player accompanying me, grinning, Balkan turbo-folk, the residents clustering around in another semicircle, clapping faster and faster …

I watched Emine's mouth move. She was so self-contained. I watched her brush hair from her eyes. A beautiful, self-made enigma. She would defy all their interpretations and expectations.

They would burn her, too, in the end.

Hogmanay morning. Luca and I on the causeway. A low, low tide and a deep, deep blue. A bitter, accusing day. We had scarves around our faces, blunting the razor cold swallowed with each breath.

He was humming. Pushing a stone into the space I'd cleared. I caught his gaze as I worked the mortar. His irises as blue as the sky. He smiled behind his scarf, the eyes crinkling. There were little beads of condensation on the fabric where his breath escaped. At breakfast, he'd said, "I'll maybe join you later." The "maybe' wouldn't have occurred to him a month ago.

"So, what's tonight's plan then?"

He stood up and inclined his head, pondering the choice already made. "I am—we are going to Bazzie's."

"Party of the year."

"You should come."

"Who said I wasn't?"

"So you are?"

"No."

"Oh. Okay then."

I made my fingers into a scissors shape, cutting an imaginary something. "Sorry for the snippiness."

"The what?"

"Being grumpy. I've never been a fan of it, New Year."

He laughed. "I wouldn't have guessed!"

We laid a few more stones. Ferris Island had almost been reached. A few more rows to cross the boulder jumble and we could step onto the black sandstone slab that led to shingle, then grass.

Luca took it all in. Grave as he surveyed our works. "It is nearly finished."

"Getting there."

"You must be very proud."

"Not really. I'm just filling in the blanks. My granny did the hard work."

"You have to give yourself more credit."

"You wouldn't be saying that if you'd seen my score."

He frowned.

"My credit score …? Never mind. It's a bad joke."

His phone buzzed again. The sixth time that morning. I looked away as he fiddled with the keypad, a smile on his face. There was a bird circling the lighthouse, a buzzard in elegant arcs.

"Are we finished, Patti? It's just I should be …"

I nodded, said "no problemo," still looking at the buzzard. When I looked back, he'd almost reached the mainland, hazed in brightness and outlined in black, like his bold advice to my good self.

You have to give yourself more credit.

I wandered along the causeway. I looked down at the puddles, the little hints of my reflection. Me but not me. Like the trial, when it came, the singular versions of me being offered up by prosecution and defence. I studied the jurors. I wondered about the capability for malice.

I stamped violently in a causeway puddle, shattering my reflection. I did a little skip and splashed into another. I remembered a letter from Sandy to Granny C. He was recounting one of their evenings. They'd been dancing, "tipsy dancing' he called it, which still made me giggle. I broke into the most bungling of Charleston's, all straining high kicks and awkward duck flaps. The ghost couple danced alongside me, the three of us slap-sticking along the causeway, arms intertwined, you just wouldn't *believe* our million-dollar smiles!

I finished with a neat foot drag, which I thought cut quite the dash, and looked up to see, looking at me a few metres away, Shore House Daddy, Spider-Girl, and, hold the front page, the mother.

"Howdy doody."

Spider-Girl replied with a gappy-toothed smile. "I liked your dance."

"Thank you. Your front teeth! What happened?"

Her mother answered, "Hello, Patti."

Though we had never met. Shore House Daddy stepped in to provide an anonymous introduction.

"My wife."

"Janice," they said at the same time.

"She's my mummy." Spider-Girl sounded very serious.

"Hello, Mummy."

"She's not *your* mummy."

Shore House Daddy and Mummy looked a bit uncomfortable

and the parting, inevitably, was swift. I watched them walk away. I watched them glance back. They knew me, Hector had told them all about me. And what had Luca said earlier? *I wouldn't have guessed.* Because he, too, knew me. Everyone had known Patti Letham since the Trial of the Decade.

It was another reason I gave Hogmanay parties a body swerve. Pissed as farts or puritan sober, everyone conferred on themselves the right to be a nosey fucker that wouldn't cross their mind at any other time of the year. I was cornered one time, some woman shaking her head: "Now you're here in front of me, I can't believe you *did* that, I really can't."

The Trial of the Decade. It was actually called that. The front-page headline of the local paper. There was a photo beneath it, a long shot of me in Shore House garden. I'm wearing a duffel coat, my arms wrapped tight around me and my hair blowing wild. I look fresh from the nuthouse.

I remembered waiting for the jury to come back in. The strangest feeling of displacement. It wasn't me sitting in the dock smelling fresh-cut grass drifting in the open windows. I was outside, playing football with the boys I could hear in the nearby park. I was dancing through the midfield, better than all of them, a *girl*. Then a rocket, top corner from the edge of the box.

I smiled, catching the eye of the foreman of the jury.

His gaze narrowed.

The gaze of the entire courtroom narrowed, everyone staring with that now-familiar and not-totally-unobjective common curiosity, the trial having recast me as collective property.

Trial of the Decade hack, on the other hand, was tapping a pencil and frowning, searching for the elusive door to the incandescent prose that would stamp his passport to the southern dailies. His balance of impassivity and irony was all wrong; he didn't look imperious so much as constipated. He hadn't yet admitted to himself that he'd be stuck here forever, scoops more meagre than a well-scraped ice-cream tub. Less Truman Capote than Truly Kaput.

Cue the clerk of the court!

A pock-faced man of indeterminate age. Looked like the captain of a bowls team.

"All rise."

I had been impressed by the prosecution, ruthlessly set out by a female procurator fiscal so startlingly different from me, she seemed to be a new paradigm of woman. As attractive as it was alienating, a reboot in that image was never an option for the "likes of Patti Letham' as she described me, a gently imposing voice that emphasised apparently random words in her monologues and had the effect of making everyone listen closely to everything she said.

Even the decrepit sheriff appeared to defer to her now and then, the sheriff being the only one who avoided my gaze, so shortsighted he couldn't actually locate me, or perhaps made uneasy by the conflict of interest of being so ancient that he was once a friend of my grandfather's and a regular guest at family parties. My father had told me to keep schtum.

What a sensation!

Right under Truly Kaput's nose if he had the instinct to look. I decided I remembered the sheriff—he was so nice to me as a child, once gave me a bag of sweets, a hand on my cheek …

The fiscal's alternative ABC about Six Iron Night was compelling. She worked the room like a boxer. First a southpaw jab: "No. Ms Letham did not *plan* to blind Mr Ruthven, her true intent was more sinister …" dousing the wide-eyed jury with the jissom of speculation before my solicitor could object. Then a haymaker: "Malicious revenge for the absurd notion that Mr Ruthven had anything to do with the attack on the man she was having a sleazy affair with? What … *rot*! A burglary. A simple burglary gone wrong. As the police established."

She stared at me.

She was good. Looked good, too, long strawberry blonde curls. And a delicate *parfum* that clashed with a genuine hostility. I almost turned around to see if she was looking at someone else.

Maybe she was right. Maybe I had wanted to kill Frank.

I stared back at her, ignoring again my mother's advice at lunch on day one. "Patti, you must stop *staring*."

My mother was the one holding things together.

My father's moments of absence had become much more frequent since my arrest. A tendency to forget things, words slipping into silence mid-sentence. Very early one morning, I heard him leave Shore House and followed him outside, finding him in the shed, surrounded by a scatter of upended boxes. He was looking for his old train set, almost in tears.

At other times the patriarch was fully present:

"Do you know, do you *really understand*, Patti, what you're doing to our reputation, our *business*. If we were public, our shares would have bloody flatlined." Then, my mother would put a hand on his arm, a gentle reminder of the necessity of decorum no matter the provocation. She held his hand as they sat in the public gallery, two Sunday-suited manifestations of time and respect, requesting by their serious-yet-humble demeanour that all the Lethams had done for the town be taken into consideration by the good people of the jury, who, excepting one or two, worked, had worked, or in time, would work for Dalriadan Stoneware.

It was extraordinary; I believed my mother and father's performance almost as much as the procurator fiscal's.

* * *

At Hogmanay I made soup. Another Granny C. tradition. It didn't matter that for many years no first foot had come by the cottage for a plate. The soup-maker was one of my very private archetypes.

Mother Letham insisted that Luca and Emine ate something before they went out. Luca tried again to persuade me to go to Bazzie's party, concerned I was going to be all by myself and looking to Emine to back him up. She shrugged and said, "Claire and I aren't doing much either."

I had a sudden flash of Frank. He was sitting on his sofa. Emine was feeding him soup:

"Open up now."

Frank is grinning, opening his mouth.

"Just a few more …"

"Just a few more spoons."

"Auld Lang Syne' drifting in from the lounge. Frank's hand on her knee again.

"Stay awhile, pet …"

I uncorked a bottle of wine and worked my way to the dregs as I oversaw the party prep. I was trying. *"You certainly are trying,"* said Groucho Marx, waggling the cigar and raising the eyebrows. When they left, I would put on *Duck Soup*. Do it next year and look, another tradition! "Not that film again," says Emine as Luca lifts his latest shirts, asking, "Which one, whadaya think?"

They tumbled out the door in a chatter of Albanian and the fug of Mitsouko that I'd doused Emine in, so long unsprayed that one sniff was enough to trigger something forgotten that I couldn't quite place. It being the season for whims, I went upstairs to my wardrobe.

I tried again.

A Hogmanay shindig a lifetime ago.

I was wearing a dress.

The very one that I now slipped on.

Indigo blue, chiffon sheath, still pleasingly and surprisingly tight in all the right places. I over-dowsed myself with the perfume, turned in the mirror a few more times and sneezed, the third bringing me back to myself. I decided that the memory had, in truth, never happened. I undressed quickly, washed off the Mitsouko in a scalding shower and watched *Duck Soup* in my pj's and dressing gown. I opened another bottle and waited for midnight.

Granny C. Her resolute and absolute refusal to sing "Auld Lang Syne." I shouted "ha' and decided to start a fire.

Tightening my dressing gown, I weaved kitchen-wards and pulled on wellies and a purple woolly hat. The head torch found the shed and then kindlers, an old newspaper, and a pile of logs. I dumped the lot into the wheelbarrow: "Wheel-BARROW, not wheel-BARRA. One may be drunk, but one remains couth, is that the opposite of uncouth? Fa KENS, I mean, who KNOWS …»

Then the black shore in thin drizzle. On a cut-glass wind, the muted sounds of a refined Shore House party, cocktails and blinis, less "soup's on' than soupçon. I found the blackened circle of stones still there from some summer's evening just as an explosion of Shore House fireworks lit the sky and sent butterflies of colour flickering along the shining causeway.

And though no one would knock on my door tonight, I sat by the fire and watched all the others come, all the old faces of times past. I had no choice. Such was the dictatorship of New Year.

Our parties were raucous.

There were dozens of people. The tradition begun by Granny C. and Grampa was reluctantly continued by my parents after the elders moved into town. Yet although they no longer lived in Shore House, back my grandparents came every Hogmanay to hold court over the miscellaneous guests who ran an openhanded range from the great and the good to the doomed and the daft, ever frustrating the parental preference for a more discerning soiree.

Granny C.

"Everyone is welcome—every foot from first to last!"

As a little girl, I'd watch from a corner of the living room, clutching Pooh Bear and a glass of squash.

After a while, no one noticed me, especially my mother and father, trying too hard to enjoy themselves, casting looks at Granny C., centre stage, the consummate host, the evening's heart and soul yet just a beat distant. Not that she gave off vibes of aloofness, quite the opposite, her naturalness was so genuine it invited both delight and uncertainty, a collective sense of "I have no idea who this woman is who has been placed among us, but I am glad she has."

"Slainte!"

I raised the bottle.

"To Granny C. and Captain Sandy."

Soldier boy was a lucky boy. All that time he got to spend behind the veil. That woman of primary colour and presence who resisted the mottled, time-bound guarantees of this place. Sea and big sky, to be settled here was to be unsettled, and no paradox in that. I told you that once, Sandy, do you remember? I'd been reading your letters, remember …?

Then sudden laughter, close by. The hairs on my neck stood up. I turned around not to Captain Sandy arm in arm with Granny C. but a laughing someone entering the front door of Shore House.

Another tradition was unfurling in there.

Their own ghosts would dance with mine, years from now, as yet other people went through new and different motions. The light was off in Spider-Girl's bedroom. I hoped that she wasn't asleep but downstairs, sitting in the corner of the living room with Pooh Bear and a glass of squash, eager to stay up but getting sleepy, the dream factory of her own memories.

I raised the bottle again. "Good luck to her!"

"To who?"

"What the hell, Luca!"

"Sorry, sorry."

Luca plonked himself beside me. Held his hands out to the fire, rubbing them together vigorously for a few moments, then slumping back, chin pressed into his waterproof, arms folded.

"I didn't expect you back for hours." I held out the bottle.

"*Gëzuar.*"

"Cheers."

He looked at me. Looked away. "I have to be better."

"Amen to that, brother."

A flare of orange beside the Shore House wall. Then a second. Two people having a cigarette.

"I'm serious, Patti."

"So am I." I threw another log on the fire. "Problems?"

"We had an argument."

I brushed something from my knee that wasn't there. "You know the problem?" He looked up, and I pointed at the fire. "With fires? The problem is there's too many things to see in the bloody flames."

"I miss her."

I felt an instant swell of anger. An intensity that surprised me. "Then find her."

"She's gone."

"How the *fuck* do you know that!"

He leaned away from me slightly but was looking at me intently. "Why would you care?"

"Why would I *care*? Why wouldn't I? Do you think there is something wrong with me?"

"What I mean is—'

"Do they say things about me?"

"What? Who?"

"The people at The Pines. Annie and all your new friends. They must have told you all about me by now."

He looked away. "I don't know about any of that."

"You're a shit liar, Luca."

"Okay. I have been—'

"So you know about Frank. Fine. So don't you think I should have known about Emine's good deed?"

"What do you mean?"

"Reading for the blind man! You think I might not be able to *handle* that?"

He was getting to his feet.

"Luca!" Aware I was shouting. "*Luca*. You're *supposed* to have an argument at New Year. That's the *point!*'

I watched him walk away. The cigarettes by Shore House were still flaring, flaring as they watched.

"Happy New Year to you too," I shouted, letting rip with an anger even I found remarkable. "It's *Hogmanay*, lighten up, don't make it such a bloody trial, I'll tell you what a trial *really* is."

***

They were still revolving when I woke up the next day with no memory of getting back to the cottage.

My smartass words.

My headache suggested I'd finished the second bottle. This was confirmed when I forced myself outside for some air. Down by the dead fire was the bottle, the neck poking out of a pyramid of pebbles I must have built around it, clearly a Very Important Meaning that meant sod all now.

I cooked a big breakfast and ate it in the living room. No sign of Luca or Emine. I put on the New Year's Day concert from Vienna. Another nod to Granny C. We watched it one morning when I was nine, under a blanket in the living room. I forgot about the concert for years, rediscovering it in my twenties. I'd watched it ever since. Usually a hangover. Often tears.

When Emine appeared, I sent her upstairs for my duvet. We huddled on the couch. Luca joined us, ashen faced, a brief and silent asking with the eyes if we were going to mention our falling out. Rain began to slam against the window. I imagined a sickly, churning sea.

I dozed.

I was cosy.

I felt Emine briefly rest her head against me. The orchestra was playing Strauss, one of them, had to be. I drifted closer to sleep and was brought back by a crescendo of percussion. I allowed myself a tentative content, then opened my eyes to Luca. He was staring, and he didn't immediately look away. There was arrogance in that look, as if he had me all figured out. I had a sudden, devastating sense of vast distance, and nothing mapped but me.

I remembered a similar certainty.

The foreman of the jury.

The ruddy-faced earnestness of duty in a plaid shirt. One of those who made New Year such a trial of dismal wistfulness. One midnight dram *only*! He had to be up at dawn to leap into the sea in his Speedos, tut-tutting the half-cut others dressed as mermaids and superheroes.

"Have you agreed upon a verdict?"

The foreman cleared his throat, and I glanced up to Frank. Accompanied by a pretty young carer, he'd been in the gallery every day, always a pair of very dark glasses. I wanted to remove them—nice and slow—until his eyes met mine and I knew he saw me, I knew he did.

Samuel Donaldson from O'Hare and Higgins solicitors had asked before the trial how I wanted to "play the Frank card." Tapping a pen on a notepad and frowning. Seeking the angle:

"I'm thinking self-defence is no offence," he said.

"Right."

"*Right*."

He seemed pleased.

"You confronted him about Jamie being attacked. He was angry and hit you and you defended yourself. Right?"

"Right."

"There was no intent, it was instinctive, okay?"

"Okay."

"Is there anything I should know? Any bad behaviour?"

"Bad behaviour?"

"Yes. We need a monster. Do we need to create one?"

"A monster?"

"Exactly." Matter-of-fact and still scribbling on his pad. "There's a narrative out there already, Patti, stuck on repeat. We have to change the tune. We need a new story." He looked up expectantly.

"I'm just the cheating wife, right?"

"Who blinded her husband."

"Didn't you say it was self-defence?"

"Wasn't it?"

"Of course."

"Then tell people that, *sell* it. Be the victim. You get me?"

He was looking at me as if I was too naïve to see the am-dram of it all, happy hour in the jury pews and the public stalls, the pasteboard goodies and baddies, the minds made up but give 'em *more*, you never know, spill those shameful, most intimate details, you might just swing it.

"No. He wasn't a monster."

The solicitor nodded vaguely.

"Pity," he said, and went back to his notes, sketching the choreography of his upcoming dance with the procurator fiscal. They worked the trial like a rumba, something obscene about it, the conceit, throwing their poses as I gawped at myself, that stranger, the same way everyone else did, glad that I had refused to end up hot with grief for all I had surrendered.

***

January. The weather worsened, forcing us off the causeway. A frustration with the completion so close. I stared out at the elegant thirty-five metre curve, rising at low tide like a petrified salamander, grey black in the near-continuous rain, a sliver glisten in occasional sun.

Nearly there.

Nearly there and then what?

The local and national press had turned out for Granny C., a Pathé crew as well, filming her from beneath, the camera tilted upwards, socialist-realist style. Soviet grey overalls and a black neck scarf, a hand cupped over her eyes as she looked back along the finished causeway. There was an ironic smile on her face, not pride, more a light-hearted "what's the big deal?"

I saw my own headline in the local rag. Page ten, a telephoto shot. "Local oddball puts last stone in place."

Imagine they snapped me skulking in the woods at The Pines. Flask at my feet. Binoculars to hand.

I mean, there was a story.

I'd been to The Pines twice already in January. I settled the binoculars and picked out Luca in the main lounge. He put a hand on Annie's backside as she passed. She rolled big eyes with fake outrage, blowing a kiss as she hurried away. I panned right and found Emine in Frank's apartment.

At 7 p.m. on a Tuesday, she read for Frank.

She left the door open, a safeguarding requirement no doubt. After they sat down on his two-person sofa, Frank leaned in and said something. She leaned back, indulgent and smiling, and got up to close the door. Frank's insistence. It made me wonder. Made me look closer.

The way he leaned back on the sofa, eyes closed and a smirk.
She read.
He listened for a bit, still smirking.
Then moving.
Moving as I watched it happen.
A slow arm snaking around Emine that she felt and tried to ignore at first, smiling as she pulled back, his arm retracting, mouth opening in apology. She started to read again, a look over her shoulder at the door. He tried again, in for a penny, in for a pound, a hand on the knee, the thigh, Emine letting it happen, she couldn't believe it was happening. She froze as I sprung to my feet, jumping over the fence and across the open ground, bursting in just as Frank was pushing her down on the sofa. I realised I was holding a golf club.

But I was just watching through the binoculars, and Emine was just reading.

Frank hadn't moved a muscle.

I watched the usual routine when she closed the book. He felt his way across to the sideboard, opened a drawer, and held up some notes. Once more, Emine mouthed "no, no." He waved the money as she backed out of the door, laughing. The other times I had watched this scene, Frank let it go in good humour. Tonight, his hand stayed in the air when the door closed. A moment later, he scrunched up the notes and hurled them across the room.

My heart was pounding.

I put the binoculars down and raised my face to the drizzle. When I picked up the binoculars again, the curtains in Frank's apartment had been drawn and nothing had ever happened.

Car lights and an engine moved my gaze. The backshift was ending, the night workers moping in. I scanned the nurses and care assistants, hurrying to their cars or dawdling in twos, eking out the last moments of freedom. From my position in the trees up on the little hill, I could see the car park and behind it, the entrance block, the doors reached by a curve of slate paving, fringed with all-weather planting, green and ferny-looking things.

Out of the bright sliding doors came Luca, Emine, and Annie. I expected them to link arms and go full MGM, high-stepping down the path, Luca spinning around a lamp post, arm outstretched.

They were happy.

They were happy and I was sitting in the wet-black trees,

thinking about Frank, wondering about guilt and if he ever considered his own, getting angrier with all I never said, then or now.

***

When I got back to Little Cottage, three had become one. Emine was sitting on the sofa eating a bowl of noodles, watching another blooper show. She really did love that slapstick. It was one of the few times I heard her laugh, belly deep and bassy, not a laugh you'd have guessed.

"No Luca?"

She slowly looked left, then right, then back at me, as if I was the stupidest person in the universe.

"Eh. No."

"So how was your evening?"

She was instantly wary. She knew that I knew she read for Frank. I knew she knew about me and Frank.

"It was fine. He's sweet. You know … like a pet or something." She looked up with a vaguely amused frown, like, you and him, what was that all about? "But what I don't really like is the …"

"What?"

She looked embarrassed. "Eggs. He smells of *eggs* when he gets close to you. You can smell it."

I stared at her.

"I know, *horrible*, right?"

I left her to the canned laughter and went upstairs. I opened the window, the wind sucking at me, insistent, the causeway a moonlit scar in the near distance. I breathed. I smelled low tide.

Sulphur. Eggs.

Eggs on Frank's breath. Emine eating instant noodles, appalled as he comes closer, still closer as she says "no, no," standing now, making some space to swing a golf club, once, twice, the third will cause all the problems. She looks down at him, curious, he's twitching a bit. Then she sits down on the sofa and looks at the TV. She's laughing. There's a *dog* hurtling down the street on a *skateboard*; she's properly *guffawing*. I could hear her despite the wind.

It felt like another verdict being delivered.

I saw myself out on the causeway. The ragged gap where the granite setts had yet to be replaced.

I was standing.

I was looking at the ruddy-faced foreman. Then Frank, sat in the gallery with his dark glasses. Listening intently as the clerk asked the foreman what the verdict was in respect of the accused Patricia Letham. The foreman began to speak and exploded into a fit of coughing that went on and on, finally ended, then started again. This happened two more times.

"For goodness' sake, can someone please get him some water?"

Everyone turned to look at me.

The gallery faces were stunned. You'd have thought I had cracked a joke as they were tying me to the stake. *"It's not right, not right, light the fire, light the fire now and be rid, be rid!"*

Well bring it on. March me, bind me, anyway you want me. I rode with the witches, bitches, it was time to make a stir, as Miss Jameson said the day I broke down in her dusty office and told her all about Frank and Jamie: "Well, we should all make a stir at least *once* in our life."

The decrepit sheriff cleared his own throat.

"Though we may be gathered like moths to a *phlegm*," he said, "a verdict is expected, not *expectorated*."

He was indeed trying to be funny. His neck was turning a deep red as he surveyed the awkward silence, desperate for a laugh but happy with a titter, a blast of canned laughter from the blooper show, *"Good one, m'lud,"* who needs poodles bouncing on a trampoline, eh?

The foreman of the jury was nodding. Telling everyone that he was finally ready. His face was scarlet.

I looked at Frank. His carer was bending to his bandaged head. Frank nodded.

Behind him in the public gallery, my mother whispered in my father's ear. His mouth instantly closed. I wondered where he retreated on those journeys into the middle distance, when Sammy and the Blonde were filling the courtroom with alternative minutiae of my life with Frank, which were empty of every reason I was in that dock in the first place.

They were the last of me, those reasons.

My life had been emptied. The revelation of my essential weakness was the ultimate degradation. I lay under its weight until my self-disgust finally imploded. When it was too late.

"Again, sir, what is the verdict in respect of the accused Patricia Letham?"

The door to the public gallery banged open.

I felt an instantaneous elation, certain that the figure appeared in silhouette was Jamie. Then Hector stepped out of the bright spring light. He smiled at me as the foreman stammered "not proven."

***

A few days later, Luca told me they were leaving. They really were, and I didn't need to ask where they were going.

Annie got the villa by the golf club in the divorce from her smug, serial shagger of an executive husband. Don't ask how I scuttled to this butt, I just knew. Time and proximity created a weird collective unconscious round these parts. The next leap in humanity's psychic evolution was happening *right now*, here at the fart-joke end of the esoteric spectrum.

"We've imposed on you far too long, you've been so, so good to us, we are so, so grateful, I cannot say …»

On so on.

Emine's occasional nods acting as the full stops that Luca rushed over in his sweet, torrential eulogy.

I went for a walk in the dunes. I found myself outside the shack where I had met them. I heard the saw as I came back and watched them from the gate. They'd taken the wooden horse from the shed and were working the bow saw on a log. Luca had the handle end and was pretending the saw was stuck, all fake exasperation. Then he suddenly moved it back and fore, Emine yelping with laughter as her arm was jerked around like an out-of-control marionette.

I thought of Daniela. I still had her photo.

I don't think he remembered slamming it down on the table when he was drunk. He hadn't asked if I had come across it. He rarely spoke of Daniela now. One fine morning in Annie's super-modish kitchen, he'd realise it wouldn't be so easy. He'd be sipping exclusive Rwandan coffee from a hand-fired mug and *ta-da!* there she would be, sitting directly across from him, smiling, her back to the big window that looked out on the fourteenth fairway.

Luca would be shocked, speechless, and look, yonder was something else! Something small and distant outside the window was getting closer and now crashing through the glass. A golf ball. Smacking him between the eyes. An epiphany right enough. Good luck drawing an arbitrary line and moving on. Love was a concertina and always an ambush, like the hard north-easterly suddenly returned, rocking me onto my heels as I opened the gate.

My mother:

"Oh dear, she's a philosopher now."

"Best adopt the brace position, dear!"

I smiled and looked west, up towards the cemetery on the headland, and gave a jaunty salute.

Because January was finally over. Because I still had that photo of beautiful Daniela, and I still believed in her. Because that sweet-sour city of rain-light, laughter, and brass was upon me once more.

Brass.

Brassy. I have been called that.

A brassy bitch.

Brass and my mother.

Something in the sunlight flowing in the hospital window.

I see her.

She's sitting at the table in the Shore House kitchen, a neat white cotton square set out in front of her with bowls and spoons from the glass-fronted sideboard, elegant candlesticks from the dining room.

She's polishing the brass, that's what she used to say, polishing as if her life depended on it.

But smiling—as if it made her happy.

Like Glasgow.

Like Glasgow made me happy, once.

Yet how can something, somewhere, be upon me once more if it never really fucked off in the first place?

I belong to Glasgow, dear old Glasgow town. That is another lie.

I lie a lot.

I lie in this bed.

Is that why they sit me up in the bed more often now?

Do they think I can't lie when lying? Do they think I must answer truthfully to the questions they pose as they pass like shapes behind bathroom glass? My vision is less milky each time I open my eyes. Unlike Frank, the darkness will leave me. I wonder about waking daily to black.

Cool Hands Luke.

His fingers sometimes pull at my eyelids. He's getting antsy. Wants to know why I am not fully awake.

Life's a bitch, huh?

Watch me dive *dowwwwwn,* away even from Bazzie, who came today. Again? Probably. He's likely been here every day, but today's the day I notice and I turn my back, I turn my *back.* I'm sorry, Baz, truly. I can't bear your empathy. I can't begin to comprehend your generosity.

He said, "I miss you," yes, I miss you.

I wake to clarity.

I stay awhile.

Harder to stop that upwards drift now.

I look around and I move, I try to *wriggle,* but it is night and no one is here to see me look and move, no one to tell me what I should be doing. Can you imagine a freedom like mine?

Of course you fuckin' can't.

In all our millennia on this jolly little outcrop, from the first amoeba to the Cro-Magnon halfwits to the AI that will soon transcend us, the behavioural protocols have set diamond hard. We are inflexible and judgmental, terrified even now of the other about to come marauding over our lost horizons. To behave in an unexpected way is not an occasion to delight in the new, it is simply inconceivable, unacceptable, explainable only by deviance.

This degenerate is simply *refusing* to wake up.

Damn right!

I'll give in to a tyranny of expectation for Katie and Katie only, not Luke or the cleaner, who's always humming the Dambusters theme so beloved by English football morons, the orderly who smells of patchouli (and patchouli always makes me want to gag), no surrender either to the Two Fishwives, no way, who bitch all day, today about Katie, again, her boyfriend who's been shagging a dumpy brunette with a lazy eye just up from the South, the boyfriend they call Pockets because have you seen the way he's always fiddling with his balls?

Laffs!

There's jokes a-plenty in the dum-dum chamber!

Laffs on this ward as there were laffs way back then, after I was bailed, when for days on end, I visited Jamie every morning, afternoon, and evening, amusing the nurses, who called me, wait for it …

The Serial Caller.

Laffs!

Not that Jamie was amused. He lay with his back to me. He talked in monosyllables. I sat so quietly he'd think I had left, turning round to clock me with an almost inaudible "fuck sake," a contempt so much more profound for being so quiet. I finally decided to take the hint.

"This is it then?"

This it was.

Although, I returned one more time to check it really was. Jamie was again lying on his side. He must have sensed me standing there, but when he turned, it wasn't Jamie but an aged homunculus with a bulbous goitre on his neck. The poor cratur looked expectant, then disappointed. I asked the nurse where Jamie was and was told he'd been discharged the day before.

I think about it all.

I think about it all day long.

I think about when I went back to the museum and Miss Jameson took me aside and said, "Don't *ever* let the buggers get to you," an insistent solidarity in her stare that made me wonder what echoed from my present to her past. Meanwhile, fine upstanding Mr Kirk did his best to avoid me lest my Scarlet Eye induce a catastrophic erection. Resign, resign or just vanish, *pleeeeaaase*; I embarrassed him by my very presence. I imagined the Patti dreams that tortured him night on night, that forced frantic masturbation as the only release.

I did this.

I know I did, and so he hid.

The girls I worked with were less circumspect. Kate and Carla asserted their righteous outrage in my earshot. "It's shameless how she pretends nothing happened, it's not in her nature." "Her nature's abnormal then, I mean, what would you do?" "Well I wouldn't show my bloody *face*."

And now.

Now in the same wearisome way as back then, the Two

Fishwives who check my feeble vitals and change my fetid sheets speculate about why I tried to kill Frank for a second time.

They know I can hear. They want me to hear.

These days that pass.

I whisper at times, and one early morning I forget myself. Katie Nurse hears me. It's pouring down outside and I'm muttering about rain on the window. She's smiling as she hurries over, looking round as if making sure no one else has heard. She has tears in her eyes.

"You're awake," she says.

I nod.

"Please," I say.

She instantly understands. She grabs my hand, a smile giving way to a frown. "I won't tell anyone," she says, and I know she won't, the Two Fishwives will come without a scoob, not a scooby *doo*, bustling in and out with their usual witlessness. Soon as they appear, I close my eyes.

To be awake is tiring.

To sleep is to have dreams becoming less vivid. The kaleidoscope of strangeness is fading.

I have one that recurs.

It's a sitcom.

"The Patti Letham Show is filmed before a live studio audience." The Two Fishwives are world-weary nurses, Betsy and Hettie. They make jaded observations, and I deliver silent punchlines from my bed, an ironic nod to camera, the droll raise of an eyebrow, the audience howling, always a dance routine as the credits roll, Dolly Parton, "9 to 5," Betsy and Hettie shaking their wobblies.

One day I wake singing along.

I'm *belting* it out, the Two Fishwives staring at me, mouths open in astonishment and no little alarm.

One of them hurries out of the room. She's off to find Cool Hands Luke and bring the consultants a-congaing. Or maybe Hector, who knows, who cares, I'll affirm defiance in song!

I'm awake.

I'm awake and I don't care.

How long will it take for him to get here?

I'll wince like Eastwood, Hector astride a chair at the foot of the bed with an inscrutable smile, white shirt, top buttons open, the Two Fishwives asked to leave will mew like disappointed cats, hissing at Katie Nurse, who I insist must stay, her gentle paw squeezing mine:

"Good to see you back with us," Hector will say.

"Lazarus is my middle name."

"I thought it was Annabel?"

"What happened then, are you going to enlighten me?"

"Patti! You mean you don't remember?"

"Last thing I remember was a Friday night."

"Friday? You mean—'

"Friday night and the lights are loooooow, looking out for a place to goooo."

Hector listens.

"He's got a weary smile, like it's gonna be like that is it?"

"Yes, it surely is."

I've got a whole soundtrack to get through, double album. The first time I took the coach to Glasgow, I had a Walkman, a brick-like, bright yellow thing. Second time with my best friend Ada, we had a mixtape and a headphone each. Later, it was a flash car and CDs. Holding Jamie's hand.

So many songs.

I'll sing them all for you, Hector. You must learn to be patient. Settle thee back.

You, too, dear Katie Nurse. The oldies are the goldies. Let me start with my most recent of journeys. Luca and Emine have gone. I'm in the Corsa, driving south. I hit an '80s station.

Cod Liver Oil and the Orange Juice

Beside the sea you lived with the wind. I started watching it as a child, having discovered, like a secret I didn't want to reveal, that you could actually see it, that the wind simply delegated its presence to the jolly scud of cumulus, the ever-shifting calligraphy of cirrus, or the discontented waves.

It was a constant presence, the wind. I was spooked by its absence in those rare minutes, only ever minutes, of quietude, the unsettling sense of an approaching something I might not be able to resist, knowing that whatever it was, it came from the silence that the wind usually kept at bay.

I woke to that unfamiliar silence the day I left, without Luca, to go back to Glasgow to look for Daniela.

Not even a seagull, as if they, too, were unnerved by the absence of the wind. I lay in bed until I could listen to nothing no longer. I needed sound. My feet on the stairs, the kettle and the radio, upstairs again to open the creaky wardrobe and thump a case on the bed. If the wind had been an early indication that I would be ever defined by absence, this trip was the latest illustration.

It was also the day Bazzie was coming over in El Greco to take Luca and Emine's stuff round to Annie's.

I didn't say goodbye.

I put the photograph of Daniela on the dashboard of my car. I wondered what defined her.

***

Soon there was nothing but sound. FM radio. Nineteen-eighties nostalgia and my automatic singalong, the frantic wipers as a hard rain swept in fifteen miles down the road, tearing north.

It was still raining in the mountain lands. Sheets of blowsing rain, a cold wind that plastered my hair against my face as I bought a scalding coffee from a lay-by food van, an ear-to-ear grin for the young woman who served me. "Some day," I said. "Some day is every day," she replied.

I sipped my coffee as mist crept down the sodden slopes of the Monadhliaths and across the road, fuzzing the lights of the cars and the supermarket juggernauts, making dusk of mid-morning and secrets of things: signs and fenceposts, the shoebox on the passenger seat.

I flicked through Captain Sandy's letters and picked up the newspaper clipping of Granny C. on the causeway, hands on her hips. Then the dog-eared photo of her and Sandy at the Christmas dance.

Miss Jameson:

"Stop refusing, lassie! I *can* give you this, I'm the *Archivist*."

It was my last day at the museum, Miss Jameson's finger against her lip.

"*Shhh.*"

Then a hand on my arm, a squeeze, and "Oh, there's one more thing." She handed me the envelope that I now picked up from the box. Sandy Nicholson's obituary from a forces magazine.

"It's not much, Patti, but there's some interesting bits and pieces."

I re-read the obituary Miss Jameson had handed me all those years ago. We accumulated so much, and in the end, there was so little to hold on to, like a child building a Lego tower and knocking it down, who gripped like dear life to one or two pieces when you tidied it away.

I looked out the windscreen, watched the sliding rain.

I felt as if I'd been doing this my whole life. Staring out on things from the windows of a shit car.

Dear god, I remembered them, those interminable journeys. It was always my mother driving, my father at the office or barricaded in his study on the occasional weekend he took off, the thought of spending time with his family such an infuriating imposition. So always, my mother killing time on a drive somewhere, screaming at my brothers as they took turns giving each other dead arms as I watched the rain on its erratic zigzag down the glass, wondering if it knew where it was headed or was deciding as it went along.

My phone buzzed from the passenger seat, proving again the synchronicity of all things tiresome.

"Brother One' the display told me, meaning Keith.

I imagined his annoyance as he waited for the "leave a message' instruction. I gave it a few more minutes before listening back. "We're here. At the cottage. Do you ever lock your door? The kids are here too. We thought we'd make a weekend of it. Call me back." Keith had the same intonation as my father, an impatient curtness, challenging the world to explain itself.

Ah, the sweet delight of lucky escapes.

I'd had a few.

My father himself told me so on the evening of the verdict, handing me a whisky that he pulled away.

"A lucky escape, Patti."

Then he let me have the glass and, as I tipped it to my mouth, added, "Not proven is not the same as not guilty."

The spirit caught in my throat and I spluttered, watching the look on my father's face quickly shift from satisfaction to resentment as he realised I wasn't angry with him but was laughing.

My mother started with the "for goodness' sake, Patricia," until silenced by a murderous look, my father starting to say something but losing his train of thought, opening and closing his mouth, then hurrying from the kitchen, my mother rushing after him, my brothers looking at me, looking away, wanting to go after our parents but not quite sure.

We listened to them in the living room, her quiet tones and his strange, furious anxiety that soon nothing but his childhood Flying Scotsman would be able to soothe as the dementia settled.

"*Choo choo*," he'd exclaim.

Such brisk delight, a driver's cap on his head, watching the model train on its never-ending circumnavigation of the dining room table that was never again to be used for meals.

All these images. Yet they were all static.

My memories rarely moved, as if I couldn't properly acknowledge process or change, clicking round one after the other like slides on an old projector. That was the attraction of living beside the sea. In the unceasing movement of water and sky, I could convince myself, sometimes, that everything was flux but progress a given, you just had to let out enough rope.

More often, I deferred to the opposite, that I was simply running to stand still, weighed down by all those heavy archetypes of place, all the stasis of belonging, frustration, or contempt.

What said Daniela of the Dashboard?

She was generous.

That enigmatic smile as I pulled back onto the road with all the recklessness that the car's acceleration could muster. I kept a steady 85 until I hit the outskirts, the motorway that took you straight to the heart of the city. No messing, you want Glasgow, well here's Glasgow.

***

The Parkside Hotel, again.

Why not.

There was no reason the receptionist, Alicja, should remember me, but her look of such utter vacancy when I mentioned my recent stay made me wonder if it had ever happened.

In my room, I put the shoebox on the bedside table. I sat on the end of the bed, flicked on the TV and put it on mute. I lay back and looked at the ceiling. I imagined Hector and a sidekick finding me:

"Cause of death?"

"Hard to tell without the full autopsy."

"I'm thinking nostalgia."

"You always think nostalgia."

"Wanna hear my reasoning?"

"You're gonna tell me anyway."

"The head against the pillow. The angle of her gaze suggests a pining, a yearning for distance. Look at the hands. The left is facing upwards, flat but splayed, unsure yet open to being convinced, while the right is grasping the sheet. We see here the classic struggle between letting go and holding on, a conflict seen also in the combination of frown and raised eyebrow."

Nostalgia.

What a bitch.

No way I could deny it, lying there like a corpse staring at the cracks in the ceiling, which ran like the rain on the car windows into cul-de-sacs of awful choices and gleeful inevitabilities.

My mother understood.

"What now, Patti?" she'd asked, maybe the night of the verdict, maybe some other time, waiting in the dark as I walked up the path after another failed attempt to get hold of Jamie on the phone.

"What happens next?" she added.

The kitchen light caught a glint on her cheeks. Just the rain. There was never a place for tears.

I stayed awhile in Shore House.

Worn down by mother's incessant wheedling, "Can you not do this *one little thing* for your dad," I even took a job in Dalriadan Stoneware's town centre shop. "The big boss's doing," I heard the manager say. "I wouldn't give her a second glance." A judgment I saw in the eyes of every customer, even the tourists who couldn't possibly know anything about Not Proven Patti Letham. The paranoia followed me home, the parental whispers that "she isn't quite right," "let's get a psychiatrist in, we might be able to get her committed!" A part of me was worried they might actually try, but that wasn't the reason I finally left.

Truly Kaput's interview with Frank in the local rag was tagged "exclusive," as if he'd scooped the nationals. My father tossed me the paper with a look of derision. I read with burning cheeks, even though the interview was less Bernstein than Beano, a fawn-job detailing Frank's rehab.

"Sound but No Fury." A moody accompanying photo of Frank with his Zimmer at the end of the pier.

The Citylink bus south it was.

The only person I told I was leaving was Bazzie. "You better get in touch … or I *will* find you." Baz who was always there. Baz who understood the comfort in the familiarity of what made us laugh.

I picked up my phone and re-read the message he'd sent this morning before I'd left Little Cottage:

Send me a text when you get to the hotel. If you don't, you know what will happen …

I smiled again as I read the follow-up.

I WILL find you!

I remembered when I hadn't wanted to be found.

When it wasn't a photo of a pretty Albanian on the dashboard of my car but a series of Jamie snapshots in my head.

***

I walked the West End. The slow stride of the returnee, stopping to remember this street corner and something that might have happened, finding my inevitable way back to The Doublet, no Luca to interfere with the late-afternoon sale of memory's indulgences, before the offices were emptying and people staring, pissed off that I was taking up a whole table.

I retreated to an Italian restaurant with no connection to Jamie that made me sad anyway, where I ate as fast as I could, thought about my hotel room, and nursed a coffee in a chain place instead.

Just me, an ancient bag lady, and the young woman behind

the counter whose thumbs moved so extraordinarily fast on her phone. This was why the young pitied the old, they couldn't keep up anymore; wasn't it amusing to see them glance at the tattoos and the clothes that they found so inexplicable. I almost told her that the thing is, pet, I *never* could keep up.

Behind me, the bag lady started to laugh. She shuffled out. A few moments later I followed her. I could still hear her laughing as I stepped off the pavement and a car braked to a halt.

I stepped back with a jaunty salute as the car sped away. That was me. A bag lady in waiting.

A few people stared at me as I stuck a hand in the air and shouted "taxi." Such things were done in movies but never in real life. I was pleased with their attention, even more so by the Hackney cab decelerating and pirouetting over to me, still a thrill for the country girl to get into a fast black in the nighttime city, where every journey was taken with the memory of every one taken before. I placed a hand on the empty seat beside me where Jamie still sat.

I asked the driver to stop in pretty much the same place where Luca had pulled over when he had driven me here. I stood on the pavement for a few moments, waiting for the Hackney to disappear the way we had come. I pulled my coat closer. I listened to my steps on the empty street.

There was no door. I went straight into the close and that familiar tenement smell: dust, sweat, and spice hanging in the cold air, soaked into the old stone. You could be in only one place in the universe.

I wondered about Daniela being taken here for the first time. I saw her scuffing up the same stairs I now scuffed up. I glanced out the filthy landing windows at the dark and mysterious back green, looking at the doors on each landing and wondering which one she might have been locked behind. I listened at one or two and pictured someone on the other side, looking back at me through the peephole. Above me, a door opened and shut, a young couple descending swiftly nightwards, laughing as they passed Daniela's door, laughing and passing as they had a thousand times. Only when the police put that tape across the entrance would they have said things like "I knew there was something going on in that flat."

I walked to the top floor, all the way back down, then sat on the bottom step and called Bazzie.

"How's the Big Smoke?"

"Smoke and mirrors—same as ever."

"Where are you? You sound like you're in a cave."

"I'm sitting in a tenement close in the dark."

"I've seen that film, Patti. It never ends well."

"How did Luca's move go?"

"Fine. How can two folk with so little stuff have so *much*?"

"It's the way of the world, Baz, an accumulation of crap. Did you see my brothers, by the way?"

"Aw, did I miss them then?"

"Better luck next time."

I hung up. Rain angling across the close mouth. Orange light, a passerby on the other side of the street. I left the tenement and crossed the road, staring back for a few moments, certain that someone had already taken my place on the stairs and was sitting unseen in the dark, looking out at me.

Where was Daniela?

Where was Jamie? I tried to find him, too, remember? Fresh off the coach after my escape from Shore House, exhausted, feeling sick with a seedy apprehension about what happened next. I found a bed and breakfast. I couldn't decide if I was more terrified by the thought of finding him or not finding him. It took me a week to decide to head to the Southside. I knew his family lived in Shawlands and I thought all I had to do was hang around, wander the streets and pubs, and one day he'd appear. It was inevitable. It was all just a matter of time.

I left Daniela's tenement behind and walked into the drizzle. I did a little jig to all the inevitabilities I could do absolutely nothing about, a car slowing slightly to watch me, then speeding up.

"Ye dancin"?" a man yelled from a bus shelter on the other side of the street.

"No, it's just the way I'm standing."

He laughed, doffing an imaginary hat.

I curtsied.

I even considered a cartwheel. Give the punters even more of a story to tell when they got home. In for a penny, in for a pony, Patti here was quite the conjurer and detail, *detail* maketh the illusion. Another memory flickered, the details of another night.

Jamie and I huddled in our pub in the village up the coast. A hard wind rattling the window, a draft making the fire dance.

"Where shall we go?"

"We could head to London."

"Really, is that the limit of our ambition. How about Paris?"

"What the hell would we do in Paris?"

"Just be."

"Just be what?"

"Dunno. Together? Where's your sense of adventure?"

And more suggestions, such freedom. And though we didn't believe that this future we were crafting would ever come to pass, we still had a vital, pressing need to fill it with detailed and ever more pastiche scenarios before the present that was snapping at our heels finally caught up.

***

I stayed in my Parkside room for the next two days. A silence so profound it was almost comforting. I may have been the only guest. I'd go out for a breath of air or to grab some food and feel strangely exposed, as if that first evening had brought me to a kind of generalised attention. I couldn't shake the feeling I was about to hear a voice behind me say "Patti, is that you?"

I dozed at odd hours and was up half the night. I took my time organising the search for Daniela. Systematic, as if placing stones on the causeway. My feelings veered from depressed to incensed as I trawled the disturbing misogyny of sex listing websites and forums. I ended up with a list of eleven places. Luca and I had checked out one or two the last time.

That Friday, I walked halfway across the city and back, trying all the way to convince myself that this wasn't completely ridiculous. Twice, I made it to the first place on my list, close to the Mitchell Library in a line of tired three-storey sandstone buildings. The sign was discreetly placed between two others, for a property company and an accountancy. Twice, I walked on by.

The third time, I stopped and looked up. White blinds were drawn on the first- and second-floor windows, the third had the name of the accountant scrolling in an arc across the glass. A couple of letters were missing and looked like they had been for a long time. I pictured a phone that never rang and a fat man as misplaced as those letters staring at the window.

I buzzed Mary's Place and waited, turning to look at the building site across the street, the chatter of jackhammers and one of those blue sectioned chutes for discarding masonry that as a child I always wanted to slide down. Then the door clicked open, and I went up the stairs. Then another door, a tired-looking receptionist with a white smock like a dental assistant, who was surprised, then nervous, as I thrust the photo under her nose, my heart thumping.

She didn't know Daniela.

She wouldn't have told me even if she did, no melodramatic pause as she stared at the photo or quick whisper as I left, *"They're always watching—meet me in the café down the street in twenty ...»*

No one knew Daniela.

The responses to her photograph were blank or suspicious looks followed by monosyllables. Once a volley of abuse. Not that many places on the list were still operating, the others likely closed down in a recent police crackdown that punters such as 91Slim, RedKing, and BangBoy lamented in the chatrooms, chasing rumours about surviving places and new places like little man-children swapping Panini football stickers. They triggered anger—never once pity—as I thought about them, what they looked like, what they wore as they waited impatiently in Shanghai 30s with its opium den vibe that had given up halfway, or the depressing tackiness of Sandra's down the same street that looked thrown together from a garage sale of mid-eighties furniture, or the salons trying hard to make clear they were legitimate with big wide windows and expensive and minimalist Balinese or Indian décor, all tealights and petals in bowls of water and low hanging lights. The forum dwellers still got it wrong now and again, just the risks of the game, right, why not take a chance on turning over, the erection posing the question and that desperate hunt for an orgasm ended with "we don't do that here' and an instruction to "get dressed, get out."

"Times have changed, the trade's moved off-piste, s'all in flats now," wrote Rubntug. "Check out the online ads."

This I had also done.

Sites like Gumtree and sleazier ones like Adultgraft, reading the adverts, thumbnail images with a black strip across the eyes, performances reviewed in the forums, what she did or didn't do, cute or brutal descriptions of her looks, the strange and near-absolute requirement for the experience to be as artificial as possible to be the most agreeable; smiling compliance, passivity, and vulnerability, the ABC of the porno caricature, the real just blows the deal.

The men who rented the flats would read the reviews too. I imagined the additional encouragement of a slap in the face, *"You're on the clock soon as that fuckin' phone rings, got it,"* those numbers that I dialled, some not recognised, some picking up but soon hanging up.

Because women didn't go to these places, funnily enough, a female voice and the bells were ringing. Cop or journalist, auf Wiedersehen in any case, no chance to find out where to take Daniela's photo. Maybe she herself would open the door, because the world worked to a different kind of happy ending sometimes. *"At last!"* she'd say. *"How do you know who I am?"* or *"You've found me."* I imagined so many of her responses as I lay on my bed and floated through Glasgow, the city totally blacked out but for the bright-lit flats of the small ads, where every girl on the edge of a bed was Daniela, Daniela waiting, whom I'd never find.

A day and a half later, I had been to all the places on my list and been hung up on five times. That night I dreamed of Jamie. I was rushing along a dark, endless corridor, opening door after door. From each, he emerged from dazzling light, an empty smoothness where his features should be. He made a snuffling sound that may have been a laugh as he slammed each door in my face.

Again, it was ridiculous, being here. I had to get out of Glasgow but couldn't face the drive north. I paid for another night. I wandered aimlessly. I found a community woodland, a noticeboard telling me about "A Family Fairy Trail." I passed scampering kids shouting "over here, over here' and found six tiny, bright-painted wooden cut-outs of fairies stuck on the trunks of trees.

The seventh had been kicked off and stamped into little pieces. I felt like crying and looked away, up to the high flats lurking beyond the sparse trees, all the black windows. The traffic swelled. In the undergrowth there was rubbish, bits of slate and wood, masonry from long-demolished buildings. The kids wouldn't notice the junk and the parents would simply ignore it.

We saw what we wanted, and the parents had now seen me.

I left by a different exit, where another noticeboard told me the name of the woodland. The Trap Grounds. "If you have enjoyed your visit, why not become a friend of "The Trap"!" That was the thing about this city, always an ambush waiting to happen. I had a sudden image of myself, anxiously wandering round and round the woods, looking for a way out of the Trap.

Alicja didn't look up when I came into the hotel lobby, staring at something out of sight behind the desk. A phone, I assumed, but who knows, maybe someone freshly killed was down there.

In my room, I broke the silence with the radio, piano music that ended with a few moments of dead air before a sonorous voice told me "that was Chopin's piano concerto number 2." It was almost seven and I went across to the window to wait for the Man in the Long Black Coat.

He appeared as he had done for the last three nights. On the pavement on the other side of Great Western Road that I could just see beyond the plane trees. He wore an out-of-time, black homburg hat and was using a furled umbrella as a walking stick. He would stop and look in the window of the secondhand bookshop. He would walk slowly down the street until I lost sight of him. He would return fifteen minutes later carrying a plastic supermarket bag.

He did all these things. We each found our own way.

I thought about Luca.

I took out the photo of Daniela. I saw myself driving to the Southside, Govanhill, asking in all the Eastern European shops if they had seen this woman, Chopin swelling around me as I left one place and moved on, holding my jacket above my head to keep off the teeming rain, the music more and more frantic and expectant but never peaking, just abruptly cutting off.

I ran a bath and turned up the music, wary again of the silence, the voices that might boom out in this most expectant of rooms. I waited in the pause between movements, but none came.

Daniela.

I closed my eyes in embarrassment to the ridiculous fantasy; the triumphant drive north, Daniela beside me, down to the villa by the golf club, a ring of the bell and Annie frowning as she looks at the two of us, Luca and Emine appearing over her shoulder, a dawning realisation …

I sank under the water to hide.

Yet I felt released. I would gracefully accept the end of the story of Luca and Daniela. Maybe if I held my breath long enough, I would also, finally, choke off the oxygen of the sweet-whispering goblin in my ear: *Sure, Patti, someone else's end point can be yours too. Course it can …*

I sat up, gasping.

"Mahler," the presenter purred, "symphony number five."

I could get to like Mahler.

He'd fill Little Cottage, boom out the day the causeway was finished, only to be expected from the "queen of eccentricity," as the reporter describes me, furry mic in my face as I stand in Granny C."s familiar pose, hands on my hips and answering the why, the why, always the why.

I'd take the reporter way, way back.

I was feeling generous.

I'd take him to the Southside, fifteen years ago, and how it explained my reticence to go back there now.

Shawlands. Jamie's home neighbourhood. One Sunday morning, a week after Not Proven Patti Letham fled the north country, she woke up in a strange bed on that other side of Glasgow, bleak light spilling round grubby curtains, trying to re-establish a foothold in time and space:

Why can't I hear any seagulls?

The day before I'd ventured out to look for him, logging every face in a series of boozers from the scuzzed to the aspirational, then staying put in one of the latter: a cocktail and jazz bar in a deconsecrated church. There, I gave in to five-mojito euphoria and convinced myself that even if not tonight, the success of Mission to Jamie was absolutely assured.

I slipped my moorings.

I danced for hours. I studied more faces and knew I'd never recall any of them. Barely even the one now lying beside me. He smiled. "Ian," he said, realising he had to remind me. He insisted on buying me breakfast so we could "say a proper hello to each other." He held open the door of a café down the street with a chivalry I had to disabuse him of quick-smart. I fled when he went to the loo. One, two streets and still hurrying. Ian had the hang-dog persistence of the too-easily smitten. I half expected him to come running after me.

When I felt safe, I took out the list of "Wrights' in Shawlands that I had copied from the phone directory. I didn't have a map and just wandered, looking for streets on the list. I realised with a quick lurch in the stomach that I had a hit. Grant Street. Number 86 was just ahead.

I found a bus shelter on the other side of the street, diagonally opposite the house. An estate agent would have called it a "stunning mid-terrace villa." Behind black railings was a neat garden and a faded burgundy door with an arched, smoked-out window, two bay windows on the ground and first floors. The sandstone glowed in the overcast light, as if lit from within.

I waited without knowing what I was waiting for.

Maybe an old man or woman would come out. In their features I'd recognise Jamie and know this *was* the family home; he was inside, about to pop out for a newspaper, pulling his bomber jacket close, the one I'd found in a charity shop, ambling down the street with that long, over-striding gait that I gently mocked him about. The minister of silly walks, here he is a-coming! He sees me and flicks out his legs, playing up to the nickname …

"Are you ok, dear?"

I looked down. A bony, almost translucent hand on mine. A surprising heat.

I realised I was crying.

The old woman had the sharpest of blue eyes. A bus was waiting at the stop. "Ye coming, hen?" She dismissed the driver, waiting until the diesel roar had diminished before speaking again.

"Can I help you with anything?"

I put my other hand on top of the old woman's. "I'm okay, thank you," I said. "You look like my granny."

She angled her head away, eyes narrowing but the smile still there. "No dear, I look like old people."

"I'm sorry."

"No, no. No apologies. Where are you going?"

"I don't know."

"Well, you're as well not knowing with me."

We waited for the next bus in silence, then sat down together. I looked out the window as we pulled away, number 86 Grant Street half gone behind window steam and dirt, gone altogether when the bus took a right. I took the list out of my bag, scrunched it up, then smoothed it out.

"There's lots of things we're not quite ready for."

I glanced up, startled.

Granny C. was beside me. "You need to let it come to you, right? And *smile*, lassie." She nudged me, and I smelled a familiar scent of Chanel and all was well, all was well and Granny C. was right, I could smile, the stop bell now ringing as I became aware of another smile, the old woman's.

"This is my stop, dear … You seem a bit brighter."

"I am, thanks."

"Well, you take care. Mind now, it might never happen."

She pressed my hand, as Granny C. did when I was a girl and the rainy days were still free of hangovers and ambushes, no realisation, yet, that all things must pass, when all was simply childhood.

The bus reached the city centre and I got off.

I hurried in pouring rain to Buchanan Street, sitting in the despondency of a Sunday morning bus station—less-frequent departures, too much time for everyone waiting to get to wherever to glance at each other and wonder where those wherevers might be.

I took the bus to Strathfield. The countryside came surprisingly quickly, the Campsie Fells appearing now and then from the smirr, green-brown and sodden, a huge sponge waiting for the hand to reach down and squeeze. In the village, I bought a bacon roll from a café and asked the way to the church.

I knew the details.

Captain Sandy volunteered here for forty years, after the injury at El Alamein, the Military Cross, and the banking career. I found his grave underneath a big cypress that kept me dryish as I picked dead stems from an aluminium flower holder and brushed dirt from the headstone.

I traced a finger around "Captain Alexander "Sandy" Nicholson, 1907–1998. A Rest Well Earned." No wife was mentioned, but I knew that already. Sandy had never married, a line drawn that day in the west, the Applecross Inn receding behind him as he sped, alone, down the coast road.

"I knew him, you know. He was some man."

I looked up at the world's tallest, thinnest, palest minister standing under the world's biggest umbrella, almost parasol sized. I half expected him to Mary Poppins away on the rising breeze.

"He was the treasurer here when I started as the minister, until he passed. Are you one of the family?"

"No. He was a friend of our family."

"That so, that so. There's some old photograph albums in the parish office. You're welcome to look."

Another kind old woman in a world full of them brought the minister and me tea and biscuits.

"I let myself have three on a Sunday," he said. "It's a tough crowd round these parts." He laughed when I said "really' and winked when the old woman tut-tutted. His wife, his housekeeper, I didn't know, and she wasn't introduced. She brought me the photo albums one after the other, the harvest suppers, the nativities, and the Easter celebrations, year after year.

I scanned through them, studying the photos more closely when Sandy appeared. He usually wore a half-stifled grimace, not a fan of having his photo taken. Then, in one, he was beaming. A woman stood beside him, also smiling. My heart jumped. I flicked on, more slowly, and saw them in other photos, now and then across the years, holding hands in more than a few.

Captain Sandy and Granny C. Getting older together. Then, as the albums reached the mid-1980s, just him.

And now, in the Parkside Hotel all these years later, in a bath become lukewarm, I felt embarrassed by the anger I'd felt that hungover morning in Strathfield. Yet it had been shocking to see them together, the photos that made an instant present of their past. How blue must Sandy Nicholson's eyes have been to remain so bright in those images now so faded?

I thought I knew everything there was to know, the beginning, middle, and end all revealed: the 1941 Christmas fundraiser, Captain Sandy's letters, and his obituary. It felt like a betrayal, somehow, to discover that they'd kept on seeing each other until the day Granny C. died. I just couldn't get my head round the bargain they'd struck, to acknowledge the limitations of a secret life, to be as happy as they were willing to allow themselves to be.

My anger then and my embarrassment now.

Neither lasted long.

I wrapped myself in a stale-smelling towel and lay on the bed. The radio presenter was purring, purrrrring, *"And now a request, dear listeners, Patti Letham has been in touch, can you play me something about searching for parallels in other lives being a fool's errand?"* Granny C. and Sandy had never parted. Jamie Wright had never once looked back. I let them go again.

As always when I returned home, I stopped in the bus lay-by on the top road, just along from the turning for the single-track down to the shore. Taking it all in, m'lady's proprietorial return. I never sought the reverse perspective: looking up to the lay-by from Little Cottage. It was too easy to imagine a line of people strung along the ridge, peering down. Soon after moving in, I pulled the garden table closer to the cottage, closing off the angle from above.

The causeway below me. Almost finished now.

I didn't know what I thought about that yet. I just looked, shielding my eyes: the quicksilver stipple-dazzle of sun on sea, murkier sky colours closing in from the east. There were three people out on the causeway. In the brightness, I couldn't tell which way they were facing. Maybe they were looking up at me looking down at them. I waved but no one waved back.

The first of the rain started to fall. The dazzle had faded, the people on the causeway hurrying to shore. I drove down to the car park, getting out just in time for the full squall.

Soaked and cold, I stepped into kitchen gloom, the light illuminating familiarity with a dull yellowness that accentuated the emptiness of the cottage. I shouted "hello' to banish the silence, then noticed a package on the table. On top was a card printed with van Gogh's sunflowers.

Inside, in a very careful hand, Luca told me:

"Thank you for everything you have done for me and Emine." The package revealed a book called *Peaks of the Balkans*, inscribed "You gave me the sea, so I give you the high places, xxx."

I was filled with such a near-physical press of loneliness that I had to get out.

I drove to Annie's. A journey to the other side of the town, the posh end with the big houses and golf club.

The place was in darkness.

I closed my eyes …

I took a deep breath and counted one-two-three, then stepped out into the teeming rain, running across the road and up the path, no lights on but pressing the doorbell anyway, no one coming, hurrying round to the back garden instead, the kitchen behind the big windows in darkness, too, knocking to nothing and waiting a bit, pressing the handle down and the door opening, dropping into a karate pose as I stepped inside, like Clouseau going after Cato, tiptoeing across the floor, every step a comic squeak from my wet trainers, through an elegant arched doorway into a hallway, and a hallway it actually was, this was a bloody big house, Annie's ex-husband some finance honcho for a booze conglomerate, my steps leaving giveaway footprints in the thick carpet, padding along walls filled with mirrors, mirrors, so many mirrors, what a terrible gauntlet to run day on day, year on year, why torture yourself, up the curving stairway into a deeper darkness shattered by a sudden security light, a saturated scarecrow with a pale face staring back at me from another mirror who I took a moment to recognise as myself, and that another reason why I avoided the dictatorship of mirrors, then moving along and opening a bedroom door, the master bedroom, I guessed, a bed you could get lost in and many men had,"twas said, hoho, Luca the latest in a post-divorce conveyor belt of tight and saggy-bellied suitors, Annie nothing if not eclectic in taste, but lucky Luca the last, the final, the *one*, look at the dressing table and the purple-painted wall above the over-cushioned opulence of the bed, those dozens of portraits, how many years had they been a couple now, wasn't it endearing, *life-affirming,* some said, Luca and Annie in moody black and whites, Luca and Annie pulling faces, Luca and Annie jumping into a villa pool, caught mid-air, holding hands, dozens of photos from the years they'd spent together, like the family sideboard in Shore House, filling as the decades spilled, framed photos that my mother encouraged guests to look at, eager to take them through our stories, "let me tell you about it' and another tired anecdote, those photos that began to be removed after an unknown apogee was reached, one by one, as they had been accumulated, a gathering up as my father's illness brought him down, the photos a cruel reminder of time's progression to decrepitude, my mother dropping another one in a box as she listens to the *choo choo* noises from dining room, my father driving the Flying Scotsman on his endless journey …

I opened my eyes.

The car heater was making me sweat. I wiped steam from the side window. Still no lights in the house.

I fell asleep.

I dreamed I was running through a vast cemetery, huge flakes falling around me that I realised weren't snow but thousands of illuminated photographs cascading out of the black, glimpses of faces, moments; as soon as one settled on my hand, it melted like an actual snowflake.

"Patti!"

I woke with a start.

An insistent knocking on the window. I rubbed the glass and revealed a smiling Luca, rolling down the window to see Annie and Emine behind him in the pouring rain, huddled under a golf umbrella. Annie was frantically beckoning me, "Come in, come in for goodness' sake!"

I had nothing against her at all.

We sat in the kitchen. As big as I had imagined and a slate floor, dark and expensive looking. They'd been at the cinema. Annie made us hot chocolate with mini marshmallows and asked how I was doing. She showed no awkwardness, a rarity with a gift for unstudied friendliness.

It seemed an abuse of that friendliness to turn to Luca and say, "I went back to Glasgow to look for Daniela."

"What?"

He looked stunned.

"Your wife?" I added, then looked at Emine. "Your mother?'

They said nothing. I had the instant certainty that everything I'd been told was a lie. Annie's face had reddened, as if she was in on the scam. I took Daniela's photograph from my purse.

Luca stared at me, not the photo.

"She isn't my mother."

We all turned to look at Emine, who was looking at Luca, expecting him to say something, who seemed shocked into silence; this wasn't the way I was supposed to find out their story.

Annie already knew. She was reaching out and taking Luca's and Emine's hands. Her eyes were glittery, on the verge of tears. She was telling me that I had done "a good thing, a selfless thing."

Luca nodded but avoided my eyes.

"I'm sorry, Patti. I should have told you before. I don't know … Emine was already staying in the flat I found, the refugee charity. She was from Albania too. Someone told me about a farm in the north. We, how do you say … teamed up. I wasn't sure if they would have made us stay, the charity people. I left a note but felt bad. They were so good. They took us in."

"Like you did, Patti," Annie added. "So'—and here she snapped her fingers—"*naturally*, no questions asked." She paused, but not to check herself, choosing to add, "I never believe what anybody—'

"Says about me?"

I looked down at my hot chocolate. A mug from a Cologne Christmas market. Elves and presents and jolly old Santa Claus. I saw Luca, Emine, and Annie laughing, wrapped up tight against the cold, a smell of Glühwein, cinnamon. It was snowing, naturally, pouring down, big flakes like those tumbling dream photos, all the moments in all the years to come.

Then Annie:

"We're going to make an application for asylum. We have to try, right? It'll mean school too."

Another "we." Luca still nodding, a gaze mixing optimism and resignation, hope and wariness, Emine looking directly at me with something much more straightforward yet completely indefinable.

I returned to the cottage.

The same rain.

Luca's package still on the table.

The first night I had stayed here I was edgy, wandering from room to room, all the time and moments I'd missed while living elsewhere simultaneously rushing out at me from every corner.

I felt that way again.

I lay in bed with the window open. I listened to the sluggish rain so I didn't need to listen to the silence.

My phone buzzed. Luca.

I ignored it.

Then a series of text messages, apologising for not having told me the full story. I thought of him and Annie in her cosy bedroom. I thought of Daniela in another. I shuffled to the edge of the bed and put my feet on the floor. I listened to the fizz of rain becoming a scuff of footsteps coming up tenement stairs, the door opening to RedKing, 91Slim, BangBoy …

***

Luca sent a text every day for a week, then stopped. I imagined Annie saying "that's enough." She was right; I decided I liked Annie. Decisions had to be decisive! I'd always been good at that.

I remembered leaving Strathfield after that morning spent looking through the photos of Granny C. and Sandy. An overheated bus. Staring out at the mist on the hills, lifting and gone as the sun swelled. I got off at the coach station just as the northbound Citylink pulled up to its stand. In that moment, I understood that going home was an irrevocable defeat, my parents waiting with arms folded and the loaded silence of the finally vindicated.

I made the decision.

I stayed.

I found a place in Broomhill, my flatmate a flint-eyed secretary called Marcie, whose partner Joe had left his wife, Marcie's sister, for her. They rarely left the flat. I once watched a documentary about fetishes. A couple wearing bright red gimp costumes with zip-up face masks were interviewed as they sat on a floral sofa sipping tea through straws and watching TV. A very British kind of eroticism. I imagined Joe and Marcie pulling on the costumes as soon as I went out. They unnerved me, but I stayed. I needed their utter indifference.

And yet more disaffection in the job I found as an invigilator in the Gallery of Modern Art. Eight hours a day in a hard plastic chair, listening to the shuffling shoes of a million visitors.

I made up a game.

I'd focus on the shoes, quickly imagine the kind of person that went with them, and then look up. I'd award myself points according to wholly superficial and ever-changing criteria about how close I was to what I'd decided they should look like and what they actually did. Lose twenty points for a big hooter that turned out to be a cute little button nose. Gain thirty for guessing nose ring, fifty for a direct hit on a goatee! Instead of the game, I sometimes made a face or stood on the chair in a weird pose, like some kind of guerrilla installation.

"You'll never guess what I did today." My group of newly emerging friends were castaways of a similar type, coalescing off the back-of-chance encounters in various pubs and nightspots. "I saluted a man in a turban and he saluted back, so I hopped on one foot and so did he."

More laughter, more music and clubs, faces glimpsed in

strobe, in rainbow. I realised one night that I'd stopped looking for Jamie. I wasn't looking for anything but oblivion in the ecstasy, the sweat, the big beats that faded into the weekday silence of Marcie and the gallery.

It all seemed so improbable.

A life laid out in a series of barely believable set pieces. Maybe it was too much time beside the North Sea, the way it made a remoteness of everything. I looked back at myself as if I were a series of avant-garde portraits in one of the gallery's exhibitions, sifting untrustworthy moments for connections between incarnations. I was still damned if I could find them.

I stayed in Glasgow for a long time.

I left it to others to seek the connections to those elusive Patti Lethams and what she was all about.

No one stumbled across Frank Ruthven and Not Proven Patti Letham. No one was interested in your past unless you gave them a reason to be. I never did. And when I discovered during a rare and gloating phone call from my brother Keith that Jamie was flying high in London town, it was like being told about a stranger. He, too, belonged to another incarnation.

Likewise, the Patti phoned out of the blue by her mother, who, in a moment of weakness undoubtedly brought on by loneliness as my father's dementia galloped away, asked me to come home. She "missed her little girl." I thought about that little girl. I couldn't remember much about her. Out of loyalty to her ghost, I headed north for the first time in years.

It was a long, long weekend.

I slept in my old bedroom, almost spookily unchanged from when I left home to move in with Frank. I looked out the window at the same sea. A million things I hadn't thought about for a very long time came fireworking out of the black as soon as I closed my eyes, keeping me awake most of the night. On Sunday afternoon my mother, father, and I sat round the kitchen table, trying to rekindle the memories of long-gone lunches as if they might have somehow achieved a warmth over the years that was wholly absent at the time.

My father sat in silence.

He stared at my mother as she fed him. When he drooled, she would patiently and tenderly dab his chin, not at all embarrassed at having to do this in front of her daughter, which surprised me. The extent of my father's decline was shocking, but I couldn't help my scepticism. I was sure he recognised me and was just pretending he didn't. I stood up and gripped the table. "Dad, *Dad*, it's me, *Patti*," I said, over and over. I was almost shouting, and he was frightened.

"You made him worse."

My mother when she dropped me off at the station.

I didn't return. I didn't go to his funeral. The outraged messages from my brothers. I made him worse.

We tended to forget our epiphanies.

I was much less sure, all these years later, of my realisation in those silent hours in the art gallery that things could only have turned out the way they had. Maybe the vanity of certainty faded with age. Or maybe it was the sea once more, too much time spent beside that endless flux, where for so many days and years I moved the causeway slowly closer to the ragged spur on the Ferris Island shore, yet where I often felt a contrary lightness, the gossamer-thin promise of sentimental tears if I thought about it too much.

I rode the flow.

I let the big sea take me farther and farther out.

***

I finally finished the causeway in mid-February. A hazy, ambiguous morning. A nonchalant sea chattered and smattered the rocks on the north end of Ferris Island as I laid the last three stones.

I posed like Granny C. in the footage I'd seen on the Pathé movie reel, arms on her hips and a half-amused smile, white hair flowing behind her in the wind. I pictured Cap'n Sandy in a Glasgow cinema, his jaw dropping suddenly open—there was Deborah on the silver screen.

She beamed at me. I could feel her hug.

"Just you go ahead and toot your horn, Patti. False modesty is a bourgeois conceit, never mind those buggers." And a nod over my shoulder, up to the ridge above Little Cottage, those hundreds of figures strung out in a long line of silent ambiguity. As one, they peered down; as one, they turned towards the cemetery, wondering what my parents made of it:

"Well, she did it."

"She finally did."

"It cannot be denied."
"'Tis the one thing that lassie could never be."
"She got that from you."
"Oh, don't start, woman."
"Too early?"
"Let's try and get past lunchtime, eh?"

I blinked and emptied the ridge, my gaze dimmed by the shift from the dazzle of white sea to dark shore. Wasn't it always so much darker on the mainland, always a few moments for colour to leach into monochrome, detail to re-emerge from shadow. I noticed Spider-Girl in full costume, leaping from rock to rock, then onto the causeway and running towards me. Her father was hurrying behind, gotta catch her before she reaches the crazy lady!

"Have you finished then?" the little girl asked.

"I have. Finally!"

"Did it take you long?"

"Hmm. You could say I've been doing it my whole life."

"Your whole *life*!"

"I know. I'm just a daft old woman. What do you think of it?"

"I love it, I love it, I love it!"

She sprinted along the stones into the swelling light, making me scrunch up my eyes again, making them water, but not tears, they *weren't* tears, resist, Patti, *resist* the sentiment at all costs, wipe your face quick, wipe it completely clear before Shore House Daddy has a chance to wonder about those tears and take his assumptions home for discussion.

When he reached me, he didn't stop, as glad as I was that chasing Spider-Girl gave him an excuse not to. Just a fleeting "well done' as he rushed past, along the causeway into white nothing, a nothing that suddenly made me think of Frank, this finished article he would never, ever see.

I remembered the morning I started.

A blue-grey bluster of a day, walking the shore a few weeks after moving into Little Cottage. I came across a regular-shaped, half-buried stone, which I kicked at, then dug out. I started to notice others scattered along the shore. I didn't yet know they were called setts. I stacked them above the high-tide line until I had over fifty in neat lines. I don't think I made an explicit decision to rebuild the causeway, it simply began, an impulse borne of the knowledge that of all those Patti Letham incarnations, only one would ever matter round here.

You wanna stare, then here's something to stare at.

It felt like an ongoing fuck you to the whole town to put Granny C.'s causeway back together. I used a specialist Cornish firm to lay the steel lengths to line the sides and give me a crash course in setting stones. They warned me it'd be tough to do by myself, that it would take years.

That night I dreamed I was laying stones at breakneck speed, flinging them down in a blur of hands. Waves rose fifty feet on either side of the causeway, cresting but not breaking. Behind me, with each stone laid, Frank hurled them into the sea, the wave instantly crashing over the empty space. As fast as I moved, he moved even faster, until I was holding the last stone.

I gave it to him and the wave swamped me.

***

Days passed and Hector still hadn't appeared. I hadn't yet walked the full length of the causeway from mainland to Ferris Island. Perhaps I was waiting to flaunt my triumph in front of his cynicism. More likely, I didn't want to definitively acknowledge that I had finished.

Instead, it was Bazzie, always safely in control of his own consequences, who blessed the completion.

A grin at the window. The wave of a bottle.

We headed to the shore, the flat rocks where we could sit and admire my handiwork.

"Never thought you had it in you, bro!"

"Crazy, isn't it? Must be some kind of weird genetic kink."

"Trust you to get the build-a-causeway gene. Why not the become-a-postie gene?"

"Postie?"

"Fishmonger then."

We talked about that for a while, the professions that suited us, deep down, stripped of aspiration.

It tickled me pink as a boiled shrimp, that startle of my Glasgow friends every time Bazzie came to visit, the only connection to my past they would ever know. I sensed their hope, at least the first couple of times they met him, that this backwoods curiosity in the stonewashed jeans and haircut beyond mullet might shine a little light on my life before the city, which I studiously avoided telling them about. He disappointed them. Bazzie was always my protector. Yet the fact he had known a different, more formative, Patti lent a respectful indulgence for his strange turns of phrase and odd interjections, the silences ended by a soliloquy on the weakest of cues about the Kabbalah, Dundee United, Mel Brooks movies …

"What's next anyway, Pats. I hear there's an industrial chimney in Greenock needs restoring."

"Who knows, Baz. I reckon I might just start dismantling it. One stone a day until it's completely gone."

"Now *that* is much more interesting."

He was grinning, neck lost in his jacket, an overstuffed red puffer that made his head seem oddly small. I thought about continuity and disconnection as I sat beside the ever-happy Bodhisattva of the tiny bonce. I thought of my Glasgow friends and what they were doing now.

I was okay with them meeting Bazzie but always had a lingering unease that Hector might appear. One evening he'd turn up in the pub and salaciously reveal a certain other Patti Letham.

And he did visit, twice. The first time I came home to find him, Marcie, and Joe sitting round the kitchen table. Hector had a quietly unsettled look, as if he'd picked up the Fred and Rose West vibes. It vanished when he saw me, becoming something altogether more inscrutable. He was down for a course. He thought he'd drop by. I didn't ask how he knew where I lived.

The second time he appeared at the gallery. A Mondrian exhibition. The place was packed. I knew he'd seen me before I noticed him, but he kept up the pretence he hadn't. He let me watch him awhile, then, eventually, allowed his eyes to find me, coming across and crouching by my chair.

He had "something to tell me but not here." "Yes here," I said. "If you're sure," he replied, his lips brushing my ear as he told me that my brothers had been trying to contact me. My mother had died. I stared at the paintings on the huge exhibition wall opposite me, Mondrian's vivid geometries of shapes and lines beginning to swim and shift the more I stared, unhurriedly reorganising themselves right angle by right angle, trying to settle on a final meaning.

"You okay, pet?"

And, instead of Hector and Mondrian's tessellations, it was the cobble-sheen riprap of the causeway under a late-glowing sun, Bazzie looking at me curiously but with his usual affection.

"Fine. I'm fine."

"Good. Here's another to make sure."

He poured two big shots of Grouse into our mugs. I let myself ease into the slipstream of Bazzie's unencumbered naturalism, forgetting about Hector for a while, whose essence was elusiveness, always a step ahead, who even as you spoke to him, was halfway to elsewhere.

Naturally, he appeared on the morning I finally decided to walk the causeway all the way to Ferris Island. I didn't know why I chose that day, something in the morning light, perhaps, maybe a dream remnant. There I was in the brace of a wicked nor'westerly, stepping hopscotch from sett to shining sett, imagining each stone playing a different note as I placed my foot down, swirly piano I was thinking, Ludwig working his way to a crescendo.

I was working my way round the uneven ground of the southern shore of Ferris Island when I looked landwards. A figure was coming out of the Little Cottage gate. Even from a distance I knew it was Hector. Instinctively, I ducked down, slipping on seaweed and landing on my arse in a pool of water. When I looked up there was no sign of him either on shore or the causeway.

I headed for the lighthouse.

I'd always liked lighthouses. They were built to withstand yet were thin, liminal places. People could vanish utterly—a table set for dinner but the lighthouse empty. Or momentarily—Granny C. that stormy night she wasn't able to cross back to the mainland, when my father almost died. Ferris Island had always felt like a place of ritual. The last time here, I had circumnavigated sunwise, this time in the opposite direction, balancing the forces.

From the edge to the centre, seventy-odd metres to the lighthouse. I unlocked the door. The scuff marks of our footprints from that last visit with Emine and Luca were still there but fading, merging into the rest of the dust like the vanishing remnants of all the other creatures long gone. The wind was picking up, and I headed straight to the top, the lantern room.

That was where Hector found me, of course. I heard the hasp of the door, then footsteps on the stairs.

"You'll have to do better, I've already seen this film," I said, when his head appeared in the open trapdoor. I felt a brief moment of dominance that was instantly swept aside when the rest of him followed.

"Then you'll know what happens next."

He left a few moments of silence, letting me fill it with whatever I wanted, the erotic or the violent, the attraction that would always be there, the expectation I could never fuckin' shake.

"There's talk about this place being restored. You probably haven't heard. Heritage. S'all we've got left to sell."

"Maybe I'll get a job as a tour guide."

"Na. You'd be no good with a script. You're too free-form, Patti, you always were."

"What can I say, it's all my granny's doing."

"She was something, eh? Didn't the media descend when she built it? Where were they this time, I thought you had an eye for the theatre? I only found out you'd finished on the grapevine."

"Don't give me that."

"It's true."

"Well now, you must be taking your eye off the ball."

"I'm a busy man. Anyway, I'm impressed. So's Frank. I was round the other day. He made a joke, you know Frank, always laughing at himself. Know what he said? "I never thought she had it in her to finish a job.""

I just laughed. "You're so full of shit."

He just looked thoughtful, as if making up his mind, then reached inside his waterproof jacket and took out a folded newspaper. Here was the moment he'd been working towards. He'd probably sketched out a dozen options to be selected as necessary, depending on my cue.

"Eck Johnstone. Our intrepid reporter from *The Chronicle*. He's retiring. On some kind of farewell tour, following up the "stories that made me" or some crap like that. Always was a self-important bugger."

He opened the newspaper to an inside spread and held it towards me. I saw a quarter-page photo of Frank, sitting in his apartment, hands on top of his cane. Then me, a smaller mugshot box in the bottom left. But it was the headline that fixed my gaze, that Hector now read:

""I'll never understand what I did to deserve this.""

I grabbed the newspaper and let the words swim, then stared

at the photo again. I felt sick.

"Is that what I think it is?"

He followed the jab of my finger.

"Haven't you seen that before? I guess you wouldn't have. You know Frank, he's a sentimental bugger."

Beside a fruit bowl, on top of a long sideboard to Frank's left, a golf club rested on two little Y-shaped plinths.

"S' a bit odd when you think about it, Patti. Isn't it usually the hunter who insists on the trophy?"

I stared at the blankness on Hector's face. We didn't need that long-removed lantern in the space between us, we each had our own mirrors and lenses scattering us to the four directions, he watching me watching him, the shapeshifting smiles and snarls, the esteem and the mockery.

"I never stopped loving you," he said.

I started to laugh and stopped. He looked away. For a moment I believed him, same as it ever was.

***

For a week I refused The Pines. I thought about things to fill my time. "Projects," as we had to call them these days, "hobbies' were too frivolous. "Projects' had meaning and there had to be meaning.

I made lists about things that didn't need doing. I fantasised about a new start, somewhere warm and far away, a new set of friends to take me through old age like my Glasgow ones took me through my thirties. I thought about selling the cottage and even made an appointment with a ponytailed estate agent who tended to the mystical end of the sales spectrum, talking mysteriously of "demographic mood makers," "vector surges," and, twice, "psychogeography." He seemed deflated when I said, "You mean I won't have trouble selling it?"

I left the estate agent with the beginnings of resolve and immediately drove to The Pines, testing the possibility of departure by managing not to stop. I drove home too fast, forcing the point. I couldn't settle on anything, flitting all evening between "goodbye it is' and "who am I kidding."

Around 3 a.m. I went downstairs and fished the newspaper from the bin, burning it in the fireplace to make sure I couldn't read Frank's interview again. I watched the flames and pictured a new home, a pine-scented Greek island with beautiful, blue-eyed waiters, the retsina that occasionally sparked a treacherous nostalgia and a web search for "home," Google taking me down the algorithms of the unrelenting past, the newspaper interview forever there in the digital ether, nothing that could be destroyed anymore, if anything ever could.

The next evening, naturally, I drove back to The Pines. I settled myself in the trees, but Frank's apartment was empty. The binoculars revealed a games night in the lounge, Frank sitting at his own little trestle table with a nurse beside him, guiding his dabber to the numbered sheet.

I screamed "house' and a bird took off in fright.

I went home.

I still couldn't sleep. I left the cottage in the middle of the night, a crescent moon sewn onto the black like a jaunty smile. I walked up the steep single-track to the top road and looked down at Little Cottage, light weakly spilling from the kitchen into the back garden. I had stood in almost exactly the same place the day I got the key, resisting the urge to hurl it away and draw a line under the suspicion that had never quite left me that my mother was playing a joke and as soon as I let down my guard, the punchline would be delivered. Earlier that same day, as the bumptious solicitor read my mother's will that gave me sole inheritance of the cottage, my brothers also seemed convinced she was having a laugh.

"Never did trust me."

"Never did trust either one of us."

"If only she could see that we were only ... reaching out."

"We only ever wanted to connect."

"To connect, yes."

"To connect, finally, with our only daughter."

I raised my hands in a prayer and bowed towards the graveyard on the promontory, just as the headlights of a car picked me out, taking the latest Patti Letham anecdote back to town.

I returned to The Pines for the rest of the week. Each time, Frank's curtains were drawn. I went home and tried to sleep. Each morning I told myself to stop. Then, on Friday, the curtains were open.

I was lightheaded with insomnia and the weird short circuits that came with it: my skin both hot and cold, sounds completely distinct yet running liquid into each other, the *fuzzzz* of rain and the scrawking nightbirds, an overdubbed soundscape to match the over-exposed colours of The Pines, the lurid green of the emergency exits, Frank's bright-lit apartment, every light turned on despite him needing none, as if he had to know that light remained.

Emine was on the sofa. She must have changed her reading day. Briefly, I wondered why I hadn't been told. But it was Annie who was now kept up to speed with these matters.

I watched her reading.

I watched her put the book down and Frank ask for more, "just a few more pages," I could see him mouthing the words. She read for ten more minutes and then he made the usual offer of money that she again refused. I watched her leave the apartment, reappearing a few moments later in the communal area, disappearing again to exit through the main entrance.

I moved the binoculars back to Frank.

He was sitting very still in the middle of his sofa. He was looking directly ahead of himself, out the window.

I knew he could see me.

I knew he could see me put the binoculars down and climb over the low fence separating the trees from the manicured lawns of The Pines. To my left, I saw Emine cycling out of the car park on a bike that wasn't mine to a home that wasn't mine. I started to run, across the grass and between the neat rectangular beds with spring flowers whose names I didn't know apart from daffodils; how could I have got to my fifties and not know any others, they were all just colours to me, purples and reds and blues, all slowly fading into the grey of the falling dusk, just how Frank had told his interviewer his sight had faded slowly into grey, greyer, then black. "A finality' was how he described it. "My blindness was a finality."

I reached the patio outside the sliding door to his apartment. I slid it across and felt a rush of heat, the usual institutional food odours hitting me. Soup and eggs, always eggs.

Frank looked up, unsurprised. "Is that you, Hector?"

I stepped inside the room and slid the door closed behind me. I felt the blood pounding in my head.

"Who is this?"

I stood very still. I watched his face. There was no concern or alarm, he was just patiently searching an inventory based only on sound, looking for someone he would never guess.

"Hello, Frank."

He froze. Then his mouth opened. "Patti?" The smile became shy, became something else. He repeated my name, "*Patti*," the disbelief in the first becoming something else in the second.

Relief, he sounded relieved.

I had the instant realisation that he'd been waiting for this moment, that he'd been expecting it. "One day," that was how he would put it in another interview. "I knew she'd come back one day." His dead eyes. Filling with tears of vindication and self-pity. I felt sick, my stomach turning with the knowledge that he was right. I also knew that I would come here one day.

"I read the newspaper, Frank."

"How long has it been?"

"The *newspaper*."

"Yes. The interview. You read that then?"

"Do you really think that?"

"How long *has*—'

"I asked you a question."

"Do I really think that?"

"That's the one?"

"Think what?"

"What you *said*, Frank. That you will never understand what you did to deserve this."

"Is that why you're here?"

"Why else would I be here?"

"Really. That's the reason you're here? You're putting me on, right?"

"Why else would I be here?"

""Why else," she says, "why else." Well now, that I don't understand. I don't understand that at all." He started to laugh. "Everything you might have said after turning up out of the blue like this."

"What would you prefer then, Frank?"

He started laughing again. I felt his apartment start to undulate around me, my knees suddenly weak, and it was so hot, getting hotter. Frank was always turning up the heating and me turning it down, and now he was standing up and moving towards me, arms outstretched, seeking me, saying "what would I *prefer*' as I backed away and tried to slide the door open, which wouldn't budge,

Frank now finding me, his fingers scrabbling, stubby fingers, I didn't remember his fingers being so stubby, taking hold of my shoulders and his mouth opening slightly, spittle in the corners, saying, softer now, "Give me a couple of options, Patti, help me out," taking my hands and pulling them up to his face, forcing my fingers to his eyes, pushing me back against the sideboard and a bowl of fruit scattering on the floor, "Help me *see*," a hand brushing my throat and me recoiling, stepping back, reaching out a hand that found metal, the golf club on its plinth that I had seen in the newspaper, that instantly made me think about finishing the job, one last swing of the six iron to silence Frank, who repeated "Help me SEE' as I finally slid the door open, just as he stumbled, his weight and momentum propelling me backwards, the two of us falling onto the patio and another *crack*, our heads must have landed at exactly the same time, what were the chances, crazy as the paving being stained by our blood, crazy as the darkness like a curtain and a last mind flash, Granny C., sighing with such resignation, resignation but not disappointment.

"It seems so rushed," she was saying. *"Isn't it incredible, the speed with which we finally come to our conclusions?"*

Damn right, Granny!
Few things offer more final a conclusion than concrete …

It felt like sleeping.
I was finally sleeping. I wanted to sleep forever on that patio. And now they have brought me back up.
I have yielded.
Just not to any of them.

Cool Hands Luke.
He always wants to know.
Never has a man asked me so many questions about myself. He is most attentive. He likely ignores his wife.
"How are we doing today?" … "I hope you are not too bored, Patricia." … "Please do say, are you anxious at all, it can be … disorienting … Do tell me what you can remember before you woke up."
"Any particular requests?" I ask. He looks startled. Then shifty. Frank. What I did, that's what he really wants to know when he bends closer and I look into eyes that are not blue but bloodshot

green, dry skin around the nostrils, a whitehead on the chin, one by the left ear.

I feel as tired as he looks. Poor sod.

I answer his questions with a voice that startles me with its weakness, its foggy fumbling for words.

"Evwee … day in … evwee way … we are getting better and …"

He beams.

He's delighted and I'm delighted and I do believe I'm even crying, because I want to, I want to please him.

The Two Fishwives also want to ask about Frank. They have theories they would love to run past Hector. He who has undoubtedly been told of my awakening. He who has not yet appeared. He who knows I have no choice but to lie here and wait and so makes me lie here and wait.

I watch the Two Fishwives. They don't gossip much now that they know I'm coming back into land. They defer to functional things about pills and pillows and food and the opening and shutting of blinds. Now they know I'm *present*; I wonder if they wonder that I might have heard everything else they said. Then, one time, when my eyes are closed, when they think I again have slipped beyond them into sleep, I hear them say Frank isn't doing well at all.

Or maybe I am asleep.

Luca and Emine come!

They seem awkward and quickly go.

I feel they have been asked to come, but why should they be persuaded? I lack generosity, I know, I know.

My brothers come!

They've been here before, I think. I peer at Tweedledum to Tweedledee and tell them I'm fine, just fine, then switch their voices to mute, watching them talking at me, fascinated by the deliberate way they hold their arms by their sides, as if they don't trust them not to flail around or strike out. I have an elusive memory of a conversation about switching off my life support.

I decide this is true, but all my remembrances are dusty.

I let them talk.

I sift instead through my own attic as I once sifted through the attic in Shore House for what was left of Granny C.

Rain on the skylight.

There's not much left up there. My clear-outs are regular and frequent. I put stuff aside, let it accumulate for a few years and then, like an overgrown garden that's started to annoy me, chop it all back.

Not everything, I'm not so completely disinterested in myself as to leave an empty loft.

Not yet!

There are so many reincarnations left to go; I'm the Albion Rovers of spiritual enlightenment, eternally treading water in the lower leagues. I'm too well-trained, it's Miss Jameson's archival influence again, it makes me keep certain stuff, just enough to remind myself that certain things really did happen, however generously or dubiously interpreted, letters and photos and knickety-knacks that provide a Very Short Introduction to Patti Letham.

Someone, surely *someone* will want to read that one day.

All the crap we hoard. It's just fear of being forgotten. Leave nothing and you were never really here. Look, forty boxes of crud, curated by the subject herself, so *do* take care with the conclusions. In my more romantic moments, I imagine one of my brother's kids who I know so little about deciding years from now, having retained a memory of my mercurial presence, an aunt who their father never spoke about, to embark on a Patti quest, just as I did with Granny C.

What say you, Raymond or Keith?

Bend across the bed, lips to my crusty ear, tell me with great chagrin which of your kids is most like me.

Which one of them will come a-looking?

Well?

Thirty years from now, when the causeway has again been claimed by the sea, rebuilding it for Auntie P.

Cool Hands Luke comes one last time. He looks upon his works and is pleased. He tells me of a swollen brain from a severe trauma and the induced coma they placed me in.

"Induced?" I say. "Sorry, I've always been a stubborn bugger."

"Indeed'—he beams—"it took a while to bring you out of it."

I'm smiling, too, both of us delighted by the banter. Then Luke exits with professional haste.

Everyone comes!

Except Hector.

And as soon as I stop expecting him to come, he will. I submit to time and stare at the clock. I have started obsessing about the clock, mounted above the mirror on the opposite wall. I'm glad that even from a sitting position, I can't see my reflection. I have no wish to see myself. When they help me to the toilet, I make sure not to catch even the merest glimpse.

Mirrors and time. What a bitch.

What a bitch time is.

What it does.

Katie Nurse or the Two Fishwives. They, too, are time. They are 8 a.m. and 5 p.m. and a plastic cup of pills. They supervise my swallowing. They are forever just about to ask me something. Care assistants appear at regular intervals. Trays of food. They, too, supervise my swallowing.

I start to wake in the morning.

Not as early as I used to.

Almost always with the sadness of a deep loss that I cannot quite locate, let alone begin to comprehend.

Most of the machines with their alarming noises and flashing buttons have been wheeled out. I'm left alone for longer. Katie Nurse speaks more but talks less. I'm sad that as I've become more of a presence, she's begun to retreat. She, too, will assume I won't remember anything she said to me. I'll defer with sadness and will likewise assume I said nothing to her.

"Are you okay?" she asks.

"Forever blowing bubbles," I say.

She looks at me carefully, trying to decide if I'm taking the mick or this is another weird re-entry glitch.

"*Crack*," I say, clapping my palms together at the same time.

"*Crack*."

I do it again.

There are tears streaming down my face, and now the Two Fishwives have appeared at the door.

Everyone comes except Hector.

I'm left alone for longer and longer. Then, just as I begin to wonder if anyone will ever appear again, I hear that slow clip of heels, stopping at the door. I imagine him silently counting 3-2-1 …

"No need to get up, Patti!"

He's carrying a huge bouquet of flowers.

"Did you nick those from the cemetery on your way here?"

"How dare you! Wow—those are some fetching *socks*."

I look down the bed. My feet are poking out of the blanket, the compression socks revealed almost to my knees. For a brief moment, they are someone else's feet. I pull them back under the blanket.

He walks over, lays the flowers on the bedside table. He scans the room as he says, "Lot quieter than the last time I was here. You were so still it was eerie, all hooked up and no place to go, eh?"

He looks at me carefully.

He knows I'm thinking about "the last time' and wondering how many times he'd been here.

He sits down on a chair and pulls it closer. "Man, I'm dog tired, Patti." He leans back, rubbing his eyes. Then folds his arms. Quiet for a few moments as if somewhere else. "That bloody pub again. The Viking. Lucky me got the call out last night. What a town, what a fuckin' town this is."

I have a playground flash. Hector with his arm in the air, a circling finger. Starsky and Hutch's blue light. Hector-Hutch still doesn't get it, all he ever wanted was to bring order to the boys and girls.

"Someone got their ear sliced off. How do these things even begin? Know where I found it? In the dartboard. Pinned to the bullseye with a dart. A Jocky Wilson anniversary dart. You believe that?"

I'm picturing an ear pinned to a dartboard, bloody and dripping. I'm wondering if this incident happened at all. Here's another of Hector's invitations. Here's the rabbit hole. Feed your head.

"Can believe, or do?"

The finger stops revolving. He only ever wanted me to play, and I never have. He hates me for that.

"What about you then?"

"Me?"

"What can I believe?"

"That's a big old question, Hector, maybe you want to narrow it down a bit."

He leans forward. "There's a film. I can't remember the title. A married couple who starts hating each other. They end up lying dead under a big chandelier and no one knows how they got there. That was you and Frank. Out for the count on Frank's patio. So there's my question. What can I believe?"

The Pines?

Pool of blood like a Tarantino movie.

"Well, I just—"

"Can't remember?"

"That's it. *Something* happened. I know that much. It's all just so—"

"Foggy?"

"I was going to say fuzzy. But foggy works."

Hector stands up, nodding. "That's okay. The quacks said it might take a while. For it all to come back."

"Might well do. Or it might not come back at all."

"Sure." He breaks out the white dazzle, wags a jaunty finger. "I was told that might also be a possibility."

He walks across the room.

"Hector?"

"Yeah?"

"Where did you get the flowers?"

He turns around. Looks at me blankly, as if he hasn't got a clue what I am talking about. Then a shrug. "Frank's room. He was never one for flowers anyway."

Yes.

That's exactly how it went down. For Patti has so decreed and to decree is to offer finality, *truth.*

Right?

Right.

Time will tell,"tis said. But what? The stars up above may have the answer. Some nights I raise a finger to join the dots, to see what there is to be seen, the shape of things to come or those already gone?

You tell me. I said that to Frank once. Near the end. "You tell me." A question he'd asked that I can't remember now, just my straight bat right back at him like a door slamming shut.

You tell me.

Tom McCulloch is from the Highlands of Scotland and lives in Oxford with his family. He is the author of three novels: The Stillman, A Private Haunting, and The Accidental Recluse. Tom's short stories and poems have appeared in many magazines and compilations, including *Jacked*: a crime fiction anthology (Run Amok Crime) and *Romy Lives*.